W9-CCQ-216

BITTER MEDICINE

Sara Paretsky

BALLANTINE BOOKS • NEW YORK

Library of Congress Catalog Card Number: 86-33238

ISBN 0-345-34722-6

This edition published by arrangement with William Morrow and Company, Inc.

Manufactured in the United States of America

First Ballantine Books Edition: June 1988

For Kathleen

Dull sublunary lovers love
  (Whose soule is sense) cannot admit
Absence, because it doth remove
  Those things which elemented it.

But we by a love, so much refin'd,
  That our selves know not what it is,
Inter-assured of the mind,
  Care lesse, eyes, lips, and hands to misse.

Our two soules therefore, which are one,
  Though [thou] must goe, endure not yet
A breach, but an expansion,
  Like gold to ayery thinnesse beate.

—JOHN DONNE
  "A Valediction: Forbidding Mourning"

Acknowledgments

Mr. Barry Zeman, executive director of the Staten Island Hospital, supplied invaluable technical help for this book. In addition to a comprehensive tour of the hospital's obstetrical services, from emergency admitting procedures through perinatal and neonatal support, he suggested the mortality conference in Chapter XXXII. Ms. Lorraine Wilson, director of Medical Records, and Dr. Earl Greenwald, head of Obstetrics, were also most generous with their time and expertise. I am grateful, too, to an anonymous woman ten days past her delivery date who allowed me to watch her ultrasound scan.

Despite the advice of these gracious and knowledgeable people, errors have inevitably filled the text—needless to say, these are my own; no debt for mistakes should be levied on the Staten Island Hospital. In no way should any of the staff of Friendship V Hospital be taken to resemble those at Staten Island, or any other hospital—in existence or in bankruptcy. Indeed, were it possible for a layperson to describe a well-run hospital where nurses, doctors, technicians, and volunteers all were humanists with unmistakable dedication to their callings, that place would be the Staten Island Hospital.

On the legal points raised in this book, the list of creditors is well-nigh overwhelming; to list them all would double the length of the manuscript. Professor William Westerbeke of the University of Kansas was helpful on tort law and the heritable properties of malpractice suits. Ms. Faith Logsden, manager of medical underwriting with the CNA Insurance Companies, was most generous with time and advice on the course that a malpractice claim follows. Again, any faults in facts are due to my poor interpretation, not their ignorance.

Acknowledgments

And finally, a word of thanks to Capo, Peppy, and all the other golden retrievers of the world for making it a better place in which to be a human being.

Contents

Contents

I

The Land Beyond
O'Hare

The heat and the tawdry sameness of the road drugged everyone to silence. The July sun shimmered around McDonald's,
Video King, Computerland, Arby's, Burger King, the Colonel,
a car dealership, and then McDonald's again. I had a headache
from the traffic, the heat, the sameness. God knows how Consuelo felt. When we left the clinic, she had been unbearably
excited, chattering about Fabiano's job, about the money, about
the layette for the baby.

"Now Mama will let me move in with you," she crowed,
linking arms cajolingly with Fabiano.

Glancing in the rearview mirror, I didn't see any signs of
mutual joy on his face. Fabiano was sullen. "A punk," Mrs.
Alvarado called him, furious with Consuelo, the darling of the
family—that she should love such a one, that she should have
become pregnant by him. And choose to bear the child. . . .
Consuelo, always strictly chaperoned (but no one could kidnap
her and carry her home from school every day), was now
virtually under house arrest.

Once Consuelo made it clear she was going to have the
baby, Mrs. Alvarado had insisted on a wedding (white, at Holy

Sepulchre). But, honor satisfied, she kept her daughter at home with her. Fabiano stayed with his mother. The situation would have been ludicrous, had it not been for the tragedy of Consuelo's life. And to do her justice, that was what Mrs. Alvarado wanted to avoid. She didn't want Consuelo to become a slave, to a baby and to a man who wouldn't even try to find a job.

Consuelo had just finished high school—a year early because of her brilliance—but she had no skills. Anyway, Mrs. Alvarado insisted, she was going to college. Class valedictorian, homecoming queen, winner of numerous scholarships, Consuelo was not throwing those opportunities away for a life of menial, exhausting jobs. Mrs. Alvarado knew what that life was like. She had raised six children working as a cafeteria attendant in one of the big downtown banks. She was determined that her daughter become the doctor or lawyer or executive who would lead the Alvarados to fame and fortune. That *maleante*, that *gamberro* was not going to destroy her bright future.

All this I had heard more than once. Carol Alvarado, Consuelo's older sister, was Lotty Herschel's nurse. Carol had begged and pleaded with her sister to have an abortion. Consuelo's general health wasn't strong; she'd already had cyst surgery at fourteen, and was diabetic. Carol and Lotty both tried telling Consuelo these conditions made for troubled pregnancies, but the girl was adamant about having the baby. To be sixteen, diabetic, and pregnant is not a pleasant state. In August, with no air-conditioning, it must have been close to intolerable. But Consuelo, thin and sick, was happy. She'd found a perfect exit from the pressure and the glory heaped on her since birth by the rest of the family.

Everyone knew that it was fear of Consuelo's brothers that kept Fabiano searching for work. His mother seemed perfectly willing to support him indefinitely. He apparently thought if he let things slide long enough, he could slide right out of Consuelo's life. But Paul, Herman, and Diego had been breathing down his neck all summer. They had beaten him up once, Carol told me, half worried—Fabiano had a tenuous connection to one of the street gangs—but it kept him going through the motions of looking for a job.

And now Fabiano had a lead on a live one. A factory near Schaumburg was hiring unskilled labor. Carol had a boyfriend whose uncle was the manager; he had unenthusiastically agreed to help Fabiano if the young man came out for an interview.

Carol had roused me at eight this morning. She hated to bother me, but everything depended on Fabiano's making it to that interview. His car had broken down—"that bastard—he probably broke it himself to avoid the trip!"—Lotty was tied up; Mama didn't know how to drive; Diego, Paul, and Herman were all working. "V. I., I know how much an imposition this is. But you are almost family and I cannot involve strangers in Consuelo's affairs."

I ground my teeth. Fabiano was the kind of half-sullen, half-arrogant punk I used to spend my life with as a public defender. I'd hoped to leave them behind me when I became a private investigator eight years ago. But the Alvarados gave of themselves freely—a year ago Christmas, Carol sacrificed the day to look after me when I took an unplanned bath in Lake Michigan. Then there was the time Paul Alvarado baby-sat for Jill Thayer when her life was in danger. I could remember countless other occasions, great and small—I had no choice. I agreed to pick them up at Lotty's clinic at noon.

The clinic was close enough to the lake that a breeze lifted some of the terrible summer heat. But when we reached the expressway and headed for the northwest suburbs the heavy air slammed at us. My little car has no air-conditioning and the hot wind forced in through the open windows dampened even Consuelo's enthusiasm.

In the mirror I could see her looking white and wilted. Fabiano had moved to the other side of the seat, saying sullenly that the heat was too intense for closeness. We came to an intersection with Route 58.

"The turn should be close by here," I called over my shoulder. "Which side of the road are we looking for?"

"Left," Fabiano muttered.

"No," Consuelo said. "Right. Carol said the north side of the highway."

"Maybe you should be talking to the manager," Fabiano said angrily in Spanish. "You set up the interview, you know the route. Do you trust me to go in by myself or do you want to do that for me?''

"I'm sorry, Fabiano. Please forgive me. I worry for the baby's sake. I know you can handle this by yourself." He pushed aside her pleading hand.

We came to Osage Way. I turned north and followed the street for a mile or two. Consuelo had been right: Canary and Bidwell, paint manufacturers, stood back from the road in a modern industrial park. The low, white building was set in a landscape that included a man-made lagoon complete with ducks.

Consuelo revived at the sight. "How pretty. How nice it will be for you to work with these pretty ducks and trees outside."

"How nice," Fabiano agreed sarcastically. "After I have driven thirty miles in the heat I will be enchanted with ducks."

I pulled into the visitors' parking lot. "We'll go look at the lagoon while you're talking. Good luck." I put as much enthusiasm as I could into the wish. If he didn't get a job before the baby came, maybe Consuelo would forget about him, get a divorce or annulment. Despite her stern morality, Mrs. Alvarado would care for the grandchild. Maybe its birth would free Consuelo from her fears and let her get on with her life.

She bade Fabiano an uncertain farewell, wanting to kiss him but getting no encouragement. She followed me quietly down the path toward the water, her seven-month stomach making her awkward and slow. We sat in the meager shade of the new trees and silently watched the birds. Used to handouts from visitors they swam toward us, quacking hopefully.

"If it is a girl, you and Lotty must be the godmothers, V. I."

"Charlotte Victoria? What a terrible burden for a child. You should ask your mother, Consuelo. It would help reconcile her."

"Reconcile? She thinks I am wicked. Wicked and wasteful. Carol is the same. Only Paul has a little sympathy. . . . Do you agree, V. I.? Do you think I'm wicked?''

"No, *cara*. I think you're scared. They wanted you to go out by yourself to Gringoland and win prizes for them. It's hard to do that alone."

She held my hand, like a little girl. "So you will be the godmother?"

I didn't like her looks—too white, with red patches in her cheeks. "I'm not a Christian. Your priest will have a thing or two to say about it. . . . Why don't you rest here—let me go to one of those fast-food places and get us something cold to drink."

"I—don't leave, V. I. I feel so queer, my legs feel so heavy—I think the baby's starting."

"It can't be. This is only the end of your seventh month!" I felt her abdomen, not sure of what signs to check for. Her skirt was damp and as I touched her I felt a spasm.

I looked around wildly. Not a soul in sight. Of course not, not in the land beyond O'Hare. No streets, no street life, no people, just endless miles of malls and fast-food chains.

I fought down my panic and spoke calmly. "I'm going to leave you for a few minutes, Consuelo. I need to go into the plant and find out where the nearest hospital is. As soon as I do that I'll get back to you. . . . Try to breathe slowly, deep breath in, hold it, count six and breathe out again." I held her hand tightly and practiced with her a few times. Her brown eyes were enormous and terrified in her pinched white face, but she gave me a quavering smile.

Inside the building, I stood momentarily bewildered. A faint acrid smell filled the air, and above it, a hum of noise, but no lobby, no receptionist. It might have been the entrance to the Inferno. I followed the noise down a short corridor. An enormous room opened to the right, filled with men, barrels, and a thicker haze. To the left I saw a grill marked RECEIVING. Behind it sat a middle-aged woman with faded hair. She was not fat, but had the kind of flabby chins that a life of poor diet and no exercise brings. She was working on several mounds of paper in what seemed a hopeless task.

She looked up, harassed and abrupt, when I called to her. I explained the situation as best I could.

"I need to phone Chicago, need to talk to her doctor. Find out where to take her."

Light winked from the woman's glasses; I couldn't see her eyes. "Pregnant girl? Out on the lagoon? You must be mis-

taken!'' She had the nasal twang of Chicago's South Side—
Marquette Park moved to the suburbs.

I took a deep breath and tried again. "I drove her husband
out—he's here talking to Mr. Hector Munoz. About a job. She
came along. She's sixteen. She's pregnant, starting labor. I've
got to call her doctor, got to find a hospital.''

The flabby chin waggled for a moment. "I'm not sure what
you're talking about. But you want to use the phone, honey,
come on in.''

She hit a buzzer next to her desk, releasing the grill covering
the door, pointed at a phone, and returned to her mounds of
paper.

Carol Alvarado responded with the unnatural calm crisis
produces in some people. Lotty was in surgery at Beth Israel;
Carol would call the obstetrics department there and find out
what hospital I should take her sister to. She knew where I
was—she had been there several times visiting Hector. She put
me on hold.

I stood, the phone damp in my hand, my armpits wet, legs
trembling, fighting back the impulse to scream with impatience. My flabby-chinned companion watched me covertly
while shuffling her paper. I took diaphragm breaths to steady
myself and concentrated on a mental run-through of "Un bel
dì.'' By the time Carol returned to the line I was breathing
more or less normally and could focus on what she was saying.

"There's a hospital somewhere close to you called Friendship Five. Dr. Hatcher at Beth Israel said it's supposed to have
a Level Three neonatal center. Get her there. We're sending
out Malcolm Tregiere to help. I'll try to get Mama, try to
close the clinic and get out as soon as I can.''

Malcolm Tregiere was Lotty's associate. Last year Lotty
had reluctantly agreed to resume part time the perinatal practice at Beth Israel that had made her famous. If you're going
in for obstetrics, even half time, someone has to cover for you.
For the first time since opening the clinic, Lotty had taken on
an associate. Malcolm Tregiere, board-certified in obstetrics,
was completing a fellowship in perinatology. He shared her
views on medicine and had her quick intuitive way with people.

I felt a measure of relief as I hung up and turned to flabby-chins. She was agog watching me. Yes, she knew where Friendship was—Canary and Bidwell sent all their accident cases there. Two miles up the road, a couple of turns, you couldn't miss it.

"Can you call ahead and tell them we're coming? Tell them it's a young girl—diabetes—labor."

Now that the crisis had penetrated, she was eager to help, glad to call.

I sprinted back to Consuelo, who lay on the grass under a sapling, breathing shallowly. I knelt beside her and touched her face. The skin was cold and heavy with sweat. She didn't open her eyes, but mumbled in Spanish. I couldn't hear what she said, except she thought she was talking to her mother.

"Yeah, I'm here, baby. You're not alone. We'll do this together. Come on, sweetheart, come on, hold on, hold on."

I felt as though I were suffocating, my breasts bending inward and pushing against my heart. "Hang on, Consuelo. Don't die out here."

Somehow I got her to her feet. Half carrying her, half guiding her, I staggered the hundred yards or so to the car. I was terrified she might faint. Once in the car I think she did lose consciousness, but I put all my energy into following the dispatcher's hasty directions. On up the road we'd come by, second left, next right. The hospital, slung low to the ground like a giant starfish, lay in front of me. I slammed the car against a curb by the emergency entrance. Flabby-chins had done her part. By the time I had my door open, practiced hands had pulled Consuelo easily from the car onto a wheeled stretcher.

"She's got diabetes," I told an attendant. "She just finished her twenty-eighth week. That's about all I can tell you. Her doctor in Chicago is sending out someone who knows her case."

Steel doors hissed open on pneumatic slides; the attendants raced the gurney through. I followed slowly, watching until the long hallway swallowed the cart. If Consuelo could hold on to the tubes and pumps until Malcolm got there, it would be all right.

I kept repeating that to myself as I wandered in the direction taken by Consuelo's gurney. I came to a nurse's station a mile or so down the hall. Two starch-capped young white women were carrying on an intense, low-pitched conversation. Judging from a smothered burst of laughter, I didn't think it had anything to do with patient treatment.

"Excuse me. I'm V. I. Warshawski—I came in with the obstetrical emergency a few minutes ago. Who can I talk to about her?"

One of the women said she was going to check on "number 108." The other felt her cap to make sure her identity was still intact and put on her medical smile—blank yet patronizing.

"I'm afraid we don't have any information about her yet. Are you her mother?"

Mother? I thought, momentarily outraged. But to these young women I probably looked old enough to be a grandmother. "No—family friend. Her doctor will be here in about an hour. Malcolm Tregiere—he's part of Lotty Herschel's team—you want to let the emergency room staff know?" I wondered if Lotty, world-famous, would be known in Schaumburg.

"I'll get someone to tell them as soon as we have a nurse free." A perfect Ipana smile flashed meaninglessly at me. "In the meantime, why don't you go to the waiting room at the end of the hall? We prefer people off the floor until visiting hours start."

I blinked a few times—what relevance did that have to getting information about Consuelo? But it was probably better to save my fighting energy for a real battle. I retraced my steps and found the waiting room.

II

Infant Baptism

The room had that sterility hospitals seem to choose for maximizing the helplessness of people waiting for bad news. Cheap vinyl chairs in bright orange stood primly against muted salmon-colored walls; a collection of old *Better Homes and Gardens, Sports Illustrated,* and *McCall's* were strewn about on chairs and a kidney-shaped metal table. My only companion was a middle-aged, well-made-up woman who smoked endlessly. She showed no emotion, did not move except to take another cigarette from her case and light it with a gold lighter. Not being a smoker, I didn't even have that for amusement.

I had conscientiously read every word about the controversial sixth game of the 1985 World Series when the woman I'd spoken to at the nurse's station appeared.

"Did you say you came in with the pregnant girl?" she asked me.

My blood stopped. "She—is there some news?"

She shook her head and gave a little giggle. "We just discovered no one had filled out any forms for her. Do you want to come with me and do that?"

She took me through a long series of interlocking corridors to the admissions office at the front of the hospital. A flat-chested woman with a faded blond rinse greeted me angrily.

"You should have come here as soon as you arrived," she snapped.

I peered at the name badge that doubled the size of her left breast. "You should hand out little leaflets at the emergency entrance telling people your policies. I'm not a mind reader, Mrs. Kirkland."

"I don't know anything about that girl—her age, her history, who to contact in case of any problems—"

"Stop the soundtrack. I'm here. I've contacted her physician and her family, but in the meantime, I'll answer any questions that I can."

The nurse's duties weren't pressing enough to keep her from a promising daytime soap. She leaned against the doorframe, blatantly eavesdropping. Mrs. Kirkland gave her a triumphant glance. She played better to an audience.

"We assumed here that she was with Canary and Bidwell—we have a preferred-provider arrangement with them and Carol Esterhazy phoned in the emergency. But when I called her back to get this girl's Social Security number, I learned she doesn't work for the plant. She's some Mexican girl who got sick on the premises. We do not run a charity ward here. We're going to have to move this girl to a public hospital."

I could feel my head vibrating with rage. "Do you know anything about Illinois public-health law? I do—and it says you cannot deny emergency treatment because you think the person can't pay. Not only that—every hospital in this state is required by law to look after a woman giving birth. I'm an attorney and I'll be glad to send you the exact text with your subpoena for malpractice if anything happens to Mrs. Hernandez because you denied treatment."

"They're waiting to find out if we want to move her," she said, her mouth set in a thin line.

"You mean they're not treating her?" I thought the top of my head would come off and it was all I could do to keep from seizing her and smashing her face. "You get me to the head of this place. Now."

The level of my fury shook her. Or the threat of legal action. "No, no—they're working on her. They are. But if they don't have to move her they'll put her in a more permanent bed. That's all."

"Well, you give them a little phone call and tell them she'll be moved if Dr. Tregiere thinks it advisable. And not until then."

The thin line of her lips disappeared completely. "You're going to have to talk to Mr. Humphries." She stood with a sharp gesture meant to be intimidating, but it only made her look like a malevolent sparrow attacking a bread crumb. She hopped down a short corridor to my right and disappeared behind a heavy door.

My nurse-guide chose this moment to leave. Whoever Mr. Humphries was, she didn't want him to catch her lounging during working hours.

I picked up the data-entry form Mrs. Kirkland had been completing for Consuelo. Name, age, height, weight all unknown. The only items completed were sex—they'd hazarded a guess there—and source of payment, which a second guess had led them to list as "Indigent"—euphemism for the dirty four-letter word poor. Americans have never been very understanding of poverty, but since Reagan was elected it's become a crime almost as bad as child-molesting.

I was inking out the "Unknowns" and filling in real data on Consuelo when Mrs. Kirkland returned with a man about my age. His brown hair was blown dry, each hair lined up with a precision as neat as the stripe in his seersucker suit. I realized how disheveled I looked in blue jeans and a Cubs T-shirt.

He held out a hand whose nails had been varnished a faint rose. "I'm Alan Humphries—executive director out here. Mrs. Kirkland tells me you're having a problem."

My hand was grimy from sweat. I rubbed some into his palm. "I'm V. I. Warshawski—a friend of the Alvarado family, as well as their attorney. Mrs. Kirkland here says you aren't sure you can treat Mrs. Hernandez because you assumed that as a Mexican she couldn't afford to pay a bill here.''

Humphries held up both hands and gave a little chuckle. ''Whoa, there! We do have a concern, of course, about not taking too many indigent patients. But we understand our obligation under Illinois law to treat obstetrical emergencies.''

''Why did Mrs. Kirkland say you were going to move Mrs. Hernandez to a public hospital?''

''I'm sure you and she may have misunderstood each other—I hear you both got a little heated. Perfectly understandable—you've had a great deal of strain today.''

''Just what are you doing for Mrs. Hernandez?''

Humphries gave a boyish laugh. ''I'm an administrator, not a medicine man. So I can't tell you the details of the treatment. But if you want to talk to Dr. Burgoyne I'll make sure he stops in the waiting room to see you when he leaves the intensive-care unit. . . . Mrs. Kirkland said the girl's own doctor is coming out. What's his name?''

''Malcolm Tregiere. He's in Dr. Charlotte Herschel's practice. Your Dr. Burgoyne may have heard of her—I guess she's considered quite an authority in obstetrics circles.''

''I'll make sure he knows Dr. Tregiere's coming. Now why don't you and Mrs. Kirkland complete this form. We do try to keep our records in good order.''

The meaningless smile, the well-groomed hand, and he returned to his office.

Mrs. Kirkland and I complied with a certain amount of hostility on both sides.

''When her mother gets here, she'll be able to give you the insurance information,'' I said stiffly. I was pretty sure Consuelo was covered under Mrs. Alvarado's health insurance—the group benefits were a major reason Mrs. Alvarado had stayed with MealService Corporation for twenty years.

After signing a space for ''Admitter—if not patient,'' I returned to the emergency entrance, since that was where Tregiere would arrive. I moved my car to a proper parking space, prowled around in the heavy July air, pushed thoughts of the cool waters of Lake Michigan out of my mind, pushed thoughts of Consuelo attached to many tubes out of my mind, looked at my watch every five minutes, trying to will Malcolm Tregiere's arrival.

It was after four when a faded blue Dodge squealed to a halt near me. Tregiere came out as the ignition died; Mrs. Alvarado slowly emerged from the passenger side. A slight, quiet black man, Tregiere had the enormous confidence needed by successful surgeons without the usual arrogance that accompanies it.

"I'm glad you're out here, Vic—would you mind parking the car for me? I'll head on in."

"The doctor's name is Burgoyne. Follow this hallway straight down and you'll get to a nurse's station where they can direct you."

He nodded briefly and disappeared inside. I left Mrs. Alvarado standing in the entrance while I moved the Dodge next to my Chevy Citation. When I rejoined her, she flickered flat black eyes over me in a glance so dispassionate as to seem contemptuous. I tried telling her something, anything, about Consuelo, but her heavy silence made the words die in my throat. I escorted her down the hallway without speaking. She followed me into the garish sterility of the waiting room, her yellow MealService uniform pulling tightly across her generous hips. She sat for a long time with her hands folded in her lap, her black eyes revealing nothing.

After a while, though, she burst out, "What did I do that was so wrong, Victoria? I wanted only the best for my baby. Was that so bad?"

The unanswerable question. "People make their own choices," I said helplessly. "We look like little girls to our mothers, but we're separate people." I didn't go on. I wanted to tell her that she had done her best but it wasn't Consuelo's best, but even if she wanted to hear such a message, this wasn't the time to deliver it.

"And why that horrible boy?" she wailed. "With anyone but him I could understand it. She never lacked for boyfriends—so pretty, so lively, she could pick from the boys

13

who wanted her. But she chooses this—this garbage. No education. No job. *Gracias a dios* her father didn't live to see it."

I said nothing, certain that this blessing had been heaped on Consuelo's head—"Your father would turn in his grave"; "If he hadn't died already, this would kill him"—I knew the litany. Poor Consuelo, what a burden. We sat again in silence. Whatever I had to say could bring no comfort to Mrs. Alvarado.

"You know that black man, that doctor?" she asked presently. "He is a good doctor?"

"Very good. If I couldn't have Lotty—Dr. Herschel—he would be my first choice." When Lotty first opened her clinic she'd been *"esa judia"*—"that Jew"—first, then the doctor. Now, the neighborhood depended on her. They went to her for everything, from children's colds to unemployment problems. With time, I supposed, Tregiere would also be looked on as a doctor first.

It was six-thirty before he came out to us, accompanied by another man in scrubs and a middle-aged priest. The skin on Malcolm's face was gray with fatigue. He sat down next to Mrs. Alvarado and looked at her seriously.

"This is Dr. Burgoyne, who's been looking after Consuelo since she got here. We couldn't save the baby. We did what was possible, but the poor thing was too little. She couldn't breathe, even with a respirator."

Dr. Burgoyne was a white man in his mid-thirties. His thick dark hair was matted to his head with sweat. A muscle twitched next to his mouth and he was kneading the gray cap he'd taken off, pushing it from one hand to the other.

"We thought if we did anything else to retard labor it might seriously harm your daughter," he said earnestly to Mrs. Alvarado.

She ignored that, demanding fiercely to know if the baby had been baptized.

"Yes, yes." The middle-aged priest was speaking. "They called me as soon as the baby was born—your daughter insisted. We named her Victoria Charlotte."

My stomach lurched. Some age-old superstition about

names and souls made me shiver slightly. I knew it was absurd, but I felt uneasy, as though I'd been forced into an alliance with this dead infant because it bore my name.

The priest sat in the chair on the other side of Mrs. Alvarado and took her hand. "Your daughter is being very brave, but she's scared, and part of her fear is that you are angry with her. Can you see her and make sure she knows you love her?" Mrs. Alvarado didn't speak, but stood up. She followed the priest and Tregiere to whatever remote recess harbored Consuelo. Burgoyne remained in the waiting room, not looking at me, or at anything. He'd stopped working his cap over, but he had a thin face with mobile, expressive planes, and whatever he was thinking was clearly not pleasant.

"How is she?" I asked.

My voice brought him abruptly back to the present. He jumped slightly. "Are you part of the family?"

"No. I'm their attorney. Also a friend of theirs and of Consuelo's doctor, Charlotte Herschel. I brought Consuelo in because I was with her at a plant up the road when she got sick."

"I see. Well, she's not doing very well. Her blood pressure went down to the point where I was really worried she might die—that's when we took the baby so we could concentrate on stabilizing her. She's conscious now and reasonably stable, but I'm still listing her as critical."

Malcolm came back into the room. "Yes. Mrs. Alvarado wants to take her back to Chicago, to Beth Israel. But I don't think she should be moved, do you, Doctor?"

Burgoyne shook his head. "If her blood values and blood pressure remain this way for another twenty-four hours we can talk about it then. But not now . . . Will you excuse me? I've got another patient I need to look in on."

He walked away with hunched shoulders. Whatever the hospital administration might feel about treating Consuelo, Burgoyne clearly had taken her situation to heart.

Malcolm echoed my thought. "He seems to have done his best. But the situation was very chaotic up there—it's hard to come into the middle of a case and know for sure what the progress has been. Hard for me, anyway. I just wish Lotty were here.''

"I doubt she could have done more than you have.''

"She's more experienced. She knows more tricks. It always makes a difference.'' He rubbed his eyes tiredly. "I need to dictate my report while it's still fresh in my mind. . . . Can you look after Mrs. Alvarado until the family gets here? I'm on call tonight at the hospital and I have to get back—I've talked to Lotty—she's standing by if Consuelo's condition changes.''

I agreed, none too happily. I wanted to get away from the hospital, from my dead namesake, from the smells and sounds of a technology indifferent to the suffering people it served. But I couldn't abandon the Alvarados. I followed Malcolm into the hall, returning his keys and telling him how to find his car. For the first time in hours I wondered about Fabiano. Where was the father of the baby? How great would his relief be to learn that after all there was no baby, no need for a job?

III

The Proud Father

I stood at the emergency entrance for a while after Malcolm left. This wing of the hospital faced open land, with a housing development perhaps a quarter mile away. By squinting it was possible to create the illusion of being on the open prairie. I watched the softening night sky. Summer twilight, with its caressing warmth, is my favorite time of day.

At last I turned sluggish steps back down the corridor toward the waiting room. Close to the doorway I met Dr. Burgoyne coming the other way. He'd put on street clothes, and he walked with his head down, his hands in his pockets.

"Excuse me," I said.

He looked up, focused on me uncertainly, then recognized me. "Oh, yes—the Alvarados' attorney."

"V. I. Warshawski . . . Look: There's something I need to know. Earlier today the admissions clerk told me you weren't treating Consuelo because you thought she should be moved to a public hospital. Is that true?"

He looked startled. I thought I could see "Malpractice Suit" flash across the mobile ticker-tape of his face.

"When she first came in, I hoped we might be able to stabilize her so that she could get into Chicago and be treated by her own doctor in familiar surroundings. It soon became obvious that wasn't going to happen. It certainly wouldn't occur to me to ask a comatose laboring girl about her financial status.''

He forced a smile. ''How rumors spread from behind an operating-room door down to the clerical area is a mystery to me. But they always do. And they always end up garbled. . . . Can I buy you a cup of coffee? I'm pretty beat and I need to unwind a bit before I head home.''

I looked into the waiting room. Mrs. Alvarado hadn't returned. I suspected the invitation for coffee was in large part a desire to be friendly with the family lawyer to quiet any concerns about negligence or failure-to-treat. But my day with the Alvarados had worn me out and I welcomed a few minutes' conversation with someone else.

The hospital restaurant was a pleasant improvement over the dingy cafeterias most city hospitals sport. The smell of food made me realize I hadn't eaten since breakfast twelve hours ago. I had broiled chicken and a salad; Burgoyne picked at a turkey sandwich and drank coffee.

He asked what I knew about Consuelo's medical history and her family's and pried gently into my relationship with them.

''I know Dr. Herschel,'' he said abruptly. ''At least, I know who she is. I trained at Northwestern, and did my residency there. But Beth Israel is one of the best places to go for high-risk OB training. I was accepted there for one of their house-staff OB slots when I finished my residency four years ago. Even though Dr. Herschel is now only part time at the hospital, she's still a bit of a legend.''

''Why didn't you go?''

He grimaced. ''Friendship opened this hospital in 1980. They've got about twenty in the Southeast, but this was their first Midwest venture and they were pulling out all the stops to turn it into a showcase. They offered me so much—not just money, but new facilities they were planning—I couldn't turn it down.''

''I see.'' We talked a little longer, but I'd been away from my post for forty minutes. Much as I disliked the duty, I thought I should get back to Mrs. Alvarado. Burgoyne walked me to the bend in the corridor leading back to the waiting room, then headed for the parking lot.

Mrs. Alvarado was sitting motionless in one of the orange chairs when I came into the room. She answered my inquiries about Consuelo with ominous comments on divine providence and justice.

I offered to take her down to the restaurant for something to eat, but she rejected the offer. She lapsed into silence and sat waiting impassively for someone to come with news of her child. Her dignified quiet had an air of helplessness that got on my nerves—she wouldn't go to the nurses and demand information on Consuelo; she sat until permission was granted. She didn't want to talk, didn't want to do anything but sit with her sorrow wrapped around her, a sweater on top of her cafeteria uniform.

It was a relief when Carol arrived with two of her brothers around eight-thirty. Paul, a large young man of twenty-two or so, had a heavy, ugly face that made him look like a particularly menacing hoodlum. When he was in high school, I used to spend the summers bailing him out of the Shakespeare Station after he'd been picked up on suspicion. It was only when he smiled that his underlying intelligence and gentleness showed.

Diego, three years younger, looked more like Consuelo—small, with fine, slender bones. Carol shepherded them into the room in front of her and went to her mother. What started as a quiet conversation quickly exploded.

"What do you mean you haven't seen her since Malcolm left? Of course you can see her. You're her mother. Come on, Mama, this is crazy—you think you have to wait for a doctor's permission to go to her?" She swept Mrs. Alvarado from the room.

"How is she?" Diego asked me.

I shook my head. "I don't know. Malcolm didn't leave until he thought her condition had stabilized—I know he talked to Lotty, so she must be holding her own."

Paul put an arm around me. "You're a good friend, V. I.

You're like family. Why don't you go home now, get some rest? We'll look after Mama—no need for us all to stay.''

Carol returned just then and reiterated his thanks. ''Yes, Vic—go on home now—no point in all of us staying—she's in intensive care, so only one person can go in at a time, and that's only every two hours. And you know that has to be Mama.''

I was fishing my car keys from my handbag when we heard an eruption outside—a crescendo of shouting coming down the hall toward us. Fabiano stormed into the room, a nurse hurrying after him. He stopped dramatically in the doorway and turned to the nurse:

''Yes—here they are—this fine family of my wife—my Consuelo—hiding her from me. Yes, indeed.'' He stormed up to me. ''You! You filthy bitch! You're the worst of them all! You pulled this trick. You and that Jew-doctor between you!''

Paul grabbed him. ''Apologize to Vic—then leave—we don't want your face in here!''

Straining against Paul's arms, Fabiano continued to yell at me. ''My wife gets sick. She almost dies. And you steal her away. Steal her away without telling me! I find out only from Hector Munoz when I am looking for you after our meeting. You can't keep me from her. You think you can trick me—she isn't really sick—that's a lie! You just trying to keep me from her!''

I felt faintly nauseated. ''Yeah, you're awfully concerned, Fabiano. It's almost nine o'clock now. It take you seven hours to walk the two miles from the plant, or did you sit in the road crying until someone gave you a ride?''

''Spent it in a bar, by the smell,'' Diego observed.

''What do you mean? What do you know? All you want to do is keep me from Consuelo. Keep me from my baby.''

''The baby's dead,'' I said. ''Consuelo's too sick to see you. You'd better go back to Chicago, Fabiano, go back and sleep this off.''

''Yes, the baby's dead—you killed it. You and your good pal *Lotty.* You're glad it's dead—you wanted Consuelo to have an abortion—she wouldn't, so you trick her and kill the baby.''

"Paul, make him stop. Get him out of here," Carol demanded.

The nurse, who had been hovering uncertainly in the doorway, spoke up as forcefully as she could. "If you don't quiet down, you are all going to have to leave the hospital."

Fabiano continued to yell and writhe. I took his left arm and worked with Paul to frog-march him out the door. We went up the wing leading to the main entrance, the one that held the admitting office and Alan Humphries.

Fabiano was shouting obscenities loudly enough to rouse Humboldt Park, let alone Schaumburg; various people came out into the hall to see the parade go by. To my amazement, Humphries appeared, looking extremely annoyed at the disturbance—I thought he would be long gone to Nautilus training or blackened redfish.

He did a double-take at the sight of me. "You there! What's going on here!"

"This is the dead baby's father. He can't control his grief." I was panting.

Fabiano had stopped shouting. He was looking at Humphries slyly. "You in charge here, gringo?"

Humphries raised shaped eyebrows. "I'm the executive director, yes."

"Well, my baby die here, gringo. That's worth much money, no?" Fabiano had assumed a heavy Mexican accent.

"You can speak English," Paul growled, adding a threat in Spanish.

"He want to hit me because I look out for my wife and my baby," Fabiano whined to Humphries.

"Come on," I urged Paul. "Let's move this garbage. Sorry for the disturbance, Humphries—we'll get him out of here."

The administrator waved a hand. "No, no—that's okay—I can understand—very natural he should be so upset. You come in and talk to me a minute, Mr.—?"

"Hernandez." Fabiano smirked.

"Now listen, Fabiano—you talk to him, you're on your own," I warned him.

"Yeah," Paul chimed in. "We do not want to see your ass

again tonight. And I wish I would never have to see it again, you slime. *¿Comprendes?*"

"But you have to give me a ride back to Chicago," Fabiano protested, indignant. "I don't have no car out here, man."

"You can walk home," Paul snapped. "Maybe we'll all get lucky and a truck will run over you."

"Don't worry, Mr. Hernandez—I think we can arrange transportation for you after we're through talking." That was Humphries, very smooth. Paul and I watched him usher Fabiano solicitously into his office.

"What's that heap of shit up to now?" Paul demanded.

"Humphries is going to buy him off. He figures he can get Fabiano to sign a release for a couple of thousand, maybe save the hospital a big loss from a lawsuit."

"But why sue?" Paul furrowed his brow as we retraced our steps. "We know they did what they could for Consuelo and the baby."

I thought of Mrs. Kirkland's hasty remarks earlier this afternoon and wasn't so sure, but didn't say it aloud. Don't trouble trouble, and trouble won't trouble you, Gabriella used to tell me—advice I occasionally followed.

"Yes, well, my innocent young friend, anytime you have a dead baby you have a potential claim. No one, apparently not even Fabiano, likes to see a baby die. And a claim like that can cost a hospital several hundred thousand dollars, even if they are as blameless as—as you." That's probably why Humphries was staying late—worried about liability, I added to myself.

I kissed Paul good-bye at the waiting-room door. Carol and Diego came out to me.

"My God, Vic, after all you've done for us today—that that vermin should insult you so. I apologize again and again," she said.

"Don't." I kissed her lightly. "You didn't create him. Anyway, I'm glad I was here to help. I'm going home, but I will be thinking about all of you tonight."

The three of them walked me to the side exit. I left them standing in the doorway, a forlorn but valiant tribe.

IV

Ten O'Clock News

The hospital, air-conditioned to the point that my bare arms were covered with goosebumps, had been uncomfortable, but the heavy air was no better. It draped me like a sock; I had to make a conscious effort to move each muscle, to make my lungs go in and out. Pushing, cajoling my body— come on, quads, work together, hamstrings—I got to the Chevy.

For a while I leaned across the steering wheel. The events of the day had ground my mind to fine powder. Driving forty miles through the dark seemed a task beyond my ability. At last, sluggishly, I put the car into gear and set off into the night.

I never get lost driving in Chicago. If I can't find the lake or the Sears Tower, the L tracks orient me, and if all else fails, the x-y street coordinates keep me on target. Out here, though, there were no landmarks. The hospital grounds were dotted with streetlamps, but once beyond them the road was dark. No crime in the northwest suburbs, so no need for brightly lighted streets. I hadn't looked at street names in my frenzied drive to the hospital, and in the dark the little cul-de-sacs, tiny malls, car dealerships provided no clues. I didn't know where I was going, and a dread I never felt in Chicago's traffic hit me in the stomach.

I hadn't seen Consuelo since she'd passed through the double steel doors six hours ago. In my mind she appeared as I'd last seen my mother, small, fragile, overshadowed by the machinery of an indifferent technology. I couldn't help picturing the baby, a small V. I., unable to breathe, lying with a shock of black hair, lost in the medical maze.

My hands were wet on the steering wheel when I passed a sign welcoming me to Glendale Heights. Thankful for a landmark, I pulled over to the side of the road and looked at my Chicago map. It seemed I was headed more or less the right way. Ten more minutes of meandering got me to the North-South Tollway, which fed a roar of traffic onto the main eastbound expressway. The noise, the speed, the sodium lights, restored my equilibrium. At Austin Avenue, where we crossed the border, I sketched a bow to the city.

Back in the comfort of my own briar patch, the ugly images of Consuelo receded. She would be fine. It was only the heat and fatigue and unnatural sterility that had unnerved me.

My little co-op on Racine north of Belmont welcomed me with stacks of papers and a thin film of summer dust. Reality. A long shower washed the day's grime from me. A generous slug of Black Label and a peanut-butter sandwich completed my recovery. I watched an old *Kojak* rerun and slept the sleep of the just.

In my sleep I tried to find the source of an anguished wailing. I went up the stairs in my parents' old house and found my ex-husband snoring loudly. I shook him. "For God's sake, Richard, wake up—you'd rouse the dead with your noise." But when he got up the sound continued, and I realized it came from a baby lying on the floor next to the bed. I tried to comfort it, but it wouldn't stop wailing. It was baby Victoria who would not stop crying because she couldn't breathe.

I came to covered with sweat, my heart pounding. The noise continued. After a few disoriented seconds, I realized it was the front-door buzzer. The orange clock readout said six-thirty—pretty early for company.

I staggered to the intercom. "Who is it?" I asked thickly.

"Vic. It's Lotty—let me in."

I pressed the buzzer, put my front door on the latch, and went back to the bedroom to find some clothes. I was fifteen when I last wore a nightgown—after my mother died there was no one to make me put one on. I found a pair of terry-cloth shorts in a stack of used clothes next to my bed. Lotty came into the room as I was pulling a Cubs T-shirt over my head.

"I thought you would never wake up, Victoria. I was wishing I knew your skill in picking locks."

The words were light, but Lotty's face was unbearably drawn, a mask of a pietà.

"Consuelo died," I said.

She nodded. "I just got back from Schaumburg. They called at three—her blood pressure had dropped again and they couldn't raise it. I made the trip out, but it was too late. Facing Mrs. Alvarado was terrible, Vic. She gave me no reproach, but her silence was a reproach in itself."

"Fucking victim," I said inadvertently.

"Vic! Her daughter is dead, tragically dead."

"I know—sorry, Lotty. But she's a damned passive woman who runs her guilt-filled bus over the nearest passerby. I really don't think Consuelo would have gotten pregnant if she hadn't had an earful of 'Thank God your father died instead of living to see you do x or y or z.' For Christ's sake, don't let her pull you into her net—she can't be the first bereaved parent you've ever faced."

Anger glittered in Lotty's eyes. "Carol Alvarado is more than my nurse. She is a good friend and an invaluable assistant. This is her mother, not any bereaved parent."

I rubbed the heels of my hands into my blurry face. "If I wasn't so groggy—and upset myself—I wouldn't have spoken so bluntly. But, Lotty, you didn't give Consuelo diabetes. You didn't impregnate her. You treated her to the best of your ability.

"In your head now you're thinking, 'If only I'd done this

25

instead of that, if only I'd been there instead of Malcolm'—but you can't. You can't save the world. Don't go on a doctor trip about how omniscient you are and how omnipotent that should have made you. Grieve. Cry. Scream. But don't act out a play for me because of Mrs. Alvarado.''

The black brows snapped shut over the strong nose. She turned on her heel. For a moment I thought she was going to walk out on me, but she went to the window instead, stumbling on a stray running shoe as she went. ''You should clean up in here sometime, Vic.''

''Yeah, but if I did, my friends wouldn't have anything left to complain about.''

''We might find one or two things.'' She nodded a few times, her back still turned to me. Then she returned and held out her hands. ''I was right to come to you, Vic. I don't cry or scream anymore—those are skills I've long forgotten. But I need a little grieving time.''

I took her with me to the living room, away from the unmade bed, to a big chair like the one Gabriella used to hold me in when I was a child. Lotty sat with me a long while, her head pushing into the soft flesh of my breast, the ultimate comfort, spreading through giver and receiver both.

After a time, she gave a deep shuddering breath and pulled herself upright. ''Coffee, Vic?''

She went with me to the kitchen while I put water on to boil and ground beans. ''Malcolm called me last night, but he only had a few minutes, he could only give me highlights. He says they gave her ritodrine to retard the onset of labor before he arrived—they pump in steroids to help the baby's lungs develop lipids if they can hold off delivery for twenty-four hours. But it wasn't working and her blood values were getting bad, so they decided to take the baby and do the best they could and concentrate on her diabetes. It sounds right. I don't know why it didn't work.''

''I know you can do a lot with high-risk deliveries. But some of them must still have this kind of outcome.''

''Oh, yes. I haven't gone that far overboard with my doctor's omnipotence. And she may have had scarring from that cyst surgery we did two years ago. I was monitoring her pretty closely just in case . . ." Her voice trailed off and she rubbed her face tiredly. "I don't know. I'll be anxious to see the autopsy report—and Malcolm's—he says he dictated most of it in the car driving back. But he wanted to check a few things with Burgoyne before he finished it." She grinned briefly. "He was on call at Beth Israel last night after spending the day in Schaumburg—who'd be young and a resident again?"

After Lotty left I wandered aimlessly through the apartment, picking up clothes and magazines, not feeling like running, not knowing quite what to do with myself. I'm a detective, a professional private investigator. So that's what I do—detect things. But there was no action I could take now. Nothing for me to find, nothing to figure out. A sixteen-year-old girl was dead. What else was there to know?

The day dragged on. Routine phone calls, a case report to complete, a few bills to pay. The oppressive heat continued, making all activity seem futile. In the afternoon, I paid a condolence call on Mrs. Alvarado. She sat in state with a dozen or so friends and relations in attendance, including a wilted Carol. Because of the need for a postmortem, the funeral was postponed until the following week. It was to be a double funeral, for Consuelo and the baby. It didn't sound like a function I could bear to attend.

The next day I went in to the clinic to give Lotty a hand. With Carol away, she had hired a nurse from a temporary agency, but the woman didn't have Carol's skills, nor, of course, knowledge of the patients. I took temperatures and weighed people. Even with my help, the day didn't end until after six.

As Lotty bade me a tired good-night, I remarked, "This helps convince me that I made the right choice in going into law, not medicine."

"You'd be a good pathologist, Vic," she said seriously. "But I don't think you have the temperament for clinical work."

Whatever that comment meant, it didn't sound like much of a compliment—too detached and analytical to be good with people? I wrinkled my face—what a commentary on my character.

I stopped at my apartment to change into a bathing suit and cutoffs and then headed to the Montrose Avenue park—not the beach, where lifeguards assiduously keep you from going farther than knee-level into the lake, but the rocks, where the water is clear and deep. After swimming a half-mile circuit of the buoys strung out to keep boats off the rocks, I floated on my back and watched the sun set behind the trees. When the oranges and reds had faded to a purply-pink I swam slowly back to shore. Why live in Barrington when you could have the lake for nothing?

Back at home I prolonged my cocoonlike state with a long shower. I fished half a bottle of Taittinger's from the jumbled cupboard in my dining room that serves as a liquor cabinet and drank it unchilled with some fruit and pumpernickel. At ten, I decided to tune back in to the city by turning on the least offensive of Chicago's TV news shows.

Mary Sherrod's sophisticated black face filled the screen. Serious look. Top-breaking story is sad. I poured the last drops of wine into my glass.

"Police tonight say they have no suspects in the brutal murder of Chicago doctor Malcolm Tregiere."

It took the close-up of Malcolm's thin, fine face—his medical-school graduation photo—and the next few sentences for the news to register. A close-up of Malcolm's apartment. I had been there, but it hadn't looked anything like this. His family was Haitian and the place he'd rented on the fringes of Uptown had been furnished with many artifacts from his homeland. On the television screen, it looked like the aftermath of Tet—the few pieces of furniture were smashed, the masks and pictures had been pulled from the walls and shattered.

Sherrod's voice continued mercilessly. "Police suspect that housebreakers surprised young Dr. Tregiere, who had spent a grueling twenty-four hours on call at Beth Israel Hospital in Uptown and was home sleeping during the day, at a time when most apartments are vacant. He was found beaten to death at six this evening by a friend who expected to join him for dinner. By air time at ten tonight, no arrests had been made.''

The picture changed to an anorectic, hysterical woman excited about lean sausage patties. Malcolm. This didn't happen. I made it up—it was as real as the grinning woman and her frenzied children eating sausages. I turned off the TV and turned on WBBM, Chicago's all-news station. The story was identical.

My right leg felt damp. I looked down and saw I had dropped my wineglass. Champagne had soaked my jeans and the glass lay in chunks on the floor—cheap five-and-dime crystal, it didn't shatter, just fell apart.

Lotty wouldn't know, not unless the hospital had called her. She had a streak of European intellectual arrogance in her—she never read Chicago papers, never listened to Chicago news. All the information she had about the world came from *The New York Times* and *The New Statesman*. We'd argued about it before—that's swell if you live in New York or Manchester. But Chicago doesn't exist around you? You walk around with your nose in the air and your head in the clouds because you're too good for the city that gives you your living?

I realized with a start that I was screaming at Lotty in my head, screaming with a rage that had nothing to do with her and little to do with the *Times*. I had to be angry with someone.

Lotty answered on the first ring. Dr. Hatcher had phoned her from Beth Israel a few minutes earlier. The news had taken a while to reach the hospital because the friend who found him was an artist, not part of the medical community.

''The police want to talk to me in the morning. I was his supervising physician, I and Dr. Hatcher together—I guess they want to talk to us about whom he knew—but how could this be done by anyone he knew? Are you free? Can you come with me? Even on such a matter I do not like talking to the police.''

Lotty had grown up in Nazi-dominated Vienna. Somehow her parents had managed to ship her and her brother to English relatives in 1938, but men in uniform still made her uneasy. I agreed reluctantly—not because I didn't want to help Lotty but because I wanted to stay far from the Alvarados and the dead baby, and that meant from Malcolm, too.

Just as I was climbing into bed my phone rang. It was Carol, troubled about Tregiere. "Diego and Paul and I have been talking, Vic. We need your ideas. You don't think it could have been Fabiano, do you? He was so crazy the other night. You don't think he would kill Malcolm because of Consuelo and the baby, do you?"

I smiled sardonically to myself: No one was going to let me stay away from the murder. "You know, Carol, I really don't believe he would. How much did he care for Consuelo? And the baby—he was the strongest advocate for an abortion, remember? He didn't want a child, didn't want responsibilities. I think he'd be glad to be free of the whole situation."

"You would think so, yes, Vic, because you are very rational. But however much people joke about machismo, it is a real thing to some men—he may well feel that a man of honor would act such and such a way, drive himself to a frenzy, and do it."

I shook my head. "I can see him having a fantasy about it. But I can't see him doing it. Still, if you like, I'll talk to him. Didn't he hang around with one of the street gangs? Ask Paul—he'll know."

A buzz of talk in the background, then Paul's voice came on. "The Lions. He wasn't exactly a heavy member—ran errands on the fringe. You don't think he'd get them to do a killing for him, do you?"

"I don't think anything. I'm talking to the police in the morning—until then I only know what I saw on TV—and that could mean anything."

He hung up reluctantly. I frowned at the phone. Not just at the Alvarados but at the idea of getting back into the muck I'd left behind when I quit being a public defender. It was all going to rise up to greet me.

V

Station Break

I slept restlessly, haunted again by Consuelo's baby. It had rained heavily. The streets in South Chicago were flooded and I made my way to my parents' house with difficulty. When I came into the living room, a crib stood in the corner with a baby in it. She lay very still, not moving, staring at me with large black eyes. I realized it was my child, but that she had no name, that she would come to life only if I gave her my name.

I woke at five with a shudder, drenched with sweat. I lay with burning sleepless eyelids for almost an hour, then staggered out for a run to the lake. I couldn't make myself move at more than a shuffling jog.

The sun had been up for perhaps half an hour. Lake and sky were bathed in coppery red, a dull angry color you might expect at the end of the world, and the air hung heavy. The water was mirror still.

A fisherman stood about twenty feet up the rocks, paying me no attention. I took off my shoes and socks and jumped in in my shorts and T-shirt. Some action of wind and water in the night had stirred the cold depths of the lake and brought them to the surface. I gasped with shock as the freezing water hit my skin, chilling my blood, and I flailed my way back to shore. The fisherman, no doubt thinking drowning a fitting end for those who disturb the perch, continued to concentrate on his line.

The cold water left me shivering despite the heavy air, but it also cleared my head. By the time I picked Lotty up at her apartment a mile north of me on Sheffield, I felt reasonably able to confront Chicago's finest.

We drove to the Sixth Area Headquarters on Belmont near Western. Lotty looked elegant, if subdued, in a navy silk suit I had never seen before. Her usual dress was a schoolgirl-like uniform of white blouse and dark skirt.

"I bought it in 1965 for my citizenship hearing. I only wear it when I have to talk to government officials, so it is almost new," she explained, with the ghost of a smile.

I had dressed professionally myself, in a wheat-colored suit with a silk shirt about the same color. Despite our elegant getups we had to wait nearly forty-five minutes for our appointment. We sat by the duty desk watching officers bring in their first catches of the day. I read all the WANTED descriptions carefully, then went through the citations of merit.

Lotty's temper rose as the minutes ticked on, and her nervousness dissipated. She stalked up to the desk sergeant, informed him people's lives waited in the balance while she sat here, and came back to the vinyl seats with her mouth set.

"This is what it's like at the average gynecologist's office, in case you've never been," I explained. "Because they treat only women and women's time has inherently no value, it doesn't matter that the average patient wait is over an hour."

"You should consult me," Lotty said testily. "I don't keep people waiting. Unlike these cretins."

At last a young uniformed officer came for us. "Detective Rawlings is sorry you had to wait so long, but he had to interrogate another suspect."

"Another suspect? Are we suspects, then?" I asked as we followed him up a scuffed flight of stairs.

"I have no idea why the detective wants to talk to you, ma'am," the officer said stiffly.

Detective Rawlings greeted us in the doorway of a small interrogation room. He was a solidly built black man about my age. The building wasn't air-conditioned, and he had loosened his tie and taken off his jacket. As early as it was in the day, his collar and armpits were soaked with sweat. He held out a hand somewhere in between Lotty and me.

"Dr. Herschel? Sorry to keep you waiting—my seven-thirty appointment went on longer than I expected." He had a soft voice, rather husky, which tried to say—don't be afraid of me, just answer my harmless questions.

Lotty shook his hand. "This is Miss Warshawski. She's my attorney—you don't mind that she sits in with us." It was less a question than a statement, a little vent of temperament.

"Not at all, not at all. Warshawski?" He narrowed his eyes. "The name is familiar—"

"You're probably thinking of the auto-parts dealer," I said briskly. The papers have given some of my cases a lot of attention; since many police officers do not like PIs horning in on their territory, I didn't want to close the door by referring to them. "No connection between the two of us—they spell their name with a *y*."

"Maybe so. But I thought it was something else." His brow furrowed for a moment, then he shook his head and ushered us into the interrogation room.

"This isn't as friendly a setting as I'd like, Doctor, but we're short on space—I don't have an office, so I use what's available."

He took her through the motions on Malcolm Tregiere—enemies, friends, lovers, daily routine, valuables.

"He had little of value to steal," she said. "He came from a family with no money, put himself through medical school—you don't see doctors like that anymore. He was one of a kind.

"The only person who might rob him would be a collector who knew the value of his Haitian and African masks. But I understand that those were smashed indiscriminately.''

''Some were. Would you know how many pieces he had— so we could do a count and see if we need to circulate descriptions of ones that are missing?''

Lotty gave me a questioning look. I shook my head. ''I don't know, Detective—he invited me to his apartment a few times when he was having a group of people over. He might have had twenty artifacts just in the living room. I don't know about the bedroom—I never saw it. But you might expect thirty or forty items altogether.''

He scribbled industriously. Thirty to forty was the official number now.

''You're sure he had no enemies? What about angry patients?''

''Rude or arrogant doctors have angry patients. Dr. Tregiere was neither,'' Lotty said haughtily, giving a good imitation of arrogance herself. ''And his skill was extremely good—the best I have seen in many years. Already the equal of men with many more years' experience.''

''The news people thought it might be street-gang violence,'' I said.

Rawlings shrugged. ''Most of the crime in that area is probably done by gang members. Not necessarily as part of gang activity, but because all the teenagers belong to one.''

He got up and pointed at a large city map pinned to one wall. ''The Garbanzos' main turf has traditionally been here.'' He stabbed at the area southeast of Wrigley Field. ''The White Overlords run eastern Uptown. Now the last year, the Garbanzos have been moving into the Hispanic part of Uptown.'' His thick forefinger stabbed the area around Broadway and Foster. ''But the Lions, another Humboldt Park gang, say that's their turf. So the Lions and the Garbanzos have been duking it out with each other, and some with the White Overlords. So maybe one of them thought Tregiere was siding with the other. Supplying them with drugs, that kind of thing.''

''No,'' Lotty snapped, dark eyes blazing. ''Remove that

from your mind. Do not insult Dr. Tregiere by wasting time and money exploring it.''

Rawlings held up a conciliatory hand. ''Just sharing my thinking with you, Doc. There isn't anything specific to suggest it—but I've got to think of everything.''

He probably meant they hadn't seen Malcolm's name written upside down on the walls in spray paint. Always a worry to the cops, because it meant the owner's time had come. In the years I had known Malcolm, I knew he had no connection with the gangs, other than fixing bullet wounds and ODs. But who knew what he'd done as a poor youth when his mother brought him from Haiti to Chicago's streets? Maybe worth looking into.

Rawlings was asking Lotty about Tessa Reynolds, the artist who had found Malcolm last night. Lotty continued to be angry and answered contemptuously.

''They were friends. Perhaps lovers—it wasn't my business. Did they want to make a life together? Maybe. A resident is a terrible person to be involved with because their time belongs to the hospital, not to their friends or themselves. If she was jealous—which I for one never observed—it wouldn't be of another woman—he couldn't have found time for another one.''

''You don't suspect her, surely, Detective?'' I pictured Tessa, tall, flamboyant, but focused as intently as Malcolm on her work. No person mattered to her as much as her metal statues, certainly not enough to go to jail.

''She's a very strong young lady—working with all that metal and stone builds big shoulders. And someone with a lot of shoulder muscle pounded that doctor.'' He flipped some garish photographs across to us, a man with his brains battered out. Not Malcolm anymore, a corpse.

Lotty studied them intently, then passed them to me. ''A brainstorm,'' she said calmly. If he'd meant to shock her, he'd picked the wrong method. ''Whoever did this was mad with rage or inhuman. Not Tessa.''

I didn't have quite the lady's nerves of steel when it came to battered corpses, although I used to see a lot of pictures defending accused murderers. I examined these carefully, looking for—what? The blown-up black-and-whites revealed in excruciating detail the back and left side of the head—a sodden mass—and the angle of the shoulders; also a blowup of bloody streaks on the uneven wood floor—Malcolm had a few throw rugs but no big carpets.

"He was dragged into the living room?" I asked Rawlings.

"Yeah. He was cooking dinner when they broke in. You know these apartments—you want to get into one, you break down the kitchen door. So that's what they did." He tossed over another sheaf, pictures of the smashed-in door, of rice flung over the floor and stove. No doubt Gervase Fen or Peter Wimsey would immediately have grasped the vital clue revealing the identity of the murderer. But to me it looked like wreckage.

"Fingerprints? Any kind of indicators?" I asked.

Rawlings revealed a gold cap in a wide, unamused smile. "The little creeps all wear gloves these days. They don't know how to read, but they pick it up on TV. We're sweating the snitches—they're the only ones going to give us a lead if we find one."

"How many you figure were in the apartment?"

"Two, by the looks." He took the photographs back from me and pulled out one showing living-room carnage. "Punk One stood here"—he jabbed the right side of the picture with a thick forefinger—"in size-ten Adidas—left the logo on a big swadge of rice he'd picked up in the kitchen. Punk Two had bigger feet, but he didn't leave the shoe designer's name for us."

"So you don't really suspect Tessa Reynolds, Detective," I said.

The gold gleamed again. "Hey, Ms. W.—you a lawyer, you know better than that. We suspect everybody right now. Even you and the doc here."

"Not very funny, Detective." Lotty's thick brows rose again in hauteur. "I have patients waiting, so if you've nothing further?" She swept from the interrogation room: Her majesty was definitely not amused.

I followed her more slowly, hoping for some last comment from the detective. When it came, it wasn't particularly helpful: "Now that's one cold-blooded lady. Doesn't turn a hair over a murder that made me sick. I can see someone getting pissed enough to off her."

There were days when I agreed with him, but I said, "You ever catch a bullet, Rawlings, make sure they take you to Dr. Herschel—they don't come any better." I caught up with Lotty at the entrance. We walked silently back to the car.

As we headed back crosstown, Lotty said, "What do you think?"

"You mean, will they find the punks who did it? It doesn't seem likely. It all depends on how much bragging they do, how scared the snitches are of them. Your best bet is to get Hatcher and the hospital to keep up pressure on the Sixth Area commander—that'll keep top resources on the case. This looks very much like a random home invasion, and the only way you crack those is routine."

"Fabiano?"

"I know, I know—Carol and Paul both think his machismo got the better of his tepid interest in Consuelo and he murdered Malcolm to prove he was a real he-man, protecting his woman. But that little squirt? Come on."

"Nonetheless, Vic, do me a favor: Look into it." The black eyes were demanding—not friend to friend but head surgeon to neophyte.

My hackles rose slightly. "Sure, Lotty, to hear is to obey." I braked hard in front of the clinic.

"I'm being unreasonable? Yes, perhaps I am. Malcolm mattered to me, Vic. More than that sad child or her intolerable husband. I need to be sure that the police do not just sweep this under the rug—put it into their unsolved-crime book."

"File," I corrected irritably. I drummed my fingers on the steering wheel, trying to control my impatience. "Lotty, this is like—like a cholera epidemic. You wouldn't think you could cure that—you'd call in the state public-health people and leave it to them. Because they have machinery and resources for treating epidemics and you don't. Well, Malcolm's death is like that. I can check on a few things, but I don't have the technology or the people to grind through a hundred spouts, and follow up five hundred false leads. Malcolm's death is really, truly, a job for the state.''

Lotty stared at me fiercely. ''Well, to use your analogy, if one friend I loved was dying in this epidemic, I would treat him, even if I couldn't stop the plague. And that's what I'm asking on Malcolm's behalf. Maybe you can't solve the crime, maybe the epidemic of gang violence is too big for anyone, even the state, to solve. But I am asking you, friend to friend, for a friend.''

I felt as if I were choking under my silk collar. The image of the baby, gasping for air, swept across my mind again. ''Yeah, okay, Lotty,'' I muttered. ''I'll do what I can. Just don't sit up nights waiting for the fever to break.''

I barely waited for her to shut the passenger door before squealing to the corner and roaring down Irving Park Road. I cut across a madly honking van at the entrance to Lake Shore Drive and accelerated hard in front of a sweep of oncoming cars. A barrage of horns and screaming brakes made me feel momentarily effective. Then the stupidity of venting my frustration in a lethal machine overcame me. I pulled over to one of the little turnouts where you can change a flat tire and waited for my pulse to settle down.

The lake lay to my left. The polished mirror surface was streaked with a light and color that would have inspired Monet. It looked at once peaceful and inviting. But its cold depths could kill you with merciless impersonality. Soberly, I put the car into gear and headed slowly into the Loop.

VI

In the Archives

I parked in the south Grant Park garage underneath Michigan Avenue and walked over to my office. The lobby of the Pulteney building on South Wabash gave up its usual fetid smell of moldy tile and stale urine. But the building was old, put up when people built for keeps; its unair-conditioned halls and stairwells were cool behind thick concrete walls.

The elevator was broken, a twice-weekly occurrence. I had to pick my way across chicken bones and less-appetizing debris in the stairwell entrance. Nylons and heels are not the ideal footwear for the four-floor climb to my office. I don't know why I bothered, why I didn't just work out of my apartment. I couldn't afford a better building, and having an office close to the financial center because its crime was my specialty didn't seem reason enough to put up with this dump and its perpetual malfunctions.

I unlocked my office door and scooped a week's accumulation of mail from the floor. My rent included a sixty-year-old "mailboy" who picked the mail up in the lobby and delivered it to tenants—no postal employee was going to climb all those stairs every day.

I flipped on the window air conditioner and called my answering service. Tessa Reynolds wanted to speak to me. As I dialed her number, I noticed that the plant I'd bought to cheer up the room had died of dehydration.

"V. I.—you heard about Malcolm?" Her deep voice was tight, strained fine through the vocal cords. "I—I'd like to hire you. I've got to make sure they find them, get those bastards off the street."

I explained as patiently as I could what I'd told Lotty.

"Vic! This isn't like you! What do you mean, a job for the police and routine? I want to be dead certain, when that routine says there's no way to track the murderer down that *there is no way*! I want to *know* that. I don't want to go to my grave with the idea that they could have found the killer, but they didn't look, that Malcolm, after all, even though he was a great surgeon, was just another dead black man!"

I tried to pull back into the rationality that made my job possible. Tessa was not pummeling me personally. She was behaving in the way grief takes some people—with rage, and by demanding a reason for her bereavement.

"I just had this conversation with Lotty, Tessa. I'll ask what questions I can of the few sources I have. And I've already promised the Alvarados I'll talk to Fabiano. But you must not look to me to solve this crime. If I turn up any leads, they go straight to the officer in charge because he has the machinery to follow them up."

"Malcolm had such respect for you, Vic. And you're turning your back on him." A sob cracking the deep voice was all that kept me from shouting at her.

"I'm not turning my back on him," I said levelly. "I'm just telling you, my going through the motions on this is not going to accomplish what the police can. Do you think I'm made of stone, that a friend of mine is battered to death and I turn up full of detached objectivity like a Sherlock Holmes? Jesus, Tessa, you and Lotty make me feel like the bludgeoned end of a battering ram."

"If I had your skill and your contacts, Vic, I'd be glad

to be able to act, instead of sitting in my studio with a
mallet trying to chisel a statue of grief.''

The line went dead. I rubbed my head tiredly. My Polish
shoulders did not seem wide enough to handle the load on
them today. I rotated them gently to undo the knots. In the
ordinary run of things, Tessa would be right: I solve my
problems better by acting than thinking. That's what makes
me a good detective. So why did this job look so unappetizing?

The Dan Ryan El rattled by. I got up stiffly and hung my
jacket on an old coatrack in the corner. All my office furniture is used. The big oak desk and the coatrack came from
a police auction. The manual Olivetti had been my mother's. Behind the desk was a khaki metal filing cabinet, a gift
from a printing company in lieu of a fee they couldn't afford
to pay.

The cabinet holds every piece of paper I've touched since
passing the bar over a decade ago. When I left the public
defender's office, my case files stayed with the county. But
I'd saved all my notes and receipts, motivated by an obscure
fear that the county—a jealous god if ever there was one—
might audit my expense reports and demand reimbursement
for my car mileage. As time passed, it didn't seem worth
the trouble to sort them out. I put the dead plant and the
scattered pages of a report for a case just ending into the
corner and dumped the contents of the cabinet's bottom
drawer onto the desk top.

I found old gasoline receipts, names and addresses of
witnesses whose identities now meant nothing to me, a detailed brief defending a woman who had killed the man who
raped her after he was released on bond. My hands turned
black and grimy from the decade-old dust and my silk shirt
changed from pale beige to gray.

At one o'clock I went to the corner deli for a corned-beef
sandwich—not the best choice on a hot muggy day. I
brought two cans of diet soda back with me to cut the salt.
Finally, toward the end of the afternoon, I found the scrap
I was looking for, stuck between two pages listing my bond-
court assignments for February 1975.

Sergio Rodriguez, boy punk. He'd been arrested numerous times in his young life, for progressively more antisocial acts. Finally at eighteen he'd made it into adult court on aggravated assault charges. It had been my happy job to defend him. He was a good-looking youth with a lot of charm and a lot of violence. What I had was his mother's phone number. She'd believed the charm, not the violence, but felt I'd done the best I could for her poor railroaded baby.

We'd gotten the sentence down from ten years to two-to-five as a so-called first offense. Sergio came out from Joliet about the time I went into business for myself.

When I defended him he'd been a lowlife in a Humboldt Park gang called the Venomous Aliens. When he got out of jail, with his graduate prison degree in gangs and violence, he'd moved quickly into a position of power. He'd helped change the Aliens' name to the Latin Lions, and claimed that they were a private men's club like the Kiwanis and the non-Latin Lions. I'd seen his picture in the *Herald-Star* a few months ago entering a courtroom where he was suing the paper for libel in calling the Lions a street gang. He'd been wearing a three-piece suit whose expensive fabric even newsprint couldn't hide. In the meantime, under his guidance, the Lions had branched out to the Wrigley Field area. Most recently, as Rawlings had said, they'd moved into the Hispanic part of Uptown.

I put Mrs. Rodriguez's phone number into my purse and surveyed the mess on my desk. Maybe it was time to ditch it all. On the other hand, I might need another obscure note someday. I swept everything back into the drawer, locked the cabinet, and left.

During the afternoon the sky had clouded over with heavy sullen clouds that seemed to shut all oxygen from the city. My beige-gray shirt became a sodden mass of sweat by the time I got home. Never wear silk in the summer, especially not for heavy cleaning jobs. I was tempted to throw it out—it looked beyond salvation.

After a cold shower, and comfortable in cutoffs and a short-sleeved shirt, I felt up to talking to Mrs. Rodriguez.

A young child answered the phone; after a few minutes of my shouted questions she called for her grandmother.

Mrs. Rodriguez's heavily accented voice came on the line. "Miss Warshawski? Ah—ah, the lawyer who worked so hard for my Sergio. How are you? How are you after all this time!"

We chatted for a few minutes. I explained I was no longer with the public defender's office, but was glad to see in the papers that Sergio was doing so well.

"Yes, a community leader! You would be proud to know him. Always he speak of you with gratitude."

I doubted that, but it provided an opportunity to ask for his phone number. "I need to talk to him about someone in his—uh—men's club. There's been some community action lately that he might be able to advise me on."

She was glad to oblige. I asked about the rest of her children—"And grandchildren, right?"

"Yes, my Cecilia's husband leave her so she come here with her two children. Is very good—good to have young people in the house again."

We hung up with mutual protestations of goodwill. What did she really think Sergio was doing? Really, deep down? I dialed the number she'd given me and let it ring a long time unanswered.

The corned-beef sandwich sat too heavily in my stomach for me to think about dinner. I took a glass of wine onto the little landing outside my kitchen door. It overlooked the alley and the small yard where some of the other tenants raised vegetables. Old Mr. Contreras from the first floor was out putting guards around his tomatoes.

He waved at me. "Big storm tonight," he called up. "Got to protect these little fellows."

I drank Ruffino and watched him work until the light failed. At nine, I tried Sergio's phone again. It still rang unanswered. The last few days had worn me out. I went to bed and slept soundly.

As Mr. Contreras had predicted, the weather broke in the night. When I went out for my morning run, the day sparkled, the leaves were deep green, the sky dark blue, birds sang furiously. The storm had ruffled up the lake; waves splashed over the rocks and whitecaps rolled briskly beyond the breakwater.

I came home the long way, past the Chesterton Hotel where the Dortmunder Restaurant serves cappuccino and croissants for breakfast. The fresh air and my long sleep renewed my confidence. Whatever superstitions had dogged me yesterday seemed irrelevant in the balance against my great skill as a detective.

Back home, I had proof that my magic powers were restored; Sergio's phone was answered on the third ring.

"Yes?" The male voice was heavy with suspicion.

"Sergio Rodriguez, please."

"Who are you?"

"This is V. I. Warshawski. Sergio knows me."

I was put on hold. The minutes ticked by. I lay on the floor on my back and did leg lifts, holding the phone to my right ear. After I'd done thirty with each leg, the heavy voice returned.

"Sergio says he don't owe you nothing. He don't need to talk to you."

"What did I say about his owing me anything? I didn't. As a favor, I would like to speak with Sergio."

This time the wait was shorter. "You want to see him, be at Sixteen-sixty-two Washtenaw tonight at ten-thirty. You be alone, no heat, and you be clean."

"Aye, aye, Captain," I said.

"Say what, man?" The voice was suspicious again.

"Gringo for 'I hear you, man.' " I broke the connection.

I lay on the floor awhile longer, staring at the neatly sworled plaster on the ceiling. Washtenaw, heart of Lion country. I wished I could go with a police battalion behind me. Better yet, in front of me. But the only thing that would accomplish would be to get me shot—if not tonight, then later. WARSHAWSKI would start appearing spray-painted upside down on garage doors in Humboldt Park. Or maybe that was too hard a name to spell. Maybe it would be just my initials.

Perhaps they'd do it even if I followed their orders. I'd

be gunned down as I left the building. Lotty would be sorry then that she'd forced me into this. She'd be sorry but it would be too late. Much moved, I pictured my funeral. Lotty was stoic, Carol sobbing openly. My ex-husband came with his suburban-chic second wife. "You were really married to her, darling? So messy and irresponsible—and hanging around with gangsters, too? I can't believe it."

The thought of plastic Terri made me laugh a little. I got up from the floor and changed from my running clothes into jeans and a bright-red knit top. I scribbled a note detailing where I was going and why and took it down to the backyard where Mr. Contreras was hovering anxiously over his tomato plants. They were heavy with ripening fruit.

"How'd they do last night?" I asked sympathetically.

"Oh, they're fine. Really fine. You want some? I got too many here, don't know what to do with them all. Ruthie, she don't really want them."

Ruthie was his daughter. She came by periodically with two subdued children to harangue her father into moving in with her.

"Sure. Give me what you don't want—I'll make you some real old-world tomato sauce. We can have pasta together this winter. . . . I have a favor to ask of you."

"Sure, cookie. Whatever you want." He sat back on his heels and carefully wiped his face with a handkerchief.

"I have to go see some punks tonight. I don't think I'm going to be in any danger. But just in case—I've written down the address and why I'm going there. If I'm not back home tomorrow morning, can you see that Lieutenant Mallory gets this? He's in Homicide at Eleventh Street."

He took the envelope from me and looked at it. Bobby Mallory had been in the police with my dad, maybe'd been his closest friend. Even though he hated my working in the detective business, if I died he'd make sure the relevant punks got nailed.

"You want me to come with you, cookie?"

Mr. Contreras was in his late seventies. Tanned, healthy, and strong for a man his age, he still wouldn't last too long in a fight. I shook my head.

"The terms were I have to come alone. I bring someone with me, they'll start shooting."

He sighed regretfully. "Such an exciting life you have. If only I was twenty years younger. . . . You're looking real pretty today, cookie. My advice, if you're going to visit some real punks, tone it down some."

I thanked him gravely and stayed talking to him until lunch. Mr. Contreras had been a machinist for a small tool-and-die operation until he retired five years ago. He thought listening to my cases was better than watching *Cagney & Lacey*. In turn he regaled me with tales of Ruthie and her husband.

In the afternoon I drove over to Washtenaw Avenue and slowly cruised past the meeting place. The street was in one of the more run-down sections of Humboldt Park, near where it borders on Pilsen. Most of the buildings were burned out. Even those still occupied were covered with spray-painted graffiti. Tin cans and broken glass took the place of lawns and trees. Cars were hoisted up on crates, their wheels removed. One was parked about two yards from the curb, partially blocking the street. Its rear window was missing.

The address where I was to meet Sergio belonged to a thickly curtained storefront. It was flanked on one side by a partially demolished three-flat, and on the left by a bedraggled liquor store. When I arrived tonight, Lions would be hidden in the ruined building, probably lounging in front of the liquor store, and signaling each other from lookouts at both ends of the block.

I turned left at the corner and found the alley that ran behind the buildings. The three ten-year-old boys playing stickball at its entrance were in all probability gang members. If I drove down the alley or talked to them, word would inevitably get back to Sergio.

I could see no way to make a reasonably protected approach to the meeting place. Not unless I crawled along the city sewers and popped up from the manhole in the middle of the street.

VII

The Lions' Den

I still had eight hours before the rendezvous. I figured if I made every golden minute count today, I could go to Lotty, Tessa, and the Alvarados on Monday and tell them, scout's honor, I'd done my best—now leave it to Detective Rawlings.

I swung up Western to Armitage, over to Milwaukee, where the expressway looms menacingly over the neighborhood on high concrete stilts. In a corner underneath it was Holy Sepulchre High School, where Consuelo had studied.

She had played tennis on the uneven asphalt courts there, looking adorable in her white shorts and shirt, breathing in the asbestos from the auto brakes overhead. I know—I'd watched her at a match one afternoon. So I could understand how Fabiano had found her enticing. He used to hang out in a bar up the street and wait for his sister while she was at tennis practice. After Consuelo joined the team, he hung out at the school watching the girls, then took to ferrying the whole team to matches. And so it went on from there. I'd heard the whole story from Paul when the news of Consuelo's pregnancy first broke.

The city has certain standards concerning bars and schools—

they can't exist side by side. I made a sweep of the area and found a couple close enough to Holy Sepulchre to be likely haunts of Fabiano's. I was in luck at the first one. Fabiano was drinking beer at El Gallo, a dingy storefront with a hand-painted, gaudy rooster on the front door. He was watching the Sox on a tiny set attached high up on the wall out of the reach of the casual burglar. About fifteen men were also in the bar, their attention held by the game. Would Ron Kittle drop yet another routine fly ball? I could see how they'd be breathless.

I pulled a stool from the end of the bar and moved it up behind Fabiano. The bartender, talking happily at the other end of the counter, paid no attention to me. I waited courteously for the inning to end, then leaned over Fabiano's shoulder.

"We need to have a little chat, Señor Hernandez."

He jerked his arm, spilling his beer, and turned around, startled. He flushed angrily when he saw me. "Shit! Get out of my face!"

"Now, now, Fabiano, that's no way to talk to your aunt."

The men on either side of him were looking at me. "I'm his mother's sister," I explained, shrugging my shoulders in embarrassment. "She hasn't seen him for days. He won't talk to her. So she asked me to find him, try to talk sense to him."

He struggled to his feet in the narrow space between my stool and his. "That's a lie, you bitch! You're no aunt of mine!"

A man farther up the bar gave an unsteady smile. "You be my aunt if he don't want you, honey."

This got a round of cheers from several others, but the man to Fabiano's left said, "Maybe she's not his aunt. Maybe she's from the collection agency, come to repo the car, huh?"

This drew louder laughter from the group. "Yeah, or the cops come to take it back to its rightful owner."

"I own it, man," Fabiano said furiously. "I have the papers right here in my pocket." He stuck a hand into his right pocket dramatically and pulled out a piece of paper.

"So maybe he stole that, too," the man to his left said.

"New car, *sobrino*?" I asked, impressed.

"I am not your nephew," he screamed, spitting at me. A man of limited imagination.

"Now that's enough." The bartender moved up. "Whether she is your aunt or not, you must not treat the lady this way, Fabiano. Not if you want to drink in my bar. And frankly, I believe she is your aunt—because no one would embarrass themselves by pretending to be related to you if they were not. So you go outside and talk to her. Your seat will be here when you get back and the rest of us can watch the game in peace for a while."

Fabiano followed me sullenly outside, pursued by cheers and catcalls from the rest of the bar. "Now you humiliate me in front of my friends. I won't take it from you, Warshawski-bitch."

"What're you going to do—have me beaten to death the way you did Malcolm Tregiere?" I asked nastily.

His face changed from sullen to alarmed. "Hey! You ain't hanging that on me. No way. I didn't touch him. I swear I didn't touch him."

A baby-blue late-model Eldorado stood a few feet from the bar entrance. It couldn't have been more than two or three years old and the body was in great condition. Since the rest of the cars on the block were a step away from the junkyard, I deduced it had to be the one the men had been ribbing him about.

"That your car, Fabiano? Pretty nice wheels for a guy who couldn't even buy his wife a ring two months ago."

I saw another movement of his mouth, and smacked it hard before he could get any saliva out. "Enough of that. I don't want to catch anything from you. . . . Tell me about the car."

"I don't have to tell you nothing," he muttered.

"No, that's right, you don't. You can tell the police. I'm going to call them now and tell them you've got yourself a new car, easily worth five-ten thousand. And I'm going to suggest to them that you collected a chunk of change from the Lions for bludgeoning Dr. Tregiere. Then *they're* going to talk to you. And while the cops are shaking you upside down, I'm going to talk to Sergio Rodriguez. And I'm going to tell him that you're driving these beautiful wheels because you're dealing dope for the Garbanzos. And then I'm going to start reading the obit pages. Because you gonna be dead meat, Fabiano.''

I turned on my heel and headed toward my car. Fabiano caught up with me as I unlocked the door. ''You can't do that to me!''

I laughed a little. ''Sure I can. What do I owe you, anyway? Tell you the truth, I'd love to read your obituary.''

''But it's a lie, man! It's a lie! I got that car legal. I can prove it.''

I shut the door and leaned against it. ''So prove it.''

He licked his lips. ''They—that man at the hospital—he gave me five thousand dollars for Consuelo. To—to say how sorry they were that the baby died and that she died, too.''

''Wait a minute while I find a Kleenex. This story is breaking my heart—five thousand? That's a hell of a price tag for your lady and her baby. What'd they ask you to do in return?''

He licked his lips again. ''Nothing. I didn't have to do nothing. Just sign a paper. Sign a paper about her and the baby.''

I nodded. A release. Just as I'd suggested to Paul. They bought him off. ''You must have told them a wonderful story. Impressed the shit out of them. No one here would figure you'd need more than five hundred to keep your mouth shut. What'd you do?—dangle threats of the Lions in front of their white suburban faces and scare 'em to death?''

''You're always on my case, man. You and that Jew-doctor and Paul. You can't believe nothing good about me. I loved Consuelo. She was having our baby. My heart's broken, man.''

I felt as though I might throw up on the spot. ''Save it for Schaumburg, honey. They con easier out there.''

A nasty smile flickered across his lips. ''That's what you think, bitch.''

My foot itched to reach up and kick him in his tiny testicles, but I restrained myself. ''Back to Dr. Tregiere, Fabiano. You swore you didn't touch him.''

He glared at me. ''I didn't. You can't lay that on me.''

''But you watched someone else touch him.''

''No way, man. No way did I have anything to do with the dude's death. I got a dozen guys say they saw me when the dude was being killed.''

"You know what time he was being killed? Or you got a dozen guys who say they saw you no matter what time he was being killed?"

"I don't have to take any more of this shit from you, Warshawski. You trying to lay a murder rap on me, you damn well not going to do it."

He turned on his heel and walked back into the bar. I stood by my car a moment, frowning at the painted rooster. I didn't like it. I wished I had a stronger lever so I could pry the truth out of him. He was holding back on something, but whether it was Malcolm's death or not I had no way of telling.

I got back in the Chevy and headed northeast toward home. Should I turn him over to Rawlings or not? I fidgeted around with it off and on all afternoon, while watching the Cubs lose an aggravating game against New York and afterward swimming lazily around the buoys off Montrose Harbor. I couldn't go to Lotty and wash my hands of it until I knew for certain.

At nine-thirty I dressed in dark clothes that were easy to move in. Instead of running shoes, I put on the heavy rubber-soled oxfords I wear for industrial surveillance. I couldn't run as fast in them, but if I had to kick someone at close quarters, I wanted it to count.

On Saturday night, Humboldt Park was shaking. Cars cruised up and down North Avenue, honking horns, blaring radios at top volume. Girls in improbably high heels and lacy blouses teetered arm in arm in laughing groups. Young men and drunks surged around them, whistled, yelled, and moved on.

I drove to Campbell, four blocks from the rendezvous. It was a quiet, decently maintained street, with a sign at either end spelling out the rules: no radios, no graffiti, no honking horns. The well-kept buildings testified to the willingness of neighbors to enforce the sign. I parked under a streetlight. If I got this far in a chase, someone might even call the cops.

I headed west across lots. One block from Campbell, the neighborhood deteriorated again. I picked my way carefully over broken bottles, splintered boards, car tires, objects too strange to be identified in the dark. Most of the occupied structures were little bungalows, not apartment buildings. Many of these had dogs in the back who lunged angrily on their leashes or against the fences that restrained them, when they heard me. A couple of times heads appeared in windows, peering to see what hoodlum was prowling about.

When I climbed the last fence between me and Washtenaw, my mouth was dry, my heart beating uncomfortably fast. I could feel the little hairs at the back of my neck standing up under the collar of my knit shirt. I hovered in the shadow of the derelict building across the street, trying to make out where the sentries were. Trying to control the weak feeling in the backs of my knees. C'mon, Warshawski, I muttered to myself, fish or cut bait. It ain't the size of the dog in the fight that counts, but the size of the fight in the dog.

Much cheered by these admonitions, I moved from my shelter out into the street, past the cars perched precariously on old juice crates, and came to the front of the heavily curtained store. No one shot at me. In the dark, though, I could sense the presence around me of many Lions.

I rapped smartly on the glass door. It opened promptly, the width of a chain. A gun barrel appeared. Naturally. The heavy drama of the gangs, the alleviation of the relentless boredom of life on the streets.

"It's V. I. Warshawski, reporting as commanded, clean in thought, word, and deed."

I felt someone come up behind me and braced myself against an expected touch; I couldn't afford to follow my reflexes and kick. Hands patted me down clumsily.

"She's clean, man," the youth behind me twanged. "I didn't see no one wit' her."

The door shut while the chain was removed, then reopened. I walked into a dark room. The doorman took my arm and guided me across bare floors that echoed our footsteps against empty walls. We went through some heavy drapery concealing a door. My escort tapped a complicated tattoo and more chains were scraped back.

Sergio Rodriguez sat in splendor on the other side. Wearing a blue silk shirt opened to the fourth button and a quantity of gold chains around his neck, he leaned back in a large leather desk chair behind a slab of mahogany. The carpet was thick underfoot, the air, cooled by a window unit, redolent of reefer. A large box in one corner was tuned loudly to a Hispanic station. When I came in, someone turned down the volume.

Three young men were with Sergio. One wore a T-shirt, revealing tattoos all the way up his arms. On the left forearm was a peacock, whose elaborate tail feathers probably covered track marks. The second had on a long-sleeved pink shirt that clung to his slender body like a leotard. He and Tattoo both ostentatiously carried guns. The third was Fabiano. As far as I could see he was unarmed.

"Bet you didn't expect to see me here, bitch." He smirked importantly.

"What'd you do—run straight to Daddy after talking to me?" I asked. "You really must be scared of Sergio asking too many questions about that Caddy."

Fabiano lunged toward me. "You bitch! You wait! I show you what fear is! I show you—"

"Okay!" Sergio said in his husky voice. "You be quiet. I handle the talk tonight. . . . So, Warshawski. It's been a long time. A long time since you worked for me, huh?"

Fabiano retreated to the back of the room. Pink Shirt moved with him, guarding him a little. So the gang didn't trust Fabiano, either.

"You've done very well, Sergio—meetings with aldermen, meetings with the Office of Community Development—your mother is very proud of you." I kept my voice level, expressing neither contempt nor admiration.

"I'm doing okay. But you—you're not any better off than when I saw you last, Warshawski. I hear you're still driving a beater, still living by yourself. You should get married, Warshawski. Settle down."

"Sergio! I'm touched—after all these years. And I thought you didn't care."

He smiled, the same breathtaking, angelic smile that had dazzled me ten years ago. It was how we'd gotten the sentence reduced.

"Oh, I'm a married man now, Warshawski. Got me a nice wife, a little baby, good home, good cars. What you got?"

"At least I don't have Fabiano. He one of yours?"

Sergio waved a negligent arm. "He runs a few errands from time to time. What's your beef with him, anyway?"

"I don't have a beef with him. I'm overcome with admiration for his style, and empathy for his grief." I turned to pick up a folding chair—only Sergio got to sit in comfort—and saw Fabiano make an angry gesture, while Pink Shirt laid a calming hand on him. I pulled the chair up next to the desk and sat.

"I would like to know for sure that his grief didn't take the regrettable form of beating Malcolm Tregiere's brains out."

"Malcolm Tregiere? The name is vaguely familiar. . . ." Sergio rolled it around his tongue like a sommalier trying to recall an elusive vintage.

"A doctor. Killed in Uptown a couple of days ago. He treated Fabiano's girlfriend and her baby last Tuesday before they died."

"Doctor! Oh, yeah, now I remember. Black dude. Someone broke into his apartment, right?"

"Right. You wouldn't happen to know who that was, would you?"

He shook his head. "Not me, Warshawski. I don't know nothing about it. Black doctor, minding his own business, got nothing to do with my business."

That sounded final. I turned and looked at the other three. Tattoo was rubbing the tailfeathers on his left arm. Pink Shirt was staring vacantly into space. Fabiano was smirking.

I turned my chair sideways so I could see all four of them at once. "Fabiano doesn't agree. He thinks you know a lot about it—isn't that right, Fabiano?"

He sprang away from the wall. "You fucking bitch! I didn't say nothing to her, Sergio, nothing at all."

"Didn't say nothing about what?" I asked.

Sergio shrugged. "About nothing, Warshawski. You gotta learn to mind your own business. Ten years ago I had to spill my guts to you. I don't need to do that no more. I got a real lawyer, one who don't act like I was a worm or something when I need help, not a broad who gotta earn a living because she can't get a husband."

He shook me momentarily—not about the husband, but

about the worm. Had I treated my clients that way? Or just Sergio, who had badly beaten an old man and whined when I wanted to talk to him about it instead of flirting with him.

I was mentally off-balance and saw Tattoo coming only a second before he hit me. I rolled low off the chair onto his legs, upending him in a crash against the desk. I kept rolling and bounced to my feet. Pink Shirt was on me, trying to pin my arms. I kicked hard against his shin. He grunted, dropped back, and tried to slug me this time. I took the blow on my forearm, came in close, and kneed him in the abdomen.

Tattoo was behind me, grabbing my shoulders. I relaxed in his hands, turned sideways, and slammed my elbow into his rib cage. He loosened his hold enough that I could wriggle free, but Sergio had joined the fight. He yelled orders to Pink Shirt, who seized my left wrist. Sergio tackled me around the waist and I fell ungracefully, with him landing on top of me.

Fabiano, who had done nothing during the brief struggle, kicked me in the head. It was merely a gesture; he couldn't kick too hard without landing his foot on Sergio. Sergio tied my hands behind me and stood up.

"Turn her over."

I got a close-up of the tattoos, then looked up into Sergio's dazzling smile.

"You thought you did me such a good deed, back in that courtroom, getting me off a ten-year stretch to two? Well, you were never inside, Warshawski. If you'd been inside, you would have worked a little harder for me. Now you can see what it's like—what it feels like to be in pain, to have someone you hate telling you what to do."

My heart was beating so fast I thought I might suffocate. I shut my eyes for a count of ten and tried to speak calmly, keeping my voice steady with an effort. "You remember Bobby Mallory, Sergio? I left a letter for him with this address, and your name. So if my body shows up in the city dump tomorrow, not even your expensive mouthpiece will be able to buy you out of trouble."

"I don't want to kill you, Warshawski. I got no reason to kill you. I just want you to mind your own business, and leave mine to me. . . . Sit on her legs, Eddie."

Tattoo obliged.

"I don't want to ruin you in case you ever get a man, War-shawski, so I'm just going to leave a little reminder."

He took out a knife. Smiling angelically, he knelt down and held it close to my eyes. My mouth felt like paper and my body was shaking with cold. Shock, I thought clinically, it's shock. I willed myself to breathe carefully, deep breath in, hold for five, breathe out. And I forced myself to keep my eyes open, to stare at Sergio.

Through the haze of fear I saw he was looking petulant: I didn't seem scared enough. The thought cheered me and helped keep my breathing steady. His hand moved away from my eyes, jerked below my line of vision. Then he stood again.

I could feel a stinging on my left jaw and neck, but the pain in my arms, tied underneath me, was such that it overrode any other feeling.

"Now, Warshawski. *You* stay out of *my* face." Sergio was breathing heavily, sweating.

Tattoo jerked me to my feet. We went through the elaborate ritual of getting the inner door unlocked. My hands still tied, I was led through the outer room and out the front door onto Washtenaw.

VIII

Needle Work

It was well after midnight when I unlocked the lobby door in my building. The blood had clotted on my face and neck, which seemed reassuring. I knew I should get to a doctor, get the wounds treated properly so as not to scar, but a vast lethargy enveloped me. All I wanted to do was go to bed and never get up again. Never try again to—to do anything.

As I headed up the stairs, the ground-floor apartment door opened. Mr. Contreras came out.

"Oh, it's you, cookie. I been thinking twenty times I should call the cops."

"Yeah, well, I don't think they could have done much for me." I started climbing again.

"You got hurt! I didn't see at first—what did they do?"

He hurried up the stairs behind me. I stopped and waited for him, my hand reflexively touching the dried blood on my jaw.

"It's nothing, really. They were pissed. It's kind of complicated. The guy has been carrying a grudge against me all these years." I gave a little laugh. "It's *Rashomon*. Everyone sees it differently. I saw myself helping this goon get off a heavy sentence he deserved. I saw myself overcoming my hatred of his behavior and his attitude to help him. He saw me being contemptuous and forcing him to do time. That's all.''

Mr. Contreras ignored me. "We're getting you to a doctor. You can't go around looking like this. You come back down here with me. This is no time for you to be going off by yourself. Oh, I should never have waited. I should have called them right away when I got worried.''

His strong, rough fingers pulled importunately on my arm. I followed him back downstairs into his apartment. His living room was crowded with old, sagging furniture. A large chest, draped in a blanket, stood in the middle of the floor. We walked around it to a mustard-colored overstuffed armchair. He sat me down, clucking softly to himself.

"How you even got home like this, doll! Why didn't you at least call me—I would have come for you.'' He bustled away for a few minutes and returned with a blanket and a mug of hot milk. "I used to see a lot of accidents when I was a machinist. You gotta keep warm, and stay off booze. . . . Now, we gonna get you to a doctor. You want to go over to the hospital or you got someone to call?''

I felt as though I were far away. I couldn't answer. Couldn't think. Doctor or hospital? No choice. I didn't want either. I held the mug of milk and sat silent.

"Listen, cookie.'' A little desperation in his voice. "I'm not as strong as I used to be. I can't knock you out and carry you. You gotta help. Come on, talk to me, doll. Or you want me just to call the cops? I should be doing that anyway, why am I asking you? I should just call them.''

That roused me a little. "No, wait. Don't call. Not yet. I have a doctor. Call her. She'll come.'' I dialed Lotty's number so often, I knew it better than my own. So why couldn't I remember it? I frowned in effort, and my jaw twinged. Finally, helpless, I said, "You'll have to look it up. She's in the book. Lotty Herschel. Charlotte Herschel, I mean.''

I leaned back in the chair, carefully clutching the mug of

milk. The heat felt good on my cold hands. Don't drop this. It's Daddy's coffee. He likes to drink it while he's shaving. Carry it carefully. He likes his little girl to bring it to him. His eyes crinkle up behind the white foam on his face. You know he's smiling, smiling to see you.

Mother is telling Daddy to bring a lamp, shine it on her little girl's face. Something happened. A fall, that's right, she fell off her bicycle. Mother is worried. A concussion. Bad fall. Iodine burns where the skin was scraped.

I struggled awake. Lotty was swabbing my face, frowning in absorption. "I'm giving you a tetanus shot, Vic. And we're going up to Beth Israel. This is not a dangerous cut, but it's a bit deep. I want a plastic surgeon to see it. Get it put together properly so it doesn't scar."

She took a syringe from her bag. Wet swab on the arm, sting. I stood up with her arm supporting the small of my back. Mr. Contreras was hovering at one side, holding a blue suede jacket that looked familiar.

"I took your keys and went up to your apartment," he explained, holding out both jacket and keys for me.

My arms still ached. It hurt to move them into the jacket sleeves and I accepted his help gratefully. He shepherded me tenderly out of the building into Lotty's Datsun. He stood watching on the curb until Lotty put the car into gear and squealed up the street. Her frantic speed was not a sign that my condition was dangerous—she always drives wildly.

"What happened to you? The old man says you went up against some punks?"

I made a nasty face in the dark, and got a stab of pain in response. "Fabiano. Or one of his pals. You wanted me to look into Malcolm's death. I looked into Malcolm's death."

"Alone? Going off alone and leaving a heroic message for Lieutenant Mallory? What possessed you?"

"Thanks for the sympathy, Lotty. I can really use it." A torrent of images cascaded through my head—Sergio as a worm, me as the evil witch in *The Silver Chair* turning into a worm, my terror in that little back room, and a nagging fear that my face would be permanently scarred. An overwhelming fatigue made it hard for me to remember what I was talking about. I made myself speak. "I told you—police job."

"So what were you trying to prove by going off alone instead of turning what you knew over to the police? Sometimes, Victoria, you are unbearable!" Lotty's Viennese accent became noticeable, as always when she was upset.

"Yeah, you're probably right." The soreness in my face merged with the throbbing in my shoulders into one giant white tom-tom of pain. It pounded harder when the car hit a bump and then eased off a little. Up and down. Like the old Ferris wheel at Riverview.

For a moment I thought I was riding the Ferris wheel, but that wasn't true. I was on my way to the hospital. My mother was sick. She might be dying but Dad and I were being brave for her sake. After winning the state high-school basketball championship, the other girls on the team and I had sneaked off with several pints of whiskey. The ten of us drank it all and were vilely sick. Now I had to go see my mother. She needed me alert and cheerful, not aching and hung over.

"I guess I'm pretty stupid sometimes, too." The sharp voice cut through the fog. Lotty. Not Gabriella. It was me cut up and sore.

"You're in terrible shape. Whatever prompted you to go off on your own, you don't need quarreling tonight. Come on, *Liebchen*. On your feet. That's right. Lean on me."

I stood up slowly, shivering unbearably in the warm air. Lotty called out a command. A wheelchair appeared. I sank down into it and was pushed inside.

I quit trying to stay awake. White lights blurred behind my drugged lids. Pricks in my face—they were stitching me back together. Something cold on my back. The muscles eased down.

"Will I live, Doc?" I mumbled.

"Live?" A man's voice echoed me loudly. I woke up a bit more and looked at him, an older man with a lined face and gray hair. "You were never in danger of dying, Miss Warshawski."

"That's not what I meant to ask. What I really want to know—my face—how bad will I look?"

He shook his head. "It won't be noticeable. Provided you stay out of direct sunlight for several months and keep on a healthy diet. Your boyfriend may see a faint line when he kisses you, but if he's that close he probably won't be looking."

Sexist asshole, I said, but to myself. No point in biting the hand that sews you.

"I'm admitting you for what's left of the night. Just so you get some rest instead of jolting around in a car anymore. The police want to talk to you, but I've asked them to wait until tomorrow."

Maybe he wasn't so bad after all. I thanked him for patching me up. When I looked around for Lotty, he told me she had left after they decided to keep me overnight. I let myself be wheeled to an elevator, up several floors, and down a hallway to a patient room. A nurse undressed me, got a gown on me, and lifted me into bed as easily as if I were a baby, not a hundred-thirty-pound-plus detective.

"Just tell them not to wake me for morning blood pressure," I mumbled, and fell down a hole into sleep.

IX

Police at the Bar-B-Q

With the help of some good dope I slept until two Sunday afternoon. I couldn't believe it when I finally woke up: No one had roused me. The immutable hospital routine had let me be. It's good to have friends in high places.

An intern came in at three to check on me. She moved my arms and legs and shone an ophthalmoscope into my eyes.

"Dr. Pirwitz left discharge orders saying you can go home this afternoon if you feel up to it."

Dr. Pirwitz? I supposed he was the gray-haired surgeon. I'd never asked his name while he was putting me together.

"Good. I feel up to it." My jaw ached horribly and my shoulders were stiff enough that I winced when I moved them. But they would heal faster in the comfort of my own home than in a hospital.

She scribbled on my chart. Even if the patient only says, yeah, I feel like leaving, you have to leave an indelible trail on the chart.

"Okay. You're all set. Just take this paper with you to the

nursing station and they'll complete your discharge." She gave a cheerful smile and left.

I staggered out of bed and moved zombielike to the bathroom. Dressing was a process that made me aware of the myriad muscles in my arms and legs. Who would have thought there were so many?

I was putting on my shoes when Mr. Contreras appeared, hesitant, in the doorway. He was clutching a sheaf of daisies. His face cleared when he saw I was dressed.

"I came at one, but they told me you were sleeping. Oh, my, doll, have you seen your face? You look like you been in a barroom brawl. Well, it'll clear up. We'll get you home, put some raw steak on it—worked wonders on my black eyes when I was young."

I hadn't looked at my face. In fact, I'd carefully avoided the mirror when I'd washed up in the little bathroom.

"I'll take your word for it," I said grumpily. Now I couldn't resist going to the mirror above a sink on the side wall. I had not seen Sergio's handiwork last night. A dark line ran from about an inch below my left eye to my jawline. Transparent plastic clips pulled it together. In itself it didn't appear particularly terrible. It was the radiating swelling in purples and yellows and my bloodshot left eye that made me look like a wife-abuse casualty. I pulled the knit shirt away from my neck and saw a similar line, with some discoloring, running down to my collarbone.

"Who wills the end wills the means," I said grandly, not sure whether it was Sergio's means or my own headlong dive into his territory I was talking about.

"Don't worry, doll—it'll heal, you'll be good as new. You'll see. . . . I brought you these in case you was gonna be laid up awhile." He thrust the daisies at me.

I thanked him. "They're letting me leave now, so I'll take them home with me."

He followed me down the hall with a steady commentary on fights he'd been in as a machinist, the time his nose got broken, how he'd lost his left canine—pulling back his mouth with a stubby forefinger to show me the cap—what his wife had to say the time he came home drunk at four

A.M. with a black eye plus the man who'd given it to him in tow, happily singing "When Irish Eyes Are Smiling."

The checkout process went smoothly. Trying to attract paying customers in a run-down city neighborhood, Beth Israel maintained a high level of professionalism in all aspects of its operations. At least so Lotty always averred. The nurse who checked the doctor's orders and the clerk who processed my discharge both treated me with a smiling courtesy far different from Mrs. Kirkland's at Friendship. They gave me some special cleansers and salves, told me to come back in a week to get the stitches out, and sent me on my way.

The Cubs were playing a doubleheader against the hated Mets—Chicagoans can't forgive New York the '69 season. A year or so ago February some PR moron staged a reunion game between the '69 Cubs and Mets down in Arizona. Ron Santo refused to play—the only real Cub in the bunch. This year, it was even worse, with Chicago playing bush-league ball and the Mets coasting through the season.

Mr. Contreras obligingly tuned to WGN so I could hear Dwight Gooden fan Moreland, get Trillo to ground out and Davis to pop up in the infield. I was just as happy to be in a car and not in the stands, although as we drove by Wrigley Field the sun and the faint strains of the organ seemed inviting.

Mr. Contreras insisted on coming up to the third floor with me to make sure I got settled in comfortably. In addition to the daisies, he had bought a large steak and a bottle of whiskey, Bell's, which is too thin and sour for my taste. I was touched by the gesture and invited him to sit down and have a glass with me.

I sat on my little back porch with the whiskey and a radio tuned to the game while Mr. Contreras grilled a steak on our communal barbecue down in the yard. He was proud of his prowess as a chef, learned in the years since his wife had died. A couple of young Korean children belonging to one of the second-floor units cautiously played ball while he cooked: Mr. Contreras's joviality vanished in a hurry at threats to his tomatoes. Or property in general. Or his neighbors.

I was chewing in small, painful bites, made tolerable by a thin haze of whiskey, when the police arrived. I got up lazily on hearing the downstairs buzzer and called down through the intercom. When Detective Rawlings announced himself I vaguely remembered Dr. Pirwitz's saying the police wanted to see me. Hospitals report all assault cases routinely; the victim and the cops take it from there.

Detective Rawlings exuded a spurious geniality. He was in jeans and a T-shirt, which made the jacket he wore to hide his gun a bit incongruous. He had a uniformed man with him displaying the woodenness common to uniformed men when they fear their senior officers may embarrass them.

"Got yourself cut up a bit, huh, Ms. Warshawski?" Rawlings asked.

"Not so as anyone would notice. At least the surgeon didn't seem to think so. I'll have to tell him it didn't fool you."

"Guess I've seen too many knife wounds in my time. I don't fool so easy—at least over them. Now over the difference between a private eye and a lawyer, that stumps me sometimes. Which are you, Ms. W.—lawyer or detective?"

Mr. Contreras moved protectively to my side, but didn't make any effort to intervene. I politely introduced him to Rawlings before answering.

"Both, Detective. I'm a member of the Illinois bar in good standing. And I'm a licensed private investigator. Also in good standing. At least with the State of Illinois."

I returned to the armchair. Rawlings sat down on the couch at right angles to me. The uniformed man stood next to him, notebook at the ready. Mr. Contreras positioned himself behind my chair. Principals and seconds. When the handkerchief drops, both principals should be prepared to fire one shot.

"Why didn't you tell me you were a dick the other day, Warshawski?"

"The other day I wasn't. I came with Dr. Herschel in my

capacity as her attorney. She grew up with Storm Troopers hovering over her and has a permanent fear of men in uniform—unreasonable in Chicago, of course, but nevertheless . . .''

Rawlings narrowed his eyes at me. "You know, your name sounded so familiar the other day. After you left I asked the station sergeant. He remembered your dad, but that wasn't who I was thinking of. So I was talking to a buddy of mine downtown yesterday afternoon and mentioned you—Terry Finchley—and he told me how you were a private eye and all. And how his lieutenant, Bobby Mallory, starts herniating when you get near a case. And I was a little pissed at you. Thought about calling you, reading you the riot act, ordering you off my turf."

"What stopped you?"

"Oh, I don't know. Terry said you're a pain in the ass but you get results. I thought I'd see if you'd find something for me. I can tell already he was right about the first half. Now we'll see about the second. Who gave you the beauty marks?"

I shut my eyes. "I was a public defender a hundred years or so ago. Finchley tell you that? I ran into one of my former clients last night. He wasn't happy with my work. Can't please everybody, I guess."

"This has nothing to do with Malcolm Tregiere's death?"

"I don't think so. I could be wrong, but I think it was a private grudge."

"Where'd this happen?"

"Near North Side."

"How far—or near, maybe I should say."

"North Avenue," I said briefly. "Washtenaw."

"Humboldt Park? Now what the hell were you doing down there, Warshawski?"

I opened my eyes to see Rawlings leaning forward on the couch in his intensity. He appeared angry, but I might have been mistaken. Mr. Contreras was muttering to himself. Maybe he didn't like Rawlings calling me by my last name, of perhaps he thought the detective shouldn't swear at me.

"Talking to a disgruntled former client, Detective."

"The hell you were. The hell you say you were. That's Lion country. Those bastards are thumbing their noses at me every day *right here in my territory*"—a jabbing finger accented the words—"and I am *damned* if you are going to join them."

More clucking sounds from Mr. Contreras.

"It's like this, Rawlings," I said, putting all my on-my-honor-I-will-try sincerity into my voice. "Dr. Herschel has a nurse. The nurse had a kid sister. The sister became pregnant. A total write-off named Fabiano Hernandez was the father. Sister and infant died unfortunately last Tuesday out in Schaumburg—nothing sinister—complications of diabetes, pregnancy, and youth.

"Well, Hernandez has been seen cruising the streets in a car he certainly cannot afford, since he's unemployed—a chronic condition. So the family wanted to know what he was up to. They are very proud. They didn't want to be affiliated with a bum like Fabiano to begin with, and they don't want him making hay out of their sister's death. So they asked me to check it out. And he sort of hangs on Sergio Rodriguez's coattails. He went whining to Rodriguez who felt he owed me something for not getting him off the hook way back when. That's all there is to it."

Rawlings sucked in his cheeks. "And this had nothing—*nothing*—to do with Malcolm Tregiere's death?"

"Not as far as I know, Detective."

"Tregiere treat the dead girl?"

Police work makes you suspicious of everyone. Either Rawlings was very shrewd or someone had been squealing up the pipeline.

I nodded. "Dr. Herschel was her physician. But she sent Dr. Tregiere out to Schaumburg—she couldn't go herself."

"So did the punk kill him because he let his wife die?"

"Because he *thought* Tregiere let his wife die? I don't think so. He wanted out—he wanted to drop her when she refused to get an abortion. It was only because two of her brothers are substantial hulks that he was induced to stick with her. He's not a fighter. He spits at people, but he's pretty weak physically."

"How about the brothers? Sounds as if they cared enough about the girl to protect her."

I thought of Paul and his older brother, Herman. Either certainly could mangle a man Tregiere's size single-handedly, and what Diego lacked in size he made up for in ferocity. But I shook my head.

"They're all sane men. The one they might've killed was Fabiano. If they didn't touch him when their sister got pregnant, they wouldn't go after Dr. Tregiere—anyway, they liked him. They felt he'd done everything he could in a losing battle."

Rawlings snorted. "Don't be naïve, Warshawski. There are twenty-five bodies in the morgue right now put there by people who supposedly liked them." He got up. "We're going to go pick up Mr. Rodriguez, Warshawski. You want to swear out a complaint?"

The thought made my stomach turn over slightly. "Not especially—I don't want to add to his grudge count against me. Besides, you know he'll be back on the street in twenty-four hours."

"Look, Warshawski. He'll be back on the street, sure. And maybe he'll feel he owes you a bigger score. But I am sick of punks like him. The more times I hassle him, the more careful he may be."

I touched my left jaw involuntarily. "Yeah, yeah. You're right. I know you're right. Go ahead. Pick him up. I'll come down and say my lines in the play."

I walked to the door with him, the uniformed man trailing behind. Rawlings turned on the landing to look at me.

"If I find that you were withholding on Malcolm Tregiere, I am going to haul your ass in for obstruction so fast it's going to be smoking."

"Yeah, yeah. Drive carefully." I shut the door and locked it.

Mr. Contreras shook his head. "Disgusting the way he talked to you, cookie. And you have to sit and take it. You oughta call a lawyer is what you oughta do."

I laughed a little, getting violent feedback from the

stitches in my face. "Don't let it trouble you. I wouldn't last a minute on the street if a little tough talk got to me."

We went back to dinner, now cold but still tasty. Mr. Contreras had grilled some fresh tomatoes along with the meat. They were easy to chew and had the rich flavor that only homegrown tomatoes have these days. I'd eaten three when the phone rang, Lotty calling to check up on me. And to remind me that Consuelo's funeral was tomorrow. And Victoria Charlotte's.

Then Paul phoned, and finally Tessa, who'd heard about my action-packed night from Lotty. She was far more sympathetic.

"Jesus, Vic—if I'd known you'd get yourself badly hurt I would never have pushed you so hard. I wasn't thinking—I should have realized anyone who would beat Malcolm's brains out wouldn't think twice about hurting you."

I responded with a Sam Spade toughness I was far from feeling, telling her it was a good sign when you got a little reaction on the street: It meant you were hitting the right nerve. It sounded good, but it didn't mean anything. I had no idea whether the Lions had killed Malcolm. And if they had, I had no idea why.

After Tessa hung up, I told Mr. Contreras that I was getting a little worn down and needed to rest. He obligingly cleaned up the dishes and took the remains of the steak downstairs for his cat.

"Now, listen, doll—I may be a hundred years old, but I got good ears. Anyone comes gunning for you, I'll hear 'em coming and head 'em off."

"Anyone comes gunning for me here, you call the police. And stay inside with your door locked."

He cocked a defiant eyebrow at me, prepared to argue the point at length. I bade him a firm good-bye and bolted my own doors, back and front. Any door can be broken down by someone who wants to badly enough, but I had extra-heavy ones installed when I moved in, with good locks. I've been attacked at home too many times to treat the prospect lightly.

X

Doctor in Mourning

I lay down with the radio turned low to the game. At first I could vaguely hear Harry Caray's inane screaming, but as I relaxed the noise faded to a buzz and I lapsed into a feverish dream.

I was outside the high, cyclone fence surrounding my high school's athletic field, watching a baseball game. Bill Buckner was on third. He turned and saw me and beckoned to me to climb the fence to join him. I started to climb but my right leg was paralyzed. I looked down and saw the mute mournful face of the baby staring at me as she clutched my pantleg. I couldn't dislodge her without hurting her and she would not let go of my jeans. The scene switched, but wherever I went, whatever else was going on, the baby clung to me.

I knew I was sleeping and wanted desperately to climb out of the quicksand of dreams. Whether because of the three scotches or the drugs they'd given me at the hospital, I couldn't make myself wake up. A ringing phone became part of a nightmare about hiding from SS guards, with the baby clinging to my shirt and wailing. I finally wrenched

70

myself from sleep into consciousness and groped with a leaden arm for the receiver.

"H'lo," I said thickly.

"Miss Warshawski?"

It was a light tenor that was vaguely familiar. I struggled to rouse myself, clearing my throat.

"Yes. Who is this?"

"Peter Burgoyne, from Friendship Hospital in Schaumburg. Have I called at a bad time?"

"No. No. I've just been sleeping. I wanted to wake up. Hold on."

I got sluggishly to my feet and staggered to the bathroom. I took off my clothes, which I hadn't changed when I came back from the hospital, and stood under a cold shower, letting water run through my hair and over my sore face. I knew Burgoyne was waiting, but I took an extra minute for a shampoo—clean hair is the key to an alert mind.

Wrapping myself in a large terry-cloth robe, I padded with a semblance of energy back to the bedroom. Burgoyne was still attached to the other end of the line.

"Sorry to keep you waiting. I was in an accident last night—I've been sleeping off some drug the hospital gave me."

"Accident! Car wreck? I assume you weren't hurt badly or you wouldn't be home?"

"No, just cut up a bit around the face. An ugly sight but not a mortal condition."

"Well, maybe I should call another time," he offered dubiously.

"No, no, this is fine. What's up?"

When he saw Malcolm's death in the papers he'd been devastated. "What a blow for you after the girl and her baby died. And now you've been in an accident, too. I'm sorry."

"Thanks. It's good of you to call."

"Look. . . . I want to go to the girl's funeral. Maybe I shouldn't, but I feel pretty depressed that we couldn't save her."

"It's tomorrow," I said. "Holy Sepulchre Church at Kennedy and Fullerton. One o'clock."

"I know—I checked with the family. The thing is, I feel awkward going by myself. I wondered—do you think—were you going?"

I ground my teeth. "Yeah, sure, I'll go with you," I said unenthusiastically. "Do you want to meet at the church, or would you rather come to my apartment?"

"You're sure you're up to it? You don't sound as though you really want to go."

"I don't want to go. And you're the third caller today to remind me about it. But I'll be there, so if you want a barricade I guess I can provide it."

He decided to come to my apartment at twelve-thirty—easier than looking for each other in the crowd of family, nuns, and schoolmates who would be packing the church. I gave him directions and hung up.

I wondered if Burgoyne lost many patients—if he did, he must feel chewed up all the time. Maybe the relatively high standard of living in the northwest suburbs meant that he didn't have a lot of high-risk pregnant women using his beautiful neonatal-care center. Maybe Consuelo was the first pregnant teenager he'd treated since leaving Chicago. Or maybe he really hadn't started treating her right away because he thought she was an indigent Mexican.

I called Lotty to let her know I wouldn't be going to the funeral with her and went back to bed. This time I slept soundly and dreamlessly and woke a little after five the next morning.

I put on shorts and a sweatshirt and walked the two miles to the harbor to watch the sun burst over the lake. The fisherman—or some fisherman—was there again casting into the slate-still water. I wondered if he ever caught anything, but didn't want to disturb the Dutch-landscape beauty of the scene by talking to him. On the way home I tried jogging a few blocks, but the motion set up an unpleasant shaking in my face. Give it a few more days.

Mr. Contreras opened his front door as I came into the lobby.

"Just checking that it was someone who belonged here, doll. You feeling better today?"

"Much, thanks." I went on up the stairs. Morning is not my favorite part of the day—this was the first time all summer I'd been outside early enough to see the sun rise—and I wasn't in the mood for chitchat.

I went to a small safe I'd had built into the wall in the hall closet and took out my gun. I don't often carry it, but if Rawlings picked up Sergio and I signed the complaint I might need it. I cleaned the Smith & Wesson carefully and loaded it. With the clip in, it weighed over two pounds, an awkward weight if you're not used to it. I stuck it into my waistband and spent some time practicing getting it out and releasing the safety quickly. I really should go to a range regularly, but it's one of a myriad high-discipline projects I can't force myself to undertake.

After a quarter hour or so of practice I put the gun away and wandered out to the kitchen. Yogurt with fresh blueberries went down easily so I had two bowls with the morning *Herald-Star*. Gooden had shut the Cubs out in the first game, but under the smooth arm of Scot Sanderson the good guys had come back 7–2 in the second.

I put the bowl into the sink. Thanks to Mr. Contreras's work, it was the only dirty dish in the house. Maybe I should have him up for dinner every Sunday.

I surveyed the living room. Clutter to live by. But I was damned if I was going to clean house just because Burgoyne had invited himself to Consuelo's funeral. By the same logic I left the bed unmade and added my shorts and sweatshirt to several other garments draped across a chair.

I went into the bathroom to inspect the damage. The reddish-purples in my face were already trailing away to greens and yellows. When I pressed my tongue underneath the wound, it pulled against the stitches but the wound didn't gape apart. Dr. Pirwitz had been right—this was going to clear up pretty fast. It seemed to me makeup would only accentuate the horrors of the flesh; I limited my toilet to a careful washing and anointing of the wound with the salves given me at Beth Israel.

For the funeral, I picked a navy suit whose bolero jacket ended low enough on the hips to cover the gun. Its rayon-linen blend would be tolerable, if not wonderful, in the heat. With a white lawn blouse, sheer navy pantyhose, and low-heeled black pumps, I looked like a candidate for convent school.

When Burgoyne arrived a little before twelve-thirty, I buzzed him in through the street door, then went out to the landing to see what Mr. Contreras might do. Sure enough, he arrived promptly on the scene. I laughed quietly to myself as I eavesdropped.

"Excuse me, young man, but where are you going?"

Burgoyne, startled: "I'm visiting one of the tenants on the third floor."

"Warshawski or Cummings?"

"Why do you want to know?" Burgoyne used his doctor-to-hysterical-patient voice.

"I've got my reasons, young man. Now, I don't want to have to call the cops, so who are you visiting?"

Before Mr. Contreras got to the point of demanding a driver's license, I called down that I knew who it was.

"Okay, doll." Mr. Contreras's voice floated back up. "Just wanted to make sure he wasn't friends of friends you don't want calling on you, if you get me."

I thanked him gravely and waited on the landing for Burgoyne. He ran up lightly and reached the top without breathing hard. In a navy summer suit, with his dark hair washed and combed, he looked younger and happier than he'd seemed at the hospital.

"Hi," he said. "Good to see you again. . . . Who's the old man?"

"Neighbor. Good friend. He's feeling in a protective mood, but it's well-intentioned—don't let it upset you."

"No, no. It doesn't. You ready? You want to go in my car?"

"Just a second." I went inside to fetch a hat. Not for religious scruples. I was taking very seriously the idea of keeping direct summer sun off my face.

"That's quite a cut you got there." Burgoyne looked closely at my face. "Looks like you were hit by a piece of flying glass. I thought most windshields crumbled these days instead of shattering."

"I was cut by a piece of metal," I explained, double-locking the door.

Burgoyne drove an '86 Nissan Maxima. The car was beautifully appointed, with leather seats, a leather dashboard, individual six-way seat controls, and, naturally, a phone resting over the universal joint. I sank back in the bucket seat. No city sounds reached us, and the air-conditioning, which kept the car at 69 degrees, was noiseless. If I'd gone into corporate law and kept my mouth shut when I was supposed to, I'd be driving a car like this. But then I'd never have met Sergio or Fabiano. You can't have everything in this life.

"How'd you get Monday afternoon off for a funeral?" I asked idly.

He smiled briefly. "I'm in charge of OB at Friendship— I simply tell people I'm taking off."

I was impressed and said so. "You're pretty young to have moved so fast, aren't you?"

He shook his head. "Not really. I think I told you I went out there when they were just starting to build up their obstetrical service. So I have seniority. That's all. Just like being a pipefitter."

It took a scant ten minutes to cover the three miles to the church. We had no trouble finding a parking space in the derelict streets. Burgoyne carefully locked the Maxima and switched on its alarm. It might slow down the less enterprising of the neighborhood's youth, at least in broad daylight.

Holy Sepulchre had been built sixty years ago as part of a large Polish community. In its heyday, close to a thousand people attended the main Sunday mass. Now, even a multitude of Alvarados, an entire convent of nuns, and dozens of schoolgirls could not fill the nave. Unadorned stone pillars disappeared high overhead into a vaulted ceiling. A high altar attached to the wall was lit fitfully by many candles: Holy Sepulchre had stood firm against many of the changes of Vatican II. The windows had been covered with wire netting to protect the few remaining pieces of stained glass, adding to the church's dark, forbidding atmosphere. Any color was provided by the schoolgirls, who were dressed in bright pastels. I liked the Catholic custom of not wearing mourning for the funeral of a child.

Lotty was sitting by herself about two thirds of the way up the aisle, looking severe in black. I went up to sit next to her, Burgoyne trailing meekly in my wake. In a hasty undertone I performed introductions. Lotty nodded briefly.

The organ played softly as people went to the front of the church to kneel at the flower-laden coffins. Mrs. Alvarado sat in the front row with her five other children. I could see the back of her head nod stiffly as various people stopped to condole with her.

The music increased a few decibels. Under its cover, Lotty leaned her head next to my ear and muttered, "Fabiano's sitting three rows up with his mother. Take a look at him."

I followed her discreetly pointing finger, but could see only his slouched shoulders and a one-eighth view of his face. I raised inquiring eyebrows at Lotty.

"Go up to the front and catch his face on your way back."

I obediently wriggled past Burgoyne and joined the pious procession to the coffins. Casting a perfunctory glance at the flowers and the photograph on Consuelo's, and avoiding a look at the miniature box next to her, I turned to Mrs. Alvarado. She accepted my courtesies with a sorrowful smile. I gave Carol's hand a quick squeeze and turned back down the aisle.

Looking soberly at the floor, I sneaked an oblique glance at Fabiano. I was so startled that I nearly lost my composure. Someone had worked him over thoroughly. His face was badly swollen, covered in purples and blacks that made my wound look like a shaving cut.

Burgoyne got up to let me back into the pew.

"Who did that?" I demanded of Lotty.

She hunched a shoulder. "I thought you might know. His mother showed up at the clinic this morning to get a salve for him, but since he wouldn't come with her, I couldn't let

her have anything. She made him come to the funeral—
Carol told me he was going to stay away.''

One of the traditionally garbed nuns a few rows in front
of us turned to give us a basilisk glare, putting a forefinger
to her lips. We obediently lapsed into silence, but as the
processional started, Lotty muttered at me again.

''You're wearing your gun, aren't you?''

I grinned but didn't say anything, concentrating my attention on the priest.

The mass was conducted in Spanish, at such a rapid rate
that I couldn't follow it. Conseulo's schoolmates sang an
anthem, and the priest preached a sermon in Spanish, which
I picked up parts of. Consuelo's name figured a number of
times, as did Victoria Charlotte's. I gathered that we were
bemoaning the cutting off of life before it had had a chance
to flower, but that God would sort it all out at some later
date. This struck me as pretty grim counsel, but from what
I'd seen of Mrs. Alvarado it probably satisfied her reasonably well.

It took a scant forty minutes to do all this, including
giving communion to all the frilly dressed girls and the
Alvarados. The organ piped up again and the church began
to empty. Burgoyne made his way against the tide to Mrs.
Alvarado. I leaned back and rubbed my eyes.

''I've done all I think I'm up to,'' I announced to Lotty.
''Are you going to the cemetery with them?''

She grimaced. ''I'm no crazier about this charade of piety
than you are. Besides, I need to get back to the clinic.
Mondays are our busiest day and I don't have Carol to help
me. . . . Your face is looking better. How are you feeling?''

I made a face. ''Oh, more bruised in spirit than body, I
guess. I'm a little nervous of what Sergio will do after the
police pick him up. And it makes me really nervous to think
I was so far off base on him—thinking he'd be reasonably
pleased to see me, instead of bearing a grudge all these
years.''

I told Lotty what he'd said about my treating him like a
worm. ''He has a point, you know. But the thing is, if I'd
been at all sensitive to that—how I'd treated him, how he'd

77

felt about it—I wouldn't have gone off to see him alone. So it makes me wonder about my judgment."

Burgoyne reappeared at the pew, waiting politely while we gathered handbags—and in Lotty's case gloves. We strolled outside together. Burgoyne looked nervously at Lotty.

"I'm sorry we couldn't save Consuelo, Dr. Herschel. I wondered if—I'm sure Dr. Tregiere gave you a report, but maybe you have some questions? If I could see a copy of what he wrote, I might be able to fill in the gaps on what we did before he got there."

Lotty looked at him measuringly. "Dr. Tregiere was killed before he got a chance to give his report to me. So I would be most obliged if you would send me a complete record of your treatment." She fished in her handbag for a card for him, then put a reassuring hand on my shoulder.

"You'll be okay, Vic. You're fundamentally sound. Trust yourself."

XI

Artistic License

I caught up with Paul Alvarado before he got into the limousine that was to carry him to the cemetery. He and Diego, looking uncomfortable in black suits, were waiting for their mother to finish talking to one of the nuns. Paul bent over to kiss me underneath the brim of my straw hat. He took the opportunity to inspect my face.

"Lotty told Carol what happened, Vic. I'm real sorry—sorry you got messed up with that heap of garbage because of us."

I shook my head. "It wasn't because of you—I was trying to find out something about Malcolm for Lotty. . . . I saw Fabiano. Was that your handiwork?"

Paul stared at me solemnly.

"You don't know anything about it, huh? And Diego doesn't either, I suppose?"

Diego grinned. "You got it, Vic."

"Look, guys—I appreciate the spirit. But I'm nervous enough about Sergio as it is. What's he going to think when Fabiano comes whining to him?"

Paul put an arm around me. "I have a feeling, Vic, that

79

the boy is not going to go crying to the Lions. The way I heard it, he was driving that Eldorado of his too fast, braked suddenly, and went into the windshield. The way I heard it, that's what he was going to tell Sergio if he asked.''

Burgoyne was listening to the conversation with a puzzled frown. Before he could ask about these unknown people, the nun finally detached herself from Mrs. Alvarado, who moved with stately dignity to the waiting limo. Burgoyne took her hand, told her once more how sorry he was, and helped her into the car. Paul and Diego shook my hand warmly and joined their mother. Herman, Carol, and the third sister, Alicia, followed in a second car. A bevy of other close relatives took up an additional four limos; it was quite a procession. Burgoyne and I watched it down the street before getting back into his Maxima.

"Feeling better now?" I asked sardonically.

"Mrs. Alvarado is remarkably composed for a bereaved mother," he answered seriously, pulling out onto Fullerton. "It makes it much easier for people to talk to her."

"You were expecting a frantic display of Latin emotion? She's a woman with a lot of dignity."

"Those were her sons you were talking to? I wondered. . . . Maybe it's none of my business, but did someone attack you? I thought you got that cut in a car accident."

I grinned at him. "You're right—it isn't your business. An old client of mine felt he had a long-standing score to settle and took after me with a knife. It didn't have anything to do with Consuelo, so don't extend your bleeding heart to crying over me."

He looked startled. "Is that how I look to you? Being dramatic over a patient's death? Maybe I am. But this is the first obstetrical patient who's died since I've been at Friendship. Maybe it's something I should be used to, but I'm not." He turned east onto Belmont.

We drove in silence for a few blocks, I feeling a bit embarrassed by my remark, he brooding perhaps on Consuelo's death. At Ashland Avenue, the traffic gummed up suddenly—the Cubs were playing a late-starting game and happy fans were packing the streets.

"How did she actually die?" I asked. "Consuelo, I mean."

"Heart failure. Her heart simply stopped beating. I was at home. They called me, but by the time I got there, she was dead. Dr. Herschel arrived about five minutes after I'd left again. I live only fifteen minutes from the hospital."

"Wasn't there an autopsy?"

He grimaced. "Oh, yes. And the county gets involved and wants a report, too. And the state, I suppose—haven't heard from them yet. I could tell you the ugly technical details, but it boils down to the fact that her heart stopped beating. Very disturbing in a young girl. I don't understand it. Maybe her diabetes . . ."

He shook his head and inched forward to Racine. Outside my apartment he fiddled with the steering wheel for a minute, then finally said, "We haven't exactly met under ideal circumstances, but I'd like to get to know you a little better. Could we have dinner sometime? Tonight, maybe? I'm taking the rest of the afternoon off—have to run an errand in the Loop, but I could pick you up here around six-thirty."

"Sure," I said lightly. "That'd be fine."

I swung my legs carefully out of the car so as not to run the stockings and went inside. Mr. Contreras didn't appear—I supposed he was out with his tomatoes. Just as well. I could use a few minutes of silence. Upstairs I took out my gun, laid it carefully on the dresser, and stripped down to my underwear. Even though the suit was a lightweight summer weave, between it and the automatic I'd gotten extremely warm and damp by the end of the service.

I lay on the floor of the living room for a while, watching the start of the game and trying to decide what further action I could take in the matter of Malcolm's death. Since leaving Sergio's late Saturday night my head had been fogged—first by pain and humiliation, then dope. This was my first opportunity to think clearly about the situation.

Sergio was a charming sociopath. At eighteen, when I was defending him, he had told the most alarming lies with great plausibility. If I hadn't had a well-documented police report I'm not sure I would ever have realized this in time to save him from being ripped apart in court. As it was, his fury had been extreme when I questioned him. He changed stories, not for the better, and it was some time before we came up with something that would stand up under examination.

He certainly could have killed Malcolm without turning a hair and lied about it with a smile later. Or given the orders for someone else to kill him, as he probably did these days. But the only reason for him to do so would have been at Fabiano's request.

But Fabiano, while a whiner and a jerk, didn't have Sergio's psychotic outlook. And anyway, Fabiano didn't stand that well with the Lions—I couldn't picture Sergio committing murder at his behest—he'd be more likely to taunt and humiliate Fabiano. I got the feeling that Fabiano knew something about Malcolm's death. But not that he had been involved in it directly. Maybe the beating he'd gotten would soften him up. I'd have to try talking to him again.

I pulled myself to my feet and glanced briefly at the TV. The Cubs were trailing 4–0 in the second. Looked like a good day to be detecting instead of sitting in the bleachers. I turned off the set, pulled on blue jeans and a yellow cotton top, stuck the gun into a shoulder bag, and left. A glance out the kitchen window before departing showed Mr. Contreras deep in communion with his plants. I didn't interrupt them.

Tessa Reynolds's studio was in a part of town known as Ukrainian Village. Not too far from Humboldt Park, it is a working-class neighborhood making a reincarnation as an artists' quarter. Tessa had bought a three-flat with city loans when the area was just starting its comeback. She had renovated the place with scrupulous care. The top two units were rented out to artists and students. The ground floor included her studio and living quarters.

Her work space took up most of the apartment. She had knocked out the south and west walls on the first floor and replaced them with bullet-resistant sheet glass. This project had taken two years and had left her with enormous debts to design and construction friends who handled the wiring and plumbing problems. But the result was a large, light studio ideally suited for the massive metal pieces that were her primary output. The glass slid open to allow her to move finished work outside with a gantry she'd installed overhead. Buyers could bring their trucks down the alley on which her backyard faced.

I parked my car in front of the building and followed the brick walk around to the back without bothering to ring the bell. As I'd assumed, Tessa was in her studio, the glass doors open to let in the summer air. I stood in the entrance a moment—her concentration was so intense I hesitated to interrupt. She was holding a broom, but staring unseeing in front of her. An African-print scarf covered her hair, strongly accentuating her high Ashanti cheekbones. Then she caught sight of me, let the broom fall, and called to me to come in.

"I can't work these days, so I thought I'd use the time to clean up. And halfway through the sweeping I thought of what I wanted to do. I'm going to make a few sketches while it's in my mind. Help yourself to juice or coffee."

She retired to a drawing board in one corner and was busy with charcoal for a few minutes. I wandered around looking at bronze and steel bars and sheets, at massive cutting torches and metal files, and a few finished pieces. One was a fifteen-foot bronze whose jutting jagged edges gave a feeling of great energy. "For a bank," Tessa commented briefly. "Called *Economy in Action*."

She finished her sketches and came over to me. Tessa tops my five feet eight by two or three inches. She took me by the shoulders and looked down at my face. I was beginning to feel like charging admission for the show.

"They ripped you good, babe—you leave any traces on them?"

"Alas, no. Probably a few bruises, but nothing lasting . . . Could we talk about Malcolm? I've got a feeling one of the punks who attacked me knows more than he's saying, but before I tackle him again I'd like to try to get a little more information."

She pursed her lips. "Like what?"

"His mother brought him to Chicago when he was nine, didn't she? Would you know if he had any kind of history with the gangs when he was younger?"

Her eyes glittered dangerously. "You're not going to take the police line, are you—that crime victims bring their sorry fate onto themselves?"

"Look, Tessa. Between you and Lotty I'm reaching the end of a stock of patience that was small to begin with. You both want me to look into Malcolm's death. Then you want to dictate and preach at me how I go about it. If Malcolm ran with the gangs when he was growing up it's possible his past caught up with him. If he didn't, then I can eliminate that exhausting and unpleasant field of inquiry and concentrate on the present. Okay?"

She continued to stare angrily at me—Tessa hates to lose fights.

"Just as well Detective Rawlings can't see you now—he figures you're strong enough to beat someone's brains in, and if he saw that look on your face he'd know you had the will to do it, too," I told her.

That brought a reluctant smile. "Oh, okay, Vic. Have it your way."

She took me over to the corner by her drafting table where she had a couple of stools we could perch on. "I'd known Malcolm going on twelve years. We were both students at Circle, me in art, him in science. He always liked tall women, being a shrimp himself. So I knew him pretty well, what with one thing and another.

"His mama was quite a lady. Some folks say she was a witch. They say her ghost walks now that she's dead. She didn't want Malcolm running with bad boys, and I'm telling you, he did what she said—the whole block did what she said. You got a lady who can wither your privates, you do what the lady wants. So you can be confident he stayed out of the gangs."

"Wish I'd known her when I was with the county." I grinned appreciatively. "The day he was killed, you stopped by to see him. Was he expecting you?"

She raised her eyebrows, tightened her face, then decided

not to get angry. "Yep. A guy with a schedule like Malcolm's you do not drop in on on the chance he'll be home."

"So you talked to him during the day? Did he say anything that might make you think he was expecting anyone else?"

She shook her head. "I didn't talk to him—I called the hospital and they said he was home. So I called his place and got his machine. He turned it on when he was trying to sleep. He always left the time he'd be returning calls—and that was our agreement, that that would be a time he'd be home, so that was when I'd plan to see him."

"So anyone who called would get the message and know when he'd be there."

She nodded. "But, Vic—hell, even if someone left a message on the machine—hey, Malcolm Tregiere, I'm going to bash your brains in—we *know* who did it."

I cocked an eyebrow. "*We?* Speak for yourself. I don't."

She ran a strong finger lightly over my face. "Why the hell did he cut you, babe? You were asking him about Malcolm, weren't you?"

"Tessa, this is where we started. If Sergio killed Malcolm, he had to have a reason. And you just finished telling me he had no reason—that Malcolm never ran with the gangs and Sergio wouldn't know him from Adam."

She hunched her shoulders impatiently. "Maybe he didn't have a reason. Maybe he broke in and found Malcolm at home. Or thought he'd be carrying morphine. Uptown ain't a honky high-rise, Vic— people *know* who you are. They knew Malcolm was a doctor."

My temper finally got the better of me. "I don't have voodoo connections; I can't go after a guy because you've got second sight into what he did."

Tessa gave me her Ashanti Queen look, arrogant and menacing. "What are you going to do about it? Piss and moan?"

"I'm doing what I can. Which is talk to the cops. Get Sergio hauled in for assault. But we don't have one shred of evidence that he went near Malcolm. And I'm not convinced in my heart of hearts that he did."

Tessa's eyes glittered again. "So you're going to sit on your ass? I'm really ashamed of you, Vic. I thought you had more courage than to act so chicken shit."

Blood rushed to my head. "Goddamn your eyes, Tessa. Chicken shit? I put my body on the line Saturday night. I'm talking to you with thirty stitches in my face and you're calling me names. I'm not Sylvester Stallone. I can't shoot a roomful of people and ask questions later. Christ!"

I slid off the stool and headed toward the door.

"Vic?"

Tessa's voice, small and tentative, stopped me. I turned back to her, still furious. Tears glistened on her face.

"Vic. I'm sorry. I really am. I'm off my head about Malcolm. I don't know why I thought yelling at you would bring him back to life."

I went over to her and put my arms around her. "Yeah, babe."

We embraced without speaking for a while.

"Tessa. I really do want to do what I can to clear up Malcolm's death. But there's fuck all to go on. Maybe I could listen to his phone machine—if it's still around—maybe at least we'd know if someone tried threatening him. Who has his personal effects?"

She shook her head. "I think everything's still locked up in his apartment. Lotty probably has the keys—Malcolm named her his executor, next of kin, all that stuff." She smiled briefly. "Probably she was the closest thing to a witch he could find after his mother died—I always wondered if that was what drew him to her."

"I wouldn't be surprised." I gently disengaged myself. "I have a date with a rich doctor tonight—the man who worked on Consuelo with Malcolm out in suburbia last week."

Her eyes narrowed in a rueful smile. "I take it back, Vic. You on the case, girl." She hesitated, then said seriously, "Be careful with those guys, V. I. You only got the one face, you know."

XII

House Call

Burgoyne took me to a small Spanish restaurant he used to frequent in his student days. He was greeted like a long-lost son by the effusive owner and his wife—"So long since we have seen you, Señor Burgoyne—we thought you had moved away." They handpicked a dinner for us, whose tender presentation made up for deficiencies of taste. When the coffee and Spanish brandy arrived, they finally retreated to other diners and left us to talk a bit.

Burgoyne was more relaxed than he'd been in the afternoon. He apologized for his self-absorption and announced a moratorium on medical topics for the evening. I asked him instead about life in the northwest suburbs.

"It's everything they tell you about," he said, smiling. "Clean, quiet, beautiful, and dull. If the commute wouldn't be a nightmare I'd move back to the city in a flash. I'm not married, so I don't care about schools and parks and all that stuff. And I can't seem to fit into the local social scene. Aerobics and golf are the hot topics and I'm not too interested in either."

"Sounds like a problem. Why not give up your perks and move back to an urban hospital?"

He made a face. "My dad always said no one was born to the purple—anyone can get used to it. I learned in a hurry after joining Friendship that it's easier to get used to a standard of living than it is to move down from it."

"So you move from five hundred thousand a year to two hundred. You won't die, and I bet some lady would still find you attractive."

He finished his brandy. "You're probably right—except for your inflated notion of what Friendship thinks I'm worth." He grinned engagingly. "Ready to leave? Would you like a moon-lit stroll on the beach?"

As we drove to the lake, Burgoyne asked if I knew anything about police progress in investigating Tregiere's death. I told him it was likely to be a slow process if the killers weren't known to him. Terrorism, as the police categorize that kind of killing, is the hardest to resolve.

"But don't feel they're not going to keep resources devoted to it. Rawlings—the detective in charge—seems like a pretty dogged guy. And no murder case is ever considered closed. One of these days they're going to get an informant or a co-incidental crime that will break the thing open. Or maybe I'll get lucky."

He pulled into the parking lot at Montrose. We drove around slowly, looking for an open slot—the city pours onto the lake-front on warm nights. Radios blared. Children shrieked in the background behind necking couples. Bands of youths with six-packs and reefer stationed themselves with fishing gear on the rocks, prepared to intercept any passing young women.

Burgoyne found a space next to an outsize, rusting van. He waited until he'd turned off the engine before speaking again.

"You're looking into Tregiere's death?"

"Sort of. If it was a terrorist murder the police will solve it. If someone he knew killed him I may sort it out. I don't suppose he said anything significant when you were working on Consuelo, did he?"

I could feel him looking at me in the dark. "Is that supposed to be a joke?" he finally asked. "I don't know you well enough to tell when you're trying to be funny. No, all we talked about was the patient's erratic heartbeat.''

We joined the throngs and climbed down the rocks to the lake. At the water's edge the crowd diminished and we found a spot to ourselves. I slipped off my sandals and dangled my feet in the water. The lake had warmed up again and lapped against me in a gentle caress.

Burgoyne wanted to know how I proceeded with an investigation.

"Oh, I talk to people. If they get angry, then I think they know something. So I poke around and talk to more people. And after a while I've learned a whole lot of stuff and some of it starts fitting into a pattern. Not very scientific, I'm afraid.''

"A lot like medicine.'' In the moonlight I could see his knees hunched up to his chin with his arms wrapped around them. "Although we have all this incredible technology, most diagnosis is still a matter of asking a lot of questions and eliminating possibilities. . . . With Tregiere's death, who are you talking to?''

"People who knew him. People who might have known him in the wrong context.''

"That isn't how you got your face cut open, is it?''

"Well, actually, yes. But I've been hurt worse than this—this is just scary because no one wants to be disfigured.''

"What was Tregiere's relationship to Dr. Herschel?'' he asked curiously. "Was he her partner?''

"Sort of. He took the clinic three mornings a week so she could make rounds, and he had an office there for his own patients. He was board-certified in obstetrics, but was completing a fellowship in perinatology.''

"So she's pretty upset by his death?''

"Yeah, you could say that. It also puts her into a major bind with her workload.'' I swatted at some mosquitoes that were beginning their high-pitched hum around my face.

He was quiet for a minute, staring out at the lake. Then he said abruptly, "I hope she doesn't blame us for Consuelo's death.''

I tried looking at him, but couldn't make out his face in the dark. "You worry too much," I said. "Send her the report you mentioned and try to put it out of your mind."

The mosquitoes started to bite more seriously. My face, with its scent of blood close to the surface, was particularly attractive to them. I swatted a few, then told Burgoyne I thought the time had come to leave. He helped me to my feet, then put an arm around me and kissed me. It seemed perfectly natural; I swatted away another few bugs and kissed him back.

As we walked arm in arm up the rocks, he asked how much danger it would take before I dropped an investigation.

"I don't know," I said. "I don't think in those terms. There've been a couple of times when people have tried to kill me, and not in pleasant ways. So I figure my job is to think faster than they do. When I can't do that anymore, or move fast enough, then it'll be time to move to Barrington and start taking aerobics classes."

"So I couldn't suggest that you back out of it so you don't get hurt worse?" he said tentatively.

"You can suggest anything," I said, pulling my arm away. "But you don't have any claims on me and it would piss me off in a major way to have you butting into my business."

"Well, I don't want that—I like you better in your non-pissed-off state. Can we erase the last minute or so of tape?"

He took my hand again tentatively. I laughed reluctantly and put it back around his waist.

Mr. Contreras came out into the hall as I unlocked the front door. He was carrying a pipe wrench. He looked at our linked arms and spoke ostentatiously to me, ignoring Burgoyne.

"We didn't have any visitors tonight, if you know what I mean, doll. You have a good time?"

"Very, thanks." I pulled my arm away from Burgoyne, feeling a little foolish.

"I'm turning in now—just wanted to make sure you got home okay. . . . You want to make sure that front door closes all the way when you go out, young man. The catch doesn't lock unless you pull it hard. I don't want to get up in the morning and find we've got a lot of trash in the front hall because the bums could find their way in."

He looked Burgoyne over fiercely, swinging the pipe wrench

suggestively, bade me a final good-night, and retreated into his apartment.

Burgoyne gave a soft whistle of relief as we headed upstairs. "I was afraid he was going to come up with us to supervise."

"I know." I made a rueful face as I unlocked my apartment door. "I haven't felt like this since I was sixteen and my dad waited up for me."

I pulled out two of my mother's red Venetian glasses and poured a couple of brandies. We took them into the bedroom with us, where I summarily dumped everything that was on the bed onto a chair, and lay down in the crumpled sheets. Burgoyne was either too much of a gentleman, or too inflamed with my manifest charms, to comment on the chaos.

We drank and necked, but my mind was half on the glasses—it had been a mistake to get them out. Finally I took Peter's and put it carefully under the bed with mine.

"This is the only real legacy I have from my mother," I explained. "She smuggled them out of Italy in the one suitcase she could carry when she left, and I can't think about anything else when I'm worrying about them."

"Just as well," he murmured into my neck. "I can't think about two things at once, anyway."

For the next hour or so he demonstrated the value a good knowledge of anatomy can have in the right hands. My detective experience came in handy, too.

We fell asleep in a damp heap. Burgoyne's beeper woke me with a start at three—a patient had started labor but his associate was covering. At six his watch alarm twittered urgently; even a suburban doctor has to be on duty early. I woke up long enough to lock the door behind him, and went back to bed.

At nine I got up again; did some exercises to keep loose while my face healed, and dressed for work: jeans, oxfords, loose shirt, and gun. I anointed my face, put on a wide-brimmed straw hat, and went out to greet the day. Before hunting out Fabiano I drove over to Lotty's clinic to get the key to Malcolm's apartment.

XIII

Open Clinic

Lotty operates out of a storefront on Damen Avenue. Damen runs most of the length of the city, and a ride along it is a ride through the heart of Chicago's identity, past sharply segregated ethnic communities—Lithuanians from blacks, blacks from Hispanics, Hispanics from Poles—as you travel north. Lotty's clinic is on a tired part of the long avenue, with a mix of houses and small shops all straggling on the edge of decay. Most of the people who live there are retired, maintaining dilapidated bungalows on Social Security. It's a quiet area, with not much violent crime and usually plenty of street parking. But not today.

A police car blocked the intersection where I wanted to turn right, its lights flashing. Beyond it, I could see hordes of people in the streets and on the sidewalks. A mobile television van stood out above the crowd; no other cars were out. I wondered if some local saint was being honored with a parade; perhaps Lotty hadn't even opened the clinic.

I leaned out my car window to call to the uniformed men in the car. "What's going on down there?"

With usual police informativeness, the driver answered, "Street's closed, lady. You'll have to go down Seeley."

I ended up parking four blocks away and found a pay phone on a corner as I walked back over. I tried Lotty's apartment first, convinced that she hadn't come in to the clinic. When there was no answer, I rang her office. The line was busy.

I came at the building from the south. Here the crowds weren't quite as heavy, although there was another police car at the far end of the block. The air was filled with shouts coming through a bullhorn and indistinguishable chants. The sound was familiar to me from my student-protest days long ago—a demonstration. I noticed uneasily that the closer I got to the clinic, the thicker the crowd became.

I obviously wasn't going to get to the front door without a struggle, so I cut through a lot to the alley and went to the back entrance. The mob out front, playing to the cameras, hadn't come here yet. It took me considerable pounding and shouting to get a response, but Mrs. Coltrain, Lotty's receptionist, finally came to the door. She cautiously opened it the length of a chain. Her face cleared when she saw it was me.

"I've never been gladder to see you, Miss Warshawski. Dr. Herschel has her hands full and the police are no help. No help at all. If I didn't know better, I'd think they were in collusion with the marchers."

"What's going on?" I came inside and helped her reestablish the chains.

"They're out there yelling awful things. That Dr. Herschel is a murderer, that we're all going to hell. And poor Carol, just back from her sister's funeral."

I frowned. "Anti-abortionists?"

She nodded her head worriedly. "I raised six children and I'd do it again. But my husband made good money, we could afford to feed them all. Some of these women who come in—they're no more than little girls themselves. No one to help them feed themselves, let alone a child. And now I'm a murderer?"

I patted her arm sympathetically. "You're not a murderer. I know you're not happy with the idea of abortions, and I admire you for sticking with Lotty even though she includes them in her practice. And defending her, too. . . . Who's out there? Is it the Eagle Forum or IckPiff or don't you know?''

"I couldn't tell you. We had a poor young girl come in at eight this morning, and they were already waiting. How they knew who it was I couldn't say, but as soon as she arrived they started their yelling.''

The back of the clinic was used as a storeroom, everything very tidy and sterile. I followed Mrs. Coltrain through to the front. The shouting was much more audible there, and I could make out the individual screams.

"You don't care if babies die! Freedom of choice, what a lie!''

"Murderers! Nazis!''

Someone, probably Mrs. Coltrain, had drawn the blinds in the front windows. I separated two slats just enough to peer between them.

In front of the clinic, holding the bullhorn, was a thin, hyperthyroid man. His face was flushed with the earnestness of his feelings. I'd never met him before, but his picture had been in the papers and on TV numerous times: Dieter Monkfish, head of IckPiff—the Illinois Committee to Protect the Fetus. His supporters included a number of college-age young men, all fervently committed to carrying their own pregnancies to term, and a variety of middle-aged women, whose faces seemed to say: My life was made miserable by maternity, and so should everyone else's be.

Lotty came up behind me and repeated Mrs. Coltrain's greeting. "I've never been gladder to see you, Vic. What a mob! I've had a few people leafleting once or twice, but never anything like this. How did you hear about it?''

I shook my head. "I came here by chance, hoping to get Malcolm's keys from you. Then I saw the crowd in the street and got worried. Why did they all converge at once? Was anything special happening here?''

Her thick brows snapped together over the prominent nose. "I performed a therapeutic abortion this morning—

but I do three or four a month. And this was not a special case. Eighteen-year-old girl with one child, trying to get her life together a little. First trimester, of course—can't do anything else in the clinic.

"I'm telling you, Vic—I'm scared. There was a night in Vienna when a Nazi mob gathered in front of our house. They looked just like this—animals, oozing hate. They broke all the windows. My parents and my brother and I fled through the garden and hid at a neighbor's and watched them burn our house to the ground. Never did I expect to feel that same fear in America."

I gripped her shoulder. "I'll call Lieutenant Mallory. Maybe he can get some more active police up here than you seem to have. What about your patients?"

"Mrs. Coltrain called to reschedule appointments. Surely these hoodlums won't be back tomorrow. Emergencies we're routing to Beth Israel. But two women fought through the mob with their children, and I don't think I can lock up—I can't have my patients abused and not be here to help them.

"Besides, we still have the young woman who seems to be the precipitating cause of all this. She's doing fine, but she's rather shaken up, not up to walking through these frightening animals. And the police—the police just sit. They say there is no problem, no peace being disturbed. Of course, the neighborhood thinks it's better than a circus."

Carol came out to the waiting room. She'd lost weight since she'd last had her uniform on; it hung slackly across her hips and breasts.

"Hi, Vic. Protestors sent by God to keep our minds off our own troubles. What do you think?"

"For the moment, they're just harassing, playing to the TV cameras. Any warning that this might happen? Hate mail? Phone calls?"

Lotty shook her head. "Dieter Monkfish has come around a couple of times passing out leaflets, but since most of the people coming in here are women laden down with children, even he has felt a little foolish about lecturing them on the sanctity of life. Brave people send us a few anonymous hate letters every month, but no bombs or anything like that. This isn't really an abortion clinic, you know, so it doesn't attract much attention."

I went over to the reception area to use the phone. All the lights on the console were on. Mrs. Coltrain bustled up behind me to help me to a line.

"I put all the phones on hold because we were getting flooded with nuisance calls. Most of them obscene. I hope no one's trying to get through with an emergency."

I dialed the Eleventh Street police headquarters and asked for Lieutenant Mallory. A long series of clicks and transfers, and Bobby came on the line.

I dutifully asked after Eileen, their six children and five grandchildren, and explained where I was.

"They're intimidating patients away from the clinic, and the local precinct just has two cars observing the street. Can you get someone to move these people away from the front of the door?"

"No way, Vicki. Not my territory. That's something they're deciding locally. You should know by now that you can't just call the police to run errands for you."

"Bobby, darling. Lieutenant Mallory. I'm not asking you to run an errand. I'm asking for protection for a taxpaying citizen whose patients are being threatened with grievous bodily harm if they try to come into her office."

"You see anyone being threatened?"

"At the moment, the marchers have such total command of the street that no one can get close enough to be threatened."

"I'm sorry, Vicki—but it doesn't sound like a serious problem to me. And even if it was, you'd have to call the local precinct. If they try to murder anyone I'll come over."

I supposed that was his idea of a joke. If it affects women or children, it can't be serious. Furious, I tried Detective Rawlings.

He gave a sarcastic little chuckle when I finished my speech. "You give us a little grudging cooperation on a murder case, and then you want us to come running when you're in trouble? Typical, Ms. W., typical. Citizens won't help us, then they shriek and howl at the first hint of danger—where're the police?''

"Spare me the public-spirit lecture, Detective. As I recall, I've agreed to press charges against your pal Sergio—against my better judgment. You pick him up yet?''

"We're still looking," he admitted. "But he won't have gone too far. Someone told me that little punk Fabiano got all beat up—you know anything about it?''

"What I heard, he was driving too fast and smashed into his tough Eldorado windshield. Least, that's what they told me at the funeral yesterday. . . . Can we get the street cleared here a bit?''

"I'll talk to my watch commander, Warshawski. Not my call. But don't expect any miracles unless they start blowing up the place.''

"Exactly the moment at which help will be most useful," I agreed sardonically, and hung up.

"What we need are some federal marshals," I told Lotty and Carol. "But maybe we can patch something together instead. Protection, not confrontation. Can Paul and Herman help out? And I suppose Diego?''

Carol shook her head. "They had to lose too much time from work last week because of Consuelo. I thought of them, but I can't ask it of them—they could well lose their jobs.''

I bit my thumb while I thought. "Can we meet people at either end of the street and have an escort bring them down the alley?''

Lotty hunched a shoulder. "It's better than nothing, I suppose—though I don't know how people will find out where to come.''

"Word of mouth, I suppose. Let's reopen the switchboard—if patients call, give me a couple of hours to get some help together and start seeing them at noon.''

I spent the next half hour on the phone. Unable to get the Streeter brothers, who usually help me with heavy jobs, I reluctantly thought of my downstairs neighbor. As I'd feared, Mr. Contreras was delighted with a bugle call to action and promised to line up a few of his machinist pals—

also retired but still, he assured me, glad to have a chance to use their muscles.

The rest of the morning I sat in Lotty's office answering the barrage of calls. Most were from people worried about the clinic, not phoning for medical care. The legitimate patients I switched to Mrs. Coltrain. Unless someone had a serious problem, she urged them to call back later in the week. For some, Lotty listened to symptoms over the phone and called prescriptions in to a pharmacy. Emergencies were sent to Beth Israel.

The rest of the time I deflected obscene phone calls. The love of fetal life prompted people to the most incredible language. A little before noon, weary of the entertainment, we put the phones back on hold while I went out of the area to a hardware store to buy a whistle. A few loud blasts into an obscene caller's ear might leave a more lasting impression. I also stopped at a grocery for some food in case we had to sit through a real siege.

At noon the first of the escorts arrived. Mr. Contreras was dressed in work clothes and had a pipe wrench slung on his belt. He introduced me to Jake Sokolowski and Mitch Kruger, both also carrying weapons. Sokolowski and Kruger were close to Mr. Contreras's age but didn't look as fit—one had a beer belly the size of a pregnant elephant's and the other shook a little, from alcohol judging by the veins in his nose.

"Do me a favor, guys: Try not to start a riot," I told them. "This is a medical clinic and we don't want a lot of maniacs firing guns or rocks at it. We just want you to help patients get down the alley and into the back door. Carol will come with you to help you locate the right people."

The plan was that Carol would wait at the top of the street. If she saw any of Lotty's patients whom she recognized, she'd explain the situation to them. If they still wanted to see the doctor, she'd get the machinists to escort them in through the back. She took the eager men out into the alley while I did sentry duty at the back door. If anything went wrong and the escorts came back under attack, I would try to help out.

For a short while, things went smoothly. We took the opportunity to get the abortion patient out; Carol found her a cab and sent her peacefully home. But the crowd out front continued to grow, and the few patients who came in through the barricades become more and more nervous. Around one-thirty, the mob finally figured out that we were using the back entrance and poured into the alley with signs and megaphones.

Lotty reluctantly decided the time had come to shut down for the day when one woman, six months pregnant and suffering from toxemia, was physically barred from entering. Lotty went out in person to try to reason with the crowd, a move that I felt might prove disastrous.

She used her trick of expanding her five-foot body into a major physical force and addressed the crowd, which quieted a bit at first.

"This woman is trying to preserve her own life, and that of her fetus. If you prevent her from receiving medical care, you may well be responsible for her death. Surely with your philosophy of life you should encourage her to look after her body, not stand in her way."

She was received with jeers and shouts of "Murderer." One brave young man came up to spit at her.

I found a Polaroid camera in Lotty's office, which she used for taking pictures of mothers who came in to show off their new babies. I went out into the alley and started taking pictures of faces in the mob. They weren't organized enough to make a grab for the camera. Instead, they backed up the alley several yards. Anonymous haters don't like their identities made public.

Carol used the momentary lull to bustle the toxemic woman into a cab, directing it to Beth Israel.

"Better take this chance to shut things up and get out. Otherwise we're facing major trouble that we're not equipped to handle," I muttered to Lotty.

She soberly agreed. Mrs. Coltrain was visibly relieved—though prepared to stay until the bitter end, she had been more upset since the machinists had arrived. Mr. Contreras and his friends were not as happy.

"C'mon, doll," he urged. "Don't give up the ship so easily. So we're outnumbered—we can still give them a run for their money."

"We're outnumbered about fifty to one," I said tiredly. "I know you guys once took on an entire police force and pushed them to their knees, but none of us here is ready for broken legs, teeth, heads, or whatever. We need to get real help, help from the law, and it doesn't seem to be coming."

Lotty had gone back inside to lock up drugs and equipment. She brought Mrs. Coltrain and Carol back out with her, stopping at the alley door to set the code for the electronic alarm. When the crowd saw we were leaving, they swarmed up again, chanting and jeering. The seven of us formed a tight wedge and pushed our way through.

"Go home, baby killers, and don't come back!" one of them screamed, and the others took up the chant.

They moved closer, brandishing boards and bottles they'd found in the alley. Before any of us could stop him, Mr. Contreras took out his pipe wrench and headed at the nearest heckler. Sokolowski and Kruger happily followed suit. It was almost funny to see the three old men wheezing into battle, as happy as if they had sense. It would have been comical but for the animal fury of the mob. They rushed to surround the old men, wielding boards and rocks.

The alley quickly seethed with battle. I tried hauling Mrs. Coltrain to one side, but lost my balance on a loose rock. Her hand was wrenched from mine as I fell. I moved quickly to get out of the way of pounding feet. Protecting my face with my hands, I bulldozed my way to the side of the melee. I scanned the crowd worriedly, but couldn't see Lotty or Mr. Contreras.

I prudently kept my Smith & Wesson tucked into my belt and pushed my way around to the front of the building. A couple of uniformed men in riot helmets were standing talking to each other as Dieter Monkfish continued his tireless work with the bullhorn. He was loud enough that the cops were paying no heed to the rising roar from the alley.

"Three old men are being beaten up by the mob in back."

I was panting, uneasily aware of a damp oozing on my cheek.

One of them looked at me suspiciously. "You sure about this?"

"All you have to do is come look, and you'll see for yourself. Lieutenant Mallory promised to come if things turned to homicide—want to wait until this is his business?"

The one who'd spoken first reluctantly unhooked his remote radio from his belt and spoke into it.

"You stay here with her, Carl—I'll go around back and see."

He sauntered down the narrow walk separating the clinic from a neighboring house. In a few seconds Carl's radio squawked to life. Carl spoke into it, got the news, and radioed for reinforcements. In a few minutes, the area was alive with police in riot helmets.

XIV

Carnage on Damen

When Dieter Monkfish saw the riot police, he went wild. He shouted through the bullhorn to his avid followers that they were under attack and took off for the alley.

If I hadn't been concerned about Lotty and Mr. Contreras, I would have fled in the other direction. I've been once or twice in the middle of a berserk crowd the police are trying to contain. Everyone panics, the police use their sticks indiscriminately, and you are as likely to be hurt by your friends as your enemies.

I put my hand protectively to the wound on my face and thought frantically. If I was stopped with the gun in my possession, they wouldn't take time to ask for the permit and my license. And I didn't want to take any more battering than I had to just now.

The TV camera crews, excited by the possibility of real action after a long, dull day, followed Monkfish happily. I got in step with a Channel 5 cameraman and used him as an escort to return to the alley.

Nineteen sixty-eight in Grant Park was being reenacted. The police had formed a tight cordon at the north end and were pushing everyone down toward Cornelia Street to the south where their paddy wagons waited. People screamed. Bricks and boards flew through the air. A can of Coke came hurling out of the mob and hit a policeman in his helmet. Coke poured down his face. He flailed blindly in front of himself. A surge of people knocked him over. The narrow space in the alley left no room for any maneuvering; police and mob got hopelessly mixed.

I scanned the crowd helplessly, not daring to try to enter it, but still could see no sign of Lotty. I pushed myself close against the side of the building to keep from being swept into the fray. Over the howl of the animals, I heard the building alarm go off. Or maybe felt its vibrations—no one could hear anything except mayhem.

I shoved my way through the camera crews to the front of the clinic. People were hurling rocks and tire irons at the glass storefront; the alarm howled ominously. In a total rage I seized one young man's arm as he reached back to throw. I slammed the side of my fist into his wrist, jarring the bone and making him drop the rock. I kneed him in the stomach hard enough to make him gag and turned to a middle-aged woman at his left. The flab on her arms swallowed my hand, but I shook a piece of brick loose from her.

"You want your grandchildren to see you on TV, drooling hate and throwing bricks?" I spat at her.

My one-woman show was hopeless. The mob was bigger, stronger, and more mindless than I. They smashed down the storefront and streamed inside. I leaned against a parked car, gasping for air and shaking.

"I guess you were right, Warshawski. Should have had the troops here sooner."

The voice, heavy, somewhat amused, belonged to Detective Rawlings. He had come up beside me without my noticing.

"So what happens now?" I said bitterly. "A few disorderly conducts, several disturbing the peace—low bail—no prosecution?"

"Probably. Although we've got several for assaulting an officer. Man was kind of hurt back in the alley."

"Well, that's good news. Pity more police weren't attacked—maybe we'd have some real arrests instead of a few taps on the wrist."

"Don't be so angry, Warshawski. You know the story—beginning, ending, middle, how justice works in this town."

"Oh, yeah. I know the entire plot. I do hope and pray you have not come to me with the news that Sergio is under arrest, because I'm not at my most cooperative right now."

Two police personnel carriers with blue lights flashing squealed to a stop in front of us. Several dozen cops in riot helmets leaped out of the back before the wheels had stopped moving. They raced into the clinic, riot sticks at the ready. After a few moments they began reappearing with handcuffed rioters. The prisoners, all white, mostly young men and older women, appeared dazed by the turn of events. But when the television crews reappeared in front of them, they raised a ragged cheer and made the victory sign.

I left Rawlings and went over to one of the cameramen. "Be sure to get a good shot of the clinic. This is where poor women and children have come for seven years to be treated for nominal fees by one of Chicago's top physicians. Make sure your viewers see that these righteous people have destroyed a major source of health care for Chicago's poor."

Someone stuck a microphone under my mouth. Mary Sherrod from Channel 13.

"Do you work here?"

"I'm one of Dr. Herschel's attorneys. I stopped by here on routine business earlier today and found the place under siege. We tried hard to continue to operate the clinic and treat the poor women and children who depend on it. One pregnant woman, badly in need of help, was attacked by the mob and was lucky to escape without injury to herself or her fetus.

"Before you present this mayhem in such a way that your viewers think they're watching vigilance in favor of unborn fetuses, please focus on the damage. Show them what really happened." I stopped talking, overwhelmed by the thought of my small voice trying to outweigh three hundred mad fanatics, and turned abruptly away.

The crowd had dispersed. Most of the police were gone. Except for the gaping windows leading into the clinic and the mess, the whole episode might never have occurred. The street was strewn with broken glass, bricks, rocks, leaflets, empty cans of soda pop and the detritus of sack lunches—McDonald's wrappers, candy-bar remains, potato-chip bags. So the city would incur some cost—they'd have to send a crew around to clean up the mess. Eventually. In this neighborhood it wouldn't happen right away.

Rawlings had disappeared, but a couple of policemen were stationed outside the clinic. I felt a bit conspicuous and vulnerable hanging around. I thought I should go find a phone and call a board-up service and was starting to walk away when Lotty reappeared. Her white lab coat was streaked with dirt and torn in several places. She had a scrape on her right arm but was otherwise unharmed.

"Thank God you're still here, Vic. I was afraid you'd been hauled away with the mob. Your valiant friend Mr. Contreras was, his head gaping open. There was no way I could get to him and do something for it before they shoved him into one of their paddy wagons. Just like 1938 all over again. Terrible, terrible. I can't believe it."

I took her hand, but there wasn't anything I could say to her. "Where're Carol and Mrs. Coltrain?" I asked instead.

"They got away—I made sure they slid out between a couple of houses to go home. Poor Mrs. Coltrain—she tries bravely to accept my ideas of medicine, which she doesn't share. And now to be subjected to this." She shook her head, wincing.

"I guess I should find out where they were taking people and go spring Mr. Contreras," I said. "Are you going to press charges? If you don't, these outlaws will get away with a fine and a slap on the wrist."

Her face screwed up with uncertainty. "I don't know—I'll talk to my lawyer—my real lawyer—and see how much time it will take. What can I do for these windows?"

I told her we should call an emergency window-boarding service and get them covered. She went over to the policemen to explain who she was and that she wanted to go inside the building. They were starting to argue with her when Rawlings reappeared.

"It's okay, Officer. I know the doc. Let her go inside," he told them.

I followed Lotty into the building, Rawlings trailing on our heels. The inside was unbearable. In Lotty's place I would have been tempted to shut the clinic and start over again someplace else. All the furniture in the waiting area was topsy-turvy, covered with glass. Inside the offices, the shambles was indescribable. Filing cabinets had been pulled down, patient files dumped willy-nilly on the floor, medical instruments lay broken on top of them. Lotty, scrounging around in the rubble for a phone, picked a stethoscope out from under a jumbled mess of paper sheets and rubbed it over and over against her dress.

"We'd better take pictures for the insurance before you get it cleaned up," I warned her. "In fact, why don't you give me your agent's name and number and I'll call—they'll take care of getting the place boarded up."

"Yes, fine. If you do that, Vic, it will be very fine." Her voice cracked a little around the edges.

I turned to Rawlings. "Be a sport, Detective. Give Dr. Herschel a ride home. She doesn't need to be exposed to this shit anymore. I'll wait here for them to take care of the windows."

"Certainly, Ms. Warshawski." The gold tooth gleamed in an ironic smile. "We in the Chicago police department are here to serve and protect." He turned to Lotty and persuaded her to go with him.

"I'll be over tonight," I promised her. "Now just go home, take a hot bath, and relax for a little while."

XV

Amazing Who You Meet in Night Court

It was four-thirty before the emergency service finished covering the gaping front window frames. Lotty's insurance agent, Claudia Fisher, had come by to view the damage as soon as I called her. A middle-aged woman, a bit on the heavy side, she brought a Polaroid and took numerous shots both of the interior and of the outside streets.

"This is really shocking," she said. "Absolutely unwarranted. I'll get the company to pay for cleaning it up, but Dr. Herschel better find some qualified help. Someone who understands medical records and medical supplies and can get them back into shape—otherwise she'll likely have a worse mess on her hands."

I nodded. "I've thought about that. I'm going to suggest she call someone at Beth Israel, see if she can get a group of nurses and interns to come over. They could take care of it in a day, I suppose."

When the boards were finally in place, I dug Lotty's answering machine out of the carnage and left a simple message: The clinic would be closed for the rest of the week.

If there were any emergencies, people should call Lotty at home.

I took Claudia Fisher out through the back door and went off to find Mr. Contreras. My first stop was home—to bathe, get some supper, and use my phone. By the time I reached my apartment, the adrenaline-based energy of the afternoon had worn off. I moved on cement feet to the front door and up the stairs.

I ran the bath as hot as I could bear it and lay back in the tub, slowly flexing cramped muscles. The steam softened the stiff left side of my face and I could smile and frown without worrying that the stitches were pulling apart.

I dozed off in the soothing water and lay half sleeping when the ringing phone roused me. I climbed slowly from the tub, wrapping myself in a bath towel, and picked up the extension next to my bed. It was Burgoyne. He'd seen the protest on the news and was anxious about Lotty's and my welfare.

"We're okay," I assured him. "The clinic is a royal mess, though. And poor old Mr. Contreras got his head beaten in and was hauled off in a paddy wagon. I'm on my way now to find him and rescue him."

"Would you be willing to drive out to Barrington tomorrow night? Have dinner in suburbia?"

"I'll have to call you," I said. "After what I've been through today I'm not up to thinking past the next task."

"Want me to come in and spend some time with you?" he asked anxiously.

"Thanks. But I don't know how long it's going to take me to manage the legal mess at this end. I'll try to call you during the day tomorrow—want to give me your office number?"

I took it down and hung up. Putting on a gold cotton dress that looked professional enough for night court, I started on an array of phone calls. First to the local precinct, then the district command, where I was switched around five or six times. Mr. Contreras had been taken to Cook County to have his head stitched up, I finally learned, and would be brought over to night court from the hospital.

After hanging up I phoned an old friend who was still hanging on in Legal Aid. Fortunately, she was at home.

"Cleo—V. I. Warshawski."

We exchanged news of the ten months or so it'd been since we last talked, then I explained my problem.

"They threw everyone into the holding cells at the district, and they're taking them down to bond court later on this evening. Can you find out who's on duty for Legal Aid? I'm going to come down and appear as a character witness."

"Oh, jeez, Vic. I might've known you'd been involved in that clinic assault this afternoon. What a horror—I thought Chicago was being spared the violent wing of the lunatic fringe."

"I did, too. I hope this isn't the signal for a concentrated attack on the city's abortion clinics. Lotty Herschel is pretty upset—for her it's a replay of what the Nazis did to her childhood home in Vienna."

Cleo promised to call back in a few minutes with a name. My bath had taken the edge from my fatigue, but I still felt dopey. Breakfast had been many hours ago; I needed protein to restore myself. I scrounged dubiously in the refrigerator. It had been almost a week since I'd been to the store and there wasn't much that looked appetizing. In fact, there were a number of items of uncertain provenance, but I didn't feel like a cleanup job this evening. I finally settled for eggs, making a quick frittata with onions, one of Mr. Contreras's tomatoes, and the remains of a green pepper.

The phone rang as I was swallowing the last few bites— Cleo calling back with Legal Aid's man at bond court tonight: Manuel Diaz. I thanked her and headed down to Eleventh and State.

Parking presents no problems beyond the deserted south end of the Loop in the evening. By day it's an area filled with ramshackle businesses run out of warehouses and the antiquated coffee shops that serve them. At night, the Central District Headquarters is the sole source of life in the area; most of the visitors aren't driving their own cars.

I parked the Chevy close to the building and walked inside. The halls with their peeling paint and strong smell of disinfectant brought nostalgic memories of visits to my father, a sergeant until his death fourteen years ago.

I found Manuel Diaz smoking a cigarette in one of the conference rooms next to the courtroom. He was a stockily built Mexican. Although I didn't remember him, he looked old enough to have been with Legal Aid when I was there. His heavy face was scored with deep lines. A smattering of pockmarks gave his cheeks the appearance of freckles. I explained who I was and what I wanted.

"Mr. Contreras is in his seventies. He's a machinist who used to mix it up in his union days and he decided to relive his youth this afternoon. I don't know what they're going to charge him with. I saw him go after someone with a pipe wrench, but he was mauled pretty well, too."

"They haven't brought the charges over to us yet, but they probably just booked him for disturbing the peace," Diaz responded. "They arrested eighty people this afternoon, so they weren't being too particular what they charged them with."

We chatted for a while. He had been a public defender for twenty years, first out in Lake County, now in the city. He lived on the South Side, he explained, and the commute to the North Shore got to be too much for him.

"Although I miss our quiet old times out there. You get pretty jaded here—I suppose you know that."

I grimaced. "I only stayed with it for five years. I guess I'm too impatient, or too egotistical—I want to see some results from my hard labor, and as a trial lawyer I always felt somehow that the situation was no different when I finished with a client than before—or sometimes maybe things were a little worse."

"So you went into business for yourself, huh? That how you got your face cut open? Well, at least you're getting some results. I've had some pretty wild clients, but they've never attacked me with a knife."

I was spared answering by the arrival of a clerk with the charge slips. Manuel went through them with the speed of long experience, segregating the simple ones—disturbing the

110

peace, disorderly conduct, vagrancy—from the more serious. He asked a bailiff to bring all the disturbing-the-peace and disorderly cases in as a group.

Nine men came in, including Mr. Contreras and his friend Jake Sokolowski. They were by far the oldest in the group. The others, young middle-class men in various stages of disarray, looked both scared and pugnacious. Mitch Kruger, the third machinist, had disappeared—hadn't been arrested, Mr. Contreras told me later. With the bandage around his head and his work clothes torn, the old man looked like a skid-row derelict, but the fight seemed to have added new fuel to his abundant store of energy and he smiled jauntily at me.

"You come to rescue me, cookie? Knew I could count on you—that's why I didn't bother calling Ruthie. You think I look bad, you shoulda seen the other guy."

"Listen," Manuel interrupted him. "The last thing I want any of you to do is boast about your accomplishments. Just keep your mouths shut for the next couple of hours and with luck you'll all sleep in your own beds tonight."

"Sure, chief, whatever you say," Mr. Contreras agreed cheerfully. He nudged Sokolowski in his large stomach and the two of them winked and grinned like a pair of teenagers eyeing a girl for the first time.

Six of the other seven defendants had also been arrested at the clinic, fighting the good fight to protect fetuses. The remaining man had been found singing in the middle of the executive offices of the Fort Dearborn Trust earlier in the evening. No one knew how he had gotten past the security guards, and when Manuel asked him he smiled happily and announced that he had flown there.

Manuel interrogated Sokolowski and Mr. Contreras together. He decided they would argue self-defense, that they were trying to help Lotty keep her clinic open and had been attacked by the mob. When Mr. Contreras protested indignantly against so passive a role, I backed up Manuel's pleas that he remain silent.

"You were hero enough this afternoon," I told him. "You're not going to do anyone any good by mouthing off to the judge and getting thirty days or a big fine. It's not going to diminish your manhood if the judge doesn't know every single detail of your antics."

He finally agreed, reluctantly, but with a mulish expression that made me feel sorry for his long-dead wife. Sokolowski, while not as fit as his friend, was just as eager to figure as the baddest, biggest man on Damen Avenue. But when Mr. Contreras finally agreed to plead self-defense, he followed suit.

I wasn't allowed to stay for the interrogation of the six clinic invaders. After the bailiff took Mr. Contreras and Sokolowski back to the holding cell I wandered into the interior of the station to see if Lieutenant Mallory was in. I talked my way past the desk sergeant and went down the hall to the homicide detectives' area.

Mallory wasn't there, but Rawlings's pal Detective Finchley was. A lean, quiet black man, he got up politely when I came in.

"Good to see you, Ms. Warshawski. What happened to your face?"

"I cut myself shaving," I said, weary of the subject. "I thought your pal Conrad Rawlings told you all about it; thanks for the read you gave him on my character." It was Finchley who told Rawlings that I was a pain in the ass who got results. "Lieutenant Mallory gone home for the day? Would you tell him I was in? That I hoped to have a chance to discuss what happened at Dr. Herschel's clinic this afternoon?"

Finchley promised to give him the message. He looked at me straight-faced. "You are a pain in the ass, Ms. Warshawski—cut yourself shaving, my Aunt Fanny. But you care about your friends and I like that in you."

Surprised and touched by the compliment, I made my way back to the courtroom with a bit more energy. I needed it to muscle my way to a seat. While the daytime courts scattered around the city attract a certain number of observers who want to pass the time of day, the night bond courts don't meet at a convenient time—they're usually empty. But tonight a large force of anti-abortionists, all carrying roses, sat waiting for the judge.

Because so many people had been arrested for destroying the clinic, a large crowd of lawyers was seated up front waiting for their clients. A good ten or so uniformed cops were seated there, too, and a couple of the newspapers also had people in the room. I knew one of them, a junior crime reporter for the *Herald-Star*, who came over when she saw me sit down. I told her Mr. Contreras's story. It had a nice human-interest touch, which might help crowd anti-abortion coverage off the front page. Chicago's papers and TV stations are blatantly anti-choice in their news coverage.

At length the bailiff mumbled something, we all stood up, and the court was in session. As docket after docket was called, various lawyers came forward, sometimes Manuel Diaz, more often one of the private attorneys—this was an unusual session for the judge, who wasn't used to so many paying patients.

My attention wandered, but my eyes kept returning to the back of one of the lawyers' heads. He looked elusively familiar. I was wishing he would turn so I could glimpse his face, when he twitched his shoulders in an irritated gesture. It brought his name back to me immediately: Richard Yarborough, senior partner at Crawford, Meade, one of the city's largest law firms. I'd gotten used to that impatient twitch of the shoulders in the eighteen months we'd been married.

I let out a soundless whistle. Dick's time was billed at two hundred dollars an hour. Someone mighty important had been arrested today. I was speculating on it fruitlessly when I realized with a start that my name had been called. I made my way to the front of the room, said my piece to the judge, and was pleased to hear my unrepentant neighbor dismissed with a warning.

"If you are seen on the street in the future carrying a pipe wrench or any other tool of similar size, it will be construed as violent intent and will constitute violation of your bond. Do you understand me, Mr. Contreras?"

The old man ground his teeth, but Manuel and I both

looked at him gravely and he said, "Yes. Yes, sir." He clearly wanted to speak further, so I took his arm, barely waiting for the judge's "Dismissed" and gavel tap before hustling him away from the bench.

He was muttering to himself about how he'd rather go to jail than have people think he was a chicken-shit when I cut him off.

"I'm going to drive you home," I said. "But my ex-husband's here in court. It's just vulgar curiosity, but I want to find out why. Mind waiting a bit?"

As I'd hoped, the news instantly took his mind off his grievances.

"I didn't know you was married! Should have guessed. Guy wasn't good enough for you, huh? Come to me next time—don't make the same mistake twice. Like this young fellow you brought in the other night—looks like kind of a lightweight to me."

"Yes, well, he's a doctor—doesn't do too much barroom fighting. The first one's a high-priced lawyer—if I'd stuck with him I'd have a mansion in Oak Brook and three children today."

He shook his head. "You wouldn't a liked it. Take my word for it, cookie—you're better off."

The bailiff was frowning at us, so I urged Mr. Contreras to an unwilling silence. We waited through a variety of other cases, including the man who'd flown into the Fort Dearborn executive suite, who was remanded to Cook County for psychiatric evaluation.

Then the bailiff announced Docket 81523—the People versus Dieter Monkfish. Dick got to his feet and approached the bench. My brain whirled around so fast that the room spun. Monkfish and IckPiff with one of the city's priciest lawyers? I couldn't hear what passed between Dick and the judge, or the judge, the policeman, and Monkfish, but the upshot was Monkfish was released on his own recognizance, given a court date in October, and enjoined from disturbing the peace. If he complied, all charges would be dropped. He mumbled agreement, his Adam's apple working, and the play was over.

Mr. Contreras came with me to wait in the hall outside the lawyers' conference room. Dick emerged after about fifteen minutes. I stopped him before he could head down the corridor.

"Hi, Dick. Can we talk for a minute?"

"Vic, what the hell are you doing here?"

"Gee, Dick, I'm glad to see you, too. How are you?"

He glared at me. He's never really forgiven me for not appreciating him as much as he does himself.

"I'm trying to get home. What do you want?"

"Same as you, Dick—to make the wheels of justice turn more smoothly. This is Salvatore Contreras. One of your client's buddies hit him over the head with a board this afternoon."

Mr. Contreras stuck out a callused hand at Dick, who shook it reluctantly.

"You made a big mistake when you let cookie here go, young man," he informed Dick. "She's a great gal, tops in my book. If I was thirty years younger I'd marry her myself. Make it twenty, even."

Dick's face was congealing, a sure sign of anger.

"Thanks," I said to Mr. Contreras, "but we're both really better off the way we are. Could I ask you to step aside for a second? I want to ask him something he won't feel like answering in front of an audience."

Mr. Contreras obligingly moved down the hall. Dick looked at me sternly.

"Well? Now that you've gotten that old man to insult me, I'm not sure I want to answer any questions of yours."

"Oh, don't mind him. He's sort of appointed himself my father—maybe he goes about it clumsily, but he doesn't mean any harm. . . . I was surprised to see you with Dieter Monkfish."

"I know you don't agree with his politics, Vic, but that doesn't mean he isn't entitled to counsel."

"No, no," I said hastily. "I'm sure you're right. And I respect you for being willing to represent him—he can't be the most congenial of clients."

He permitted himself a careful smile. "I certainly wouldn't

invite him to the Union League Club with me. But I don't think it will come to that—he's not that type of client.''

"I guess I wondered what type of client he was. I mean, here you are, one of the top corporate lawyers in town. And there he is, a fanatic with a shoestring organization. How can they afford Crawford, Meade?''

Dick smiled patronizingly. "Not your business, Vic. Even fanatics have friends.'' He shot a glance at the Rolex weighting down his left wrist and announced that he had to get going.

Mr. Contreras came back over to me as soon as Dick walked off.

''Excuse the language, cookie, but the guy really is a prick. He tell you what you want to know?''

"A whiff of it. And yes, he really is a prick.''

We arrived at my little Chevy in time to see Dick squeal by ostentatiously in a Mercedes sports car. Yeah, yeah, I thought, you made it big, man. I get the message: If I'd been a good girl I'd get to ride in those fancy wheels instead of my little beater.

I unlocked the doors and helped Mr. Contreras into the passenger seat. As he babbled happily along at my side, I wondered. So Monkfish wasn't paying his own bill. Dick was right—it wasn't my business. Nonetheless, I was consumed with curiosity.

XVI

Who Is Rosemary Jiminez?

The next week passed in a frenzy of work. I joined a team of medical professionals in restoring Lotty's building. While they sorted records, reassembled files, and took a careful inventory of controlled drugs, Mrs. Coltrain and I did manual labor. We cleared glass, glued chairs together, and scrubbed all the examining tables with heavy disinfectant. On Friday the insurance company sent over a glazier to replace the windows. We spent the weekend on a final cleanup.

Tessa came on Sunday to paint the place. A group of her friends tagged along, and the waiting room was transformed into an African veldt, with beautiful grasses and flowers and herds of animals sniffing alertly for lions. The examining rooms were turned into undersea grottos, with soft colors and fanciful, friendly fishes.

Lotty opened for business again on Tuesday, with several reporters hovering over her patients: Did they feel it was safe? Did they worry about their children coming to a place that had been attacked? A Mexican woman drew herself up to her full five feet.

"Without Dr. Herschel, I have no child," she said in heavily accented English. "She save my life, my baby's life, when no other doctor would treat me because I cannot pay. Always I come to her."

My face healed during this time. Dr. Pirwitz took out the stitches the day we reopened Lotty's clinic. My cheek was no longer sore when I laughed and I went back to running and swimming without worrying about damaging the skin.

I continued to see Peter Burgoyne, somewhat sporadically. Often a funny and knowledgeable companion, he also worried about details in a way that could make him hard to be around. Friendship was hosting a seminar on "Treating Amniotic Fluid Embolism—the Whole Team Approach." It was his show, his chance to show off what he'd accomplished at Friendship, but I wearied of his fretting—about the paper he was presenting, or about logistics that a competent secretary should have been handling. He continued to worry about Lotty and Consuelo to a degree I found unpalatable. While his concern for my health and Lotty's progress in restoring the clinic was well meant, I saw him only once for every two or three times he called.

I continued a halfhearted inquiry into Malcolm's death, but got nowhere with it. One afternoon I took his keys from Lotty and went into his apartment. No clues leaped at me from the appalling havoc. I played the answering machine, which had somehow survived the onslaught. It was true several people had called and hung up without leaving messages, but that happens every day. I left the building depressed but no wiser.

Detective Rawlings picked Sergio up late the following Saturday—deliberately, to keep him off the street until someone found his lawyer late in the day on Sunday. The bond had been set for fifty thousand on the aggravated battery charge, but Sergio easily made bail. We had a trial date of October 20—the first in a long series of motions and continuances by which Sergio would hope to get charges dropped if I failed to show up for one of them. Rawlings told me five Lions, including Tattoo, were prepared to testify that Sergio had been with them at a wedding party all through the night in question.

I wondered uneasily what form Sergio's revenge might take and never left home without the Smith & Wesson tucked into my waistband or purse, but as the days passed without incident I thought he might be willing to wait it out in the courts.

I had a second interview with Fabiano on Wednesday of the week Lotty's clinic reopened. Once again I tracked him down in the Rooster bar near Holy Sepulchre. The swelling in his face had healed; only a few discolored bruises remained. The men in the bar greeted me warmly.

"So, Fabiano, your poor aunt returns." "When he showed up with those bruises we knew he had insulted you once too often." "Come here, Auntie, let's have a kiss—I appreciate you if this garbage doesn't."

After taking Fabiano outside with me, I went over to the baby-blue Eldorado, inspecting it ostentatiously.

"I hear you drive that car of yours too fast. Banged your face into it, huh? Car looks okay to me—must be harder than that head of yours, which is really astounding."

He looked at me murderously. "You know damn well how my face got hurt, bitch. You don't look so good yourself. You tell those Alvarados to leave me alone or they see your body in the river. Next time we don't be so easy on you."

"Look, Fabiano. If you want to fight me, fight. Don't go sniveling to Sergio. It makes you look ridiculous. Come on—you want to kill me, do it now. Bare hands—no weapons."

He looked at me sullenly, but said nothing.

"Okay, you don't want to fight. Good. That makes two of us. All I want from you is information. Information about whether your pals in the Lions had anything to do with Malcolm Tregiere's death."

Alarm suffused his face. "Hey, man, you ain't laying that on me. No way. I wasn't there, I didn't have nothing to do with it."

"But you know who did."

"I don't know nothing."

We went round and round on it for five minutes. I was convinced—from his fright and his words—that he knew something about Tregiere's death. But he wasn't going to talk.

"Okay, boy. I guess I'm going to have to go to Detective Rawlings and tell him you were involved in the murder. He'll pick you up as a material witness, and we'll see if that makes you talk."

Even that didn't shake him. Whoever he was afraid of was a worse threat than the police. Not surprising—the police could hold him for a few days, but they wouldn't break his legs or his skull.

He wasn't brave physically; I grabbed his shirt front and slapped his face a few times to see if that got me anywhere, but he knew I couldn't be berserk enough to really hurt him. I gave it up and sent him back to his beer. He left with half-tearful warnings of revenge, which I would have dismissed unthinkingly if not for his alliance with Sergio.

I stopped by the Sixth Area. Rawlings was in; I told him about my conversation with Fabiano.

"I'm convinced the jerk knows something about Malcolm's death, but he's too scared to talk. After two weeks that's all I've been able to come up with. I don't think there's one damned thing else I can do on this case."

Rawlings's heavy smile gleamed. "Good news, Warshawski. Now I can concentrate on my investigation without worrying about you creeping around a corner in front of me. But I'll pick up Hernandez and see if I can sweat him."

I had supper with Lotty that night and told her that I had done what I could about Malcolm.

"Aside from my wounds and the few bruises Fabiano got, I would say the results I've gotten on this case have been nonexistent. I'm going to have to find a paying client pretty soon."

She agreed, reluctantly, and the talk turned to her efforts to find a replacement for Malcolm. When she left, around ten-thirty, Mr. Contreras didn't even come to his door. Almost two weeks with no action had persuaded even him that the premises weren't in danger.

I was still curious about where Dieter Monkfish had gotten the money to pay for Dick's legal services, but with all the work at the clinic I hadn't had time to do anything more than phone my attorney. Freeman Carter was the partner with Crawford, Meade who handled their small criminal caseload. I had met him when married to Dick and had found him the only member of the firm who didn't believe he was doing the world as well as the legal profession a favor by participating in it. Given the size of his fees I used him only on occasions when the forces of justice genuinely threatened to flatten me.

Freeman expressed himself delighted, as always, to hear from me, wanted to know if I needed help with Sergio Rodriguez, and told me I should know better than to call asking him to divulge anything about any of the firm's other clients.

"Hey, Freeman, if I always assumed no one was going to tell me anything, I might as well go home and go to bed for the duration. Just thought I'd try."

He laughed, told me to call him if I changed my mind about prosecuting Sergio, and hung up.

On the Thursday after my second interview with Fabiano, I got a call from a real client, a man in Downers Grove who wanted help stopping drug sales on the premises of his small box factory. Before going to see him I decided to take my curiosity about Monkfish one step farther.

IckPiff's address, in the 400 block of South Wells, put it close to the Congress Expressway, the least desirable fringe of the Loop. I drove, picking my way past potholes and chunks of masonry, and parked on the street about a block from the building.

Money was not pouring into IckPiff headquarters. Their building was one of a handful of forlorn survivors of urban removal, standing on the street like uneasy pins left after the efforts of a bush-league bowler. A few winos were sitting in the doorways, blinking unsteadily in the late August sun. I stepped over the outstretched legs of one who couldn't rouse himself enough to panhandle and went into a fetid hallway.

A handwritten sheet taped to the peeling paint informed me that IckPiff headquarters was on the third floor. Other building tenants included a talent agency, a tourist agency for a tiny African country, and a telemarketing firm. The elevator, a small box set into the wall, was padlocked shut. As I climbed the stairs I didn't see anyone, but perhaps it was still too early in the day for talent agencies.

On the third floor, a faint light shone through the half glass of IckPiff's door. A poster featuring a blown-up photograph of a blob—presumably a fetus—was taped to the door with a screamer headline reading STOP THE SLAUGHTER. I pulled the blob toward me and went in.

The interior of the office was a small step up from the squalor of the lobby and stairwell. Cheap metal desks and filing cabinets; a long deal table covered with pamphlets where volunteers could collate mailings; and a battery of telephones for campaigns in the state and national legislatures made up the furnishings. Decoration was provided by wall-to-wall posters depicting the evils of abortion and the virtues of fetus protection.

A heavyset, white-haired woman was watering a scraggly plant in a dirty window when I came in. She wore a beige polyester skirt hiked up in front by her protruding stomach to reveal the scalloped end of a slip. Her legs, badly swollen, were encased in support hose and plastic sandals. I wondered with fleeting sympathy how she negotiated the stairs every day.

She looked at me with dull eyes partly hidden by the flabby creases of her face and asked what I wanted.

"State of Illinois," I said briskly. "Audit department." I flashed my private-eye license at her briefly. "You're registered as a not-for-profit organization, aren't you?"

"Why, why, yes. We certainly are. Yes." Her voice had the heavy twang of the South Side.

"I just need to take a look at your list of donors. Some questions have arisen about whether they are sheltering income with IckPiff instead of using it as a genuine tax-exempt charity.'' I hoped she wasn't an accountant—my meaningless jargon wouldn't fool anyone with a junior-college certificate.

She drew herself up proudly. "We are a genuine organization. If you've been sent here by *the murderers* to harass us I'm going to call the police."

"No, no," I said soothingly. "I have great admiration for your views and goals. This is totally impersonal—just the machinery of the state division of taxes and audits. We can't have your donors taking advantage of you, can we?"

She shuffled back to the desk on slow, painful feet. "I just need to call Mr. Monkfish. He doesn't like me showing our private papers to strangers."

"I'm not a stranger," I said brightly. "One of your public servants, you know. It won't take but a minute."

She continued dialing. With one hand over the mouthpiece she said, "What did you say your name was?"

"Jiminez," I said. "Rosemary Jiminez."

Mr. Monkfish was unfortunately at home, or at the Union League Club, or wherever it was she'd dialed. She explained her predicament in her heavy, panting voice and nodded in relief several times before hanging up.

"If you'll just wait here, Mrs. . . . what did you say your name was? He'll be right over."

"How long will it take him to get here?"

"Not more than thirty minutes."

I looked conspicuously at my wrist. "I have a noon meeting with someone from the governor's office. If Mr. Monkfish isn't here by a quarter to, I'm going to have to leave. And if I leave without the information, my boss may decide to subpoena the records. You wouldn't like that, would you? So why not let me look at the files while we're both waiting for him?"

She hesitated, so I upped the pressure, discoursing gently about police, the FBI, and subpoenas. At last she pulled out some heavy ledgers and the file cards of donors' names and addresses and let me sit at the table.

The ledgers were all handwritten and in an appalling mess. I started through them in reverse order in the hopes of finding either Dick's fee or some incoming amount big enough to pay for it, but it was hopeless. It would take hours, and I had minutes. I flipped through the file of donor cards, which at least was in alphabetical order, but I had no idea of whom to look for among the several thousand names. Out of curiosity I looked in the Y's for Dick. His name and office number were listed, along with a penciled note saying "Bills to be mailed directly to donor." I snapped the lid shut and got up.

"I think we're going to have to send in a full audit team, ma'am. Your records, if you'll forgive my saying so, are not in apple-pie order."

I slung my handbag over my shoulder and headed for the exit. Unfortunately, I had not been quite quick enough. Dieter Monkfish was coming toward me as I opened the door. His hot, bulging brown eyes burned me with their fire.

"You're the girl from the state?" His nasal baritone was bigger than he was; bigger than the crowded office, and it made my ears ring.

"Woman," I said automatically. "Didn't find what I was looking for—we're going to have to organize a full audit team, as I explained to your office manager."

"I want to see your identification. Did you ask for any, Marjorie?"

"Yes, Mr. Monkfish, of course I did."

"Yes, we went through all that," I said soothingly. "Now I have to be going. Lunch with one of the governor's assistants."

"I want to see your identification, young woman." He stood in the doorway, barring my way.

I hesitated. He was taller than I, but reedy. I suspected I could elbow my way past him. But then Marjorie might call the police and who knew where it would all end? I pulled from my bag a card with nothing but my name and address on it and handed it to him.

"V. I. Warshawski." He butchered the pronunciation. "Where's your credentials from the State of Illinois?"

I looked at him unhappily. "I'm afraid I told a little bit of a lie, Mr. Monkfish. I'm not really from the state. It's like this." I put a supplicatory hand on his sleeve. "Can I trust you? I feel like you're the kind of man who can really understand a woman's problems. I mean, look how understanding you are of women with unwanted pregnancies—that is, how well you understand the problem of being an unwanted child."

He didn't say anything, but I thought the manic fire died down a bit. I took a breath and continued, faltering a little.

"It's my husband, you see. My ex-husband, I should say. He—he left me for another woman. When I was pregnant with our last child. He—he wanted me to have an abortion, but of course I refused. He's a very wealthy lawyer, charges two hundred dollars an hour, but he doesn't pay a dime in child support. We had five beautiful children together. But I don't have any money, and he knows I can't afford to sue him." It sounded so heartbreaking I was close to tears.

"If you've come here looking for money, young lady, I can't help you."

"No, no. I wouldn't ask it of you. But—my husband is Dick—Richard Yarborough. I know he represents you. And I thought—I thought if I could find out who was paying the bill, I might persuade them to send the money to me, to feed little Jessica and Monica and Fred and—and the others, you know."

"How come your name isn't Yarborough?" he demanded, focusing on the least important part of the melodrama.

Because I wouldn't use that prick's name on a bad check, I said to myself. Aloud I quavered, "When he left me, I was so embarrassed I took Daddy's name again."

His face wavered uncertainly. Like all fanatics, he couldn't think about events except as they affected him directly. He might have given me the anonymous donor's name, but Marjorie had to stick in her two cents. She shuffled over on her uncertain legs and took the card from him.

"I thought your name was Spanish—Rosemary Him—something."

"I—I didn't want to use my real name unless I had to," I faltered.

Monkfish's eyes bulged farther. I was afraid they might pop out of his head and hit me in the face. Marjorie hadn't recognized the name, but he did—Rosemary Jiminez was the first woman killed from a back-alley abortion after the state cut off public-aid funds for poor women. She's become something of a rallying point in Illinois pro-choice circles.

"You—you're nothing but a filthy abortionist. Call the police, Marjorie. She may have stolen something."

He took my wrist and tried to pull me back into the office. I let him drag me in past the open doorway. As soon as his body was out of the way I jerked my wrist free and fled down the hallway.

XVII

The IckPiff Files

I spent the afternoon in Downers Grove hearing a horror story about blatant drug dealing in the little box factory. The owner listened while I sketched out an undercover surveillance plan involving me and a few young men working in the factory. The Streeter brothers, who had a moving and security-guard business, usually help me out on jobs like this. The owner was enthusiastic until I mentioned the fee, which runs about ten thousand a month on such an operation; he decided to spend the weekend mulling it over—deciding whether his losses from theft and downtime were less than my charges.

Even though August was sliding toward September, the days were still sweltering, especially in the late-afternoon jam of traffic on the Eisenhower. I stopped at home long enough to change from business attire into a bathing suit and spent the remainder of the daylight at the lake.

I waited until late evening to return to IckPiff. Mindful of the winos—who could be aggressive when drunk and in a group—I didn't carry a purse, but stuffed the Smith & Wesson into the belt of my jeans and stuck my wallet into a front pocket. I'd lost my picklocks last winter but I had a makeshift collection of some of the commoner kinds of keys and a plastic ruler in my back pocket.

As I drove over to Wells, I wondered why it mattered so much to me who was paying Dick's bill. I was very angry, certainly, that Monkfish was getting away scot-free with the destruction of Lotty's clinic. But would I have been as hot on the trail if some other attorney had represented him? I hated to think I suffered from residual bitterness after all these years.

I parked on the corner of Polk and Wells and covered the remaining block on foot. After dark is not a good time for women to be out alone in this area. In hot, muggy weather all the nightcrawlers come out. I knew I could outrun most of these derelicts, and in a pinch I could use the gun, but I still breathed easier when I made it into the stairwell of Monkfish's building without any more hassles than some obscene panhandling.

No lights in the stairwells. I turned on the pencil flash on my key chain so I could see as I climbed. Galloping feet behind the wainscoting told of the inevitable rats feasting on the remains of the dying building. A man lay pitched over at the turn of the second landing. He had vomited generously; it dripped down the stairs in large blobs and I stepped in one patch as I carefully climbed over his inert body.

I stood outside Monkfish's door for a few minutes, listening for signs of life within. I had no real expectation of a welcome committee—no sane person would hang around such a place after dark. Although the kindest well-wisher would not levy a charge of sanity against Monkfish.

I pulled out my collection of keys. Not worrying about the noise, I fiddled with the lock underneath the fetus poster. In deference to his neighbors, Monkfish had installed a double lock, which did not yield easily. It took about ten minutes of work to wrestle it open. Once inside I turned on the overhead light. No one who saw me enter the building was going to remember what I looked like, let alone what night I'd been here.

Stacks of envelopes lay sorted into zip codes on the deal table. They were neatly addressed by hand. Why invest in a computer when you had Marjorie? Indeed, a computer in a building like this wouldn't last a week. Marjorie was the sensible choice. I flipped open one of the envelopes to see what call to action Dieter was trumpeting this week.

"Abortion Mill Shut Down" trumpeted the typescript. "A small group of people dedicated to LIFE risked their lives and went to jail last week to stop a DEATH camp more hideous than Auschwitz." Thus Dieter rhapsodized about the destruction of Lotty's clinic. My stomach turned over; I was tempted to add arson to the breaking and entering on my charge sheet tonight.

The room held few places to secure anything. I found the ledgers and the membership list locked in Marjorie's desk drawer. Activity for the last three years seemed to be crammed into two giant books, one for receipts and one for disbursals. At least it was a system. Or so I thought until I started examining line items.

3/26—bought 20 boxes staples	$ 21.13
3/28—paid phone bill	198.42
3/31—paid electricity	12.81
4/2—cash receipts in mail	212.15

She apparently had started out with a system of disbursals and receipts and then had got in the habit of entering items in whichever log was closest to hand. No breakdown by type of expenditure.

I chewed on a pencil. I needed hours with these books and I didn't want to spend them with the rats and the drunks. Naturally the office didn't have a photocopier. Monkfish had my name and phone number. If I stole both books or cut out the last few pages from them, he would know to check on me. Inevitably, since I'd just been there making inquiries. On the other hand . . .

I gathered up the ledgers and stood the card-catalog drawer with donor names in it on top of them. I looked in my wallet. It held a twenty and seven singles. I crumpled the singles together in my fist, stuck two in my shirt pocket, and held the others tightly clasped over the top of the file drawer. Thus laden I went back downstairs, leaving the light on and the door open. My pal on the second-floor landing was still there and walking over him was even harder with the load I was carrying. I brushed his head with my left foot but didn't wake him.

Three men were camped in the hallway when I reached street level. They eyed me suspiciously, making no effort to move. I opened my fist and the wad of bills dropped. They dived for it instantly.

"Hey, that's mine," I whined. "I found it myself. You guys want money, you work for it the way I do."

I put the stack of papers on the floor and made an ineffectual grab for the cash. One of the men saw the singles in my pocket and snatched them out.

"C'mon, guys. Let me have it. There's plenty more upstairs. You want some, go get it yourself."

At that they stopped and looked at me hard.

"You got this upstairs?" one of them asked, a man of indeterminate age, perhaps white.

"There's an office open up there," I sniveled. "They left the lights on and everything. I found that in a drawer. There was a whole lot more, not locked up or anything. I didn't want to steal—I just took enough for a bottle."

Still eyeing me suspiciously, they muttered to themselves. They saw the box of name cards.

"She's got money in there," the speaker announced.

Before he could dump the contents—or steal the box—I opened it and riffled it in front of him. "Now how about my money?"

"Forget it." The speaker wore an overcoat several sizes too big and five months too warm.

His companions had backed away a little. Now they added menacing support, ordering me out of the way if I knew what was good for me. I shrank back in the malodorous doorway as they shuffled upstairs together, poking each other in the back, giggling in high, obscene cackles.

Outside, as I moved on up Wells Street toward my car, I

passed two men having an argument. One was dressed in a three-piece suit tailored for a man thirty pounds heavier, the other in a sleeveless T-shirt and dungarees.

"And I say nobody never hit better'n Billy Williams," the suit said in the tone of one clinching the matter, his face thrust close to T-shirt's.

"Hey!" I shouted at them. "There's an office open in that building with money in it. I found it and these guys tried to muscle me away."

It took a few repetitions, but they got the message and headed on down the street to Monkfish's building. I jogged swiftly to my car. The blue-and-whites come through a street like this pretty frequently; I didn't want to be picked up in the headlights.

Once in the Chevy I took off my foul-smelling running shoes and drove home barefoot. When I pulled up in front of my building I saw Peter's Maxima across the street. With a guilty start, I remembered we'd been going to have dinner together. My obsession about Monkfish and the afternoon drive to Downers Grove had pushed the date completely out of my mind.

I went into the lobby, expecting to find him there. When I didn't see him I headed up the stairs. Mr. Contreras's door opened behind me.

"There you are, doll. I've been entertaining the doc for you."

I came back down and went into the overstuffed living room. Peter was sitting in the mustard-colored armchair where Mr. Contreras had fed me hot milk the night of my injury. He was drinking a clear liquid—the foul grappa Mr. Contreras favored.

"Hi, Vic. I thought we had a date. Your neighbor took pity on me and brought me in for some grappa. We've been cursing the fickleness of women for some time now." He didn't move out of the armchair. I couldn't figure out whether this was due to anger at being stood up, or paralysis, a typical side effect of grappa.

"With good reason. I apologize. I got a bee in my bonnet or something about how Dieter Monkfish was affording my ex-husband's legal fees. And I'm afraid I was so intent on getting evidence about it that I forgot our plans."

I offered to raid my insubstantial larder for him, but Mr. Contreras had grilled ribs in the backyard and they were both content.

"So did you get your evidence? Is that it?" That was Mr. Contreras.

"I hope so. It's IckPiff's ledgers, and I had to fight off winos to get it, so they'd better be useful."

Peter sat up, sloshing his drink on his trousers. "You burglarized them, Vic?"

The sharpness in his voice nettled me. "You from the Legion of Decency or something? All I want to know is who is paying Dick's monster bill. He won't tell me, Monkfish won't tell me, and Crawford, Meade won't tell me. So I'm going to find out. Then I will return their ledgers. Even though I think they are mad lunatics whose papers should be burned I'm not going to erase a single line item. Though I may call their auditors—these are the most screwed-up books I ever saw."

"But, Vic. You can't do that. You really shouldn't."

"So call the police. Or take me to church in the morning."

As I left the room, Mr. Contreras said in an urgent undertone, "Go apologize to her. She's just doing her job— don't blow a good thing over a little incident like this."

Peter seemed to think this was sound advice. He caught up with me as I started up the stairs. "Sorry, Vic. Didn't mean to criticize. The thing is, I've been drinking more than I should. These the documents? Here, let me carry 'em for you."

He took the books from me and followed me up the stairs. I carried my malodorous shoes into the kitchen and began pouring water and Clorox on them. I was really furious, both with his criticism, and also with myself for having said anything. It's never a good idea to let people know that you've been obtaining information through questionable means. If I hadn't been startled, guilty, feeling at ease with

132

Mr. Contreras, and pissed as hell with Dick, I wouldn't have said one word about it. Goes to show.

Peter gave me a tentative, alcoholic kiss behind my ear. "C'mon, Vic. Scout's honor, I won't say anything more about your—uh—business methods. Okay?"

"Yeah, okay." I finished rinsing my shoes. My hands now smelled of Clorox, not as bad as vomit, but not good. I rubbed lemon juice into them. Not all the perfumes of Arabia. "No one likes being criticized, Peter. Least of all me. At least not on stuff that's connected with my job."

"You're right. You're absolutely right. Did I ever tell you I was descended from the General Burgoyne who did so badly for the British at Saratoga? I know just how he felt. The Americans fought dirty, and he got squeamish. So put down my idiotic objections to burglary as squeamishness. Okay, General Washington?"

"Okay." I couldn't help laughing. "Done . . . I need to get some food and there ain't a hell of a lot to eat here. Are you up to a trip to the all-night diner or have you had it for the day?"

He put both arms around me. "No, sure. Let's go. Maybe a walk'll clear my head."

Before going out I called the *Herald-Star*'s city desk and told them drunks were pawing through IckPiff's headquarters. In case that wasn't enough, I called the police, too—not 911, where all the lines are monitored, but the Central District Headquarters.

Well pleased with myself, I walked with Peter, who was still a bit unsteady, to the Belmont Diner, a twenty-four-hour place where old Mrs. Bielsen bakes her own pies and cooks fresh soups. He excused himself to make a phone call while I ate cold tomato soup—called gazpacho in upscale restaurants where it's half as good at twice the price—and a BLT on wholewheat. I was paying the bill when Peter finally returned, his narrow, mobile face troubled.

"Bad news on the delivery front?" I asked.

"No," he shook his head. "Personal problem." His face cleared and he tried for a lighter note. "I keep a boat up on Pistakee Lake. It's not a real big lake, so it's not a real big boat—twenty-footer with one sail. How about coming up tomorrow—spend the day on the water? I don't have any patients to see and I can cancel all my meetings.''

The weather was still so hot that a day in the country sounded great. And if the Downers Grove box factory hired me, this might be my last free day for some time. We went back to my apartment in good humor, Peter making a successful effort to keep his private worries at bay. Mr. Contreras popped his head out the door as we came in.

"Ah, good. You took my advice, young man. You won't be sorry.''

Peter flushed and stiffened. I felt slightly embarrassed myself. Mr. Contreras watched us go up the stairs together, hands solemnly at our sides, and finally closed his door when we disappeared around the landing. We burst into an explosion of guilty laughter when we got to the top.

XVIII

Messing About in a Boat

The Herald-Star had a nice little story about IckPiff head-lined VANDALS WRECK ABORTION FOE OFFICE. I was afraid they might relegate it to the second section, where the previous day's haul of rapists, murderers, car wrecks, and drug busts are reported, but they tucked the lead into the bottom of the front page. Dieter Monkfish attributed the break-in to the machinations of the evil baby murderers, retaliating for the destruction of Lotty's clinic, but the police said they'd found five drunks having a fight, flinging drawers open and throwing paper at each other.

The five men had been charged with breaking and entering, disorderly conduct, and vandalism. The story was nice and short—it didn't include room for comments from the drunks on mysterious ladies who might have sent them up to IckPiff in the first place.

I'd gone to the corner store for the paper and some food while Peter continued to sleep off the grappa. He staggered into the kitchen as I was finishing my second cup of coffee, wearing his underpants and my bathrobe, his eyes squinted shut. He held out a hand and said piteously: "Coffee."

I poured him a cup. "I hope you feel better than you look, General Burgoyne. Want to call off the trip to Lake Pistakee?"

"No," he said hoarsely. "I'll be okay. I just need to get used to the idea that I'm not dead. Jesus Christ, what the hell did that guy give me last night?"

He sat morosely for a while, sipping the coffee and burying his face in its steam, shuddering at the mention of food. With a heartiness typical of the virtuous sober in the face of a friend's hangover, I ate pita bread with swiss cheese, tomato, lettuce, and mustard. When Peter didn't respond to the news that the Cubs had beaten the Braves in Atlanta last night—in thirteen innings—I left him huddled by the kitchen table and went into the living room to call Lotty.

"I read about this IckPiff burglary in the morning paper, Lotty. Dieter the Mad thinks it's pro-choice monsters getting even with him for smashing up your clinic. Want me to send over the Streeter brothers to keep an eye on things in case his followers decide to come back for seconds?"

She'd read the article, too. "Just give me their number. If anyone shows up I'll call them. You don't know anything about this break-in, do you, Vic?"

"Me, boss? The paper says five drunks were up there getting ready for a ticker-tape parade." I looked at the IckPiff files where Peter had perched them on the mountain of *Wall Street Journal*s covering the coffee table.

"Yes, Vic. I can read. Also I know you. Thanks for calling—I have to run."

I sat cross-legged on the floor with the card catalog on my lap. From the background sounds, Peter had decided to revive his life-support system in the shower. I started with the A's. At a guess, there were six thousand names in the file. If I could go through ten a minute, that was ten hours. My favorite kind of work, the main reason I'm sorry the women's movement came to life before I could use my B.A. to be a secretary.

I'd gotten to Attwood, Edna and Bill, who'd donated fifteen dollars a year for the last four years, when Peter came in. He was dressed and looked more like a human being, although not one I'd trust my obstetrical care to.

"Having any luck with your files?" he asked.

"I've just begun. I figure at the steady pace I'm working I should be at the end around Thanksgiving sometime."

"Can you bear to leave them for a while? It's nine-thirty now—I need to stop at home to change, so it'll be noon or so before we get to the boat if we leave now."

"Fine with me. These will certainly keep until tomorrow." I stood up in one movement, pushing with my quadriceps. We learned how in kindergarten and I've always been proud of being able to do it—not everybody can.

Even though the line in my face was disappearing, Dr. Pirwitz had stressed keeping it out of the sun for another several months. I had bought myself a little golfing cap with a long green polarized sun bill in front—twenty-five dollars at a pro shop, but worth it. That, with white jeans, a white sleeveless shirt, a bathing suit, and my Cubs jacket—in case it got cold on the lake—and I was ready.

Peter looked at me faintly. "The Cubs jacket *and* a green golfing cap? Please, Vic. My stomach can't take it this time of day."

He also objected to the Smith & Wesson. I, too, wondered about the point in carrying it around—nothing was happening. If Sergio was seeking revenge for my filing charges, he was taking a lot longer to act than the gangs usually do. I weighed the gun in my hand, finally compromising by promising to lock it in my glove compartment for the duration of the trip.

I followed the Maxima to his home in Barrington Hills. He had a beautiful place. Not a large house, maybe eight rooms, but set on three acres, with a little wood and a creek running through it. Birds were twittering in the midday heat. The air was fresh, no hydrocarbons to clog the sinuses. I had to admit it would be hard to leave it just for the joy of practicing medicine in the city.

His dog, a golden retriever named Princess Scheherazade of Du Page but called Peppy, bounded out to meet us. Peter had a fancy electronic dog feeder set up, since he often was away on business as well as pleasure, which measured out a ration of dog food at six every evening in her large, covered kennel. She seemed perfectly happy—never bearing a grudge for long periods of abandonment.

I'd been to Peter's a few times already. The dog seemed to know me and was almost as glad to see me as him. I stayed in the yard to play fetch with her while Peter went inside to change into sailing gear. He came back half an hour later in faded jeans and a T-shirt, carrying a cooler.

"I packed us up some cheese and stuff for the boat," he called. "You don't mind if we take Peppy with us, do you?"

It was hard to see how we could keep her away. At the sight of Peter in civvies, she went wild, banging her tail madly into the side of the car, doing a little dance and panting. When he opened the door, she sprang into the backseat and sat there with a defiant grin on her face.

Lake Pistakee was another sixteen or so miles to the north. We drove slowly on country roads, the windows open, the rich air of late summer enveloping us voluptuously. Peppy kept her head out the window the whole time, giving little grunts of excitement as we got closer to the water. As soon as we stopped, she jumped through the window and bounded down to the lake.

I followed Peter out to the marina. It was a workday; despite the dozens of boats docked there, we had the place to ourselves. His was a pretty little boat, white fiberglass trimmed in red, just big enough for a couple of adults and a large dog. Peppy leaped in in front of us, slowing down the launching by running back and forth across the length of the boat while we were untying it.

We spent a delightful day on the water, swimming, picnicking, holding the boat steady while Peppy jumped over the side after a flock of ducks. The city, with Sergio, dead bodies, and Dieter Monkfish, receded into the background. Peter lapsed occasionally into a brooding silence, but whatever was bothering him he kept to himself.

At seven, as the sun set, we returned to the marina. It was crowded now with families taking to the water, escaping from the week's pressures. Children screamed shrilly. I watched one little girl carefully pick up a plastic buggy holding a large doll family to carry it over the rough aluminum docks. Cabin cruisers filled the air with whining and gasoline, and freckled young businessmen hollered at each other with beery goodwill.

We drove into the quiet of the countryside and found dinner at a little place on a side road. It wasn't much of a restaurant, the kind of place where you can get an average steak or awful quasi-French dishes and chilled red Inglenook. I drank Black Label while Peter had beer; we wrapped up the remains of our steak for Peppy and went back to Peter's house.

While he checked in with the hospital from the phone in his study, I called my answering service on the other line in the kitchen. Lotty wanted me to call; it was urgent.

I dialed her number, my heart pounding: If she had been vandalized again. And because of my stupid burglary . . . She answered on the first ring, in a most un-Lotty-like frenzy.

"Vic! . . . No, no, the clinic's all right. No one showed up today. But at noon I had a call from a lawyer. A man named"—she was apparently consulting a piece of paper—"Gerald Rutkowski. He wanted my records on Consuelo."

"I see. A malpractice claim. Who filed it, I wonder? Does Carol know?"

"Oh, yes." Lotty's voice was bitter, the Viennese accent pronounced. "It was Fabiano. His revenge for harassment by you and her brothers, she thinks. Vic, the problem is—Consuelo's file is missing."

I said reasonably, "Well, we refiled everything last week. Maybe her stuff got stuck in with some other patient's file."

"Oh, believe me, Vic, that was my first thought. My first reaction. Mrs. Coltrain and Carol and I went through every file in there, every piece of paper. There is not one document about Consuelo."

I couldn't help being skeptical—it's so easy to lose papers. I said as much, offering to go over in the morning to hunt for the file myself.

"Vic, Consuelo's file is not in the clinic. Neither is Fabiano's, or his mother's. My only hope in calling you is that you might remember doing something with papers while you were working with them. Perhaps taken them home with you inadvertently.''

''No,'' I said slowly, trying to visualize my movements while working in the clinic last week. ''I'll check my car, of course, and look through my place. But not a whole stack of documents—I don't think I could walk off with those and not know I had them. No, if they're really gone, one of the clinic vandals must have stolen them.''

Cleaning up the mess, we'd sorted records from broken glass, had cleaned and dried records sticky with spilled medication, had pulled paper from behind radiators and underneath cabinets. But we had not found any mutilated or shredded documents—nothing to indicate that files had been destroyed during the brief violent occupation.

''Why steal the Hernandez files?'' I asked aloud. ''Are any other patient records missing?''

She had spot-checked the records, but with two thousand or so patient files, it was tough to tell if any others were gone.

Peter came into the kitchen. He started to talk, then realized I was on the phone. When he heard me ask about the files, he looked concerned.

I concentrated on Lotty. ''What are they suing you for doing, or not doing?'' I asked.

''They haven't sued me. They just want the record. That means they're contemplating a suit. If they think they have grounds after looking at the record they'll file a claim. I don't know what the charge will be. Probably a combination of failure to treat her properly during the pregnancy and negligence in not supervising her care out at Friendship more closely. And if I can't turn over her patient records, I might as well concede without a fight. I can just imagine a prosecuting attorney with that.''

So could I. ''And tell us, Dr. Herschel. Do you really expect the jury to believe that your memory, unaided by any documents whatsoever—yes, we understand you *lost* them—is as reliable as Dr. X's expert testimony?''

140

"Look," I said. "This is impossible to discuss on the phone. I'm out in Barrington right now, but I could come see you at about ten-thirty or so."

"If you could come tonight, Vic, I would appreciate it very much."

I hung up and turned to Peter. "Lotty's missing some patient files. Consuelo's among others. It looks as though Fabiano Hernandez is suing for malpractice. Don't you have some record of Consuelo's treatment at Friendship? Do you think you could make a copy and get it to Lotty? She's got to be in a godawful legal spot, not being able to produce her records. If she had the file on what you did out at Friendship, it would be better than nothing."

"Sued?" he repeated angrily. "Sued by that little jackal? I'd better call Humphries. We gave that little bastard money just to avoid a suit. I can't believe it. Goddamn little bastard."

"Yes, well, it is annoying and obnoxious. But can you get a copy of Consuelo's file? I'm going over to Lotty's now. I i like to be able to tell her something useful."

He ignored me and went to the phone. I couldn't think who Humphries was at first. Then, as Peter spoke—"Alan! Sorry to get you out of bed"—I remembered: Alan Humphries, the blow-dried administrator at Friendship. He'd given Fabiano five thousand in hush money. Protection money. So would Fabiano honor that and keep Friendship out of the suit? Or had he decided the baby-blue Eldorado was so nice, he should go back to the source and get more?

Peter hung up. "So far as Alan knows, we haven't been hit with anything. But since Dr. Herschel was the primary care provider, we won't know until they actually file a claim."

I came close to punching him in the nose. "Can you think of something besides yourself for a minute? I want to know if you can get Friendship's file on Consuelo for Dr. Herschel. Did you even think to talk to Humphries about that? Or were you too absorbed in your own damned worries?"

"Hey, Vic—take it easy. This kind of damned thing, they

take an elephant gun and fire at anyone who was near the patient. Sorry to think of Friendship first, but we're just as vulnerable as Lotty. More so—the lawyers will come after us because they see we have the money.'' He hesitated and held out a hand. ''Can't you give me some of the concern you have for her?''

I took his fingers between my hands and looked at them instead of his face. ''I've known Lotty for close to twenty years. First she filled in for my mother, and then we became—friends is a weak word for it. Close, anyway. So when she has problems, they trouble me, too. When you and I have known each other twenty years, I'll probably feel the same way about you, too.''

He squeezed my hand so hard I winced. Looking at his face I was astounded to see it drained of color, the eyes shining black and fevered in the lamplight.

''I hope so, Vic. I hope I know you twenty years from now.''

I kissed him. ''You make it sound like high tragedy. No reason why we shouldn't—I ain't prone to dropping dead at a moment's notice. But I do want to head back to town now. Lotty needs me, and she wouldn't have asked me to make the long drive back if she didn't.''

''Okay,'' he agreed reluctantly. ''I'm not crazy about it, but I guess I can understand.''

''And will you look up your file on Consuelo for her?''

''Yeah, sure. I'll do it Monday. Drive carefully.''

He kissed me good-bye at the door. Convinced we were going back to the lake, Peppy followed me happily to my car. When I didn't let her into the car, she watched me haughtily from the tarmac until I was out of sight.

XIX

Uptown Blues

I ended up dragging Lotty back to the clinic so I could see for myself that the files weren't there. It's an irrational itch—when someone's lost something, you're convinced you can find it—that they've overlooked some obscure hiding place from which you'll triumphantly produce it. I pulled up rugs, looked behind radiators, under every surface, in every drawer, lifted out the hanging files to see if Consuelo and the Hernandez family had somehow slipped underneath. After a couple of hours of pulling and lifting, I had to admit that the records were gone.

"What about Malcolm's dictation—his notes after he saw Consuelo out at Friendship? Do you still have the tape?"

She shook her head. "I never got it. When his place was broken into, they must have stolen the dictating machine."

"Damned funny thing to steal if they did. They didn't take the TV or the phone machine."

"Well, maybe they couldn't carry the TV," Lotty said, not really interested. "It was a big old-fashioned one; wasn't it? He got it secondhand from one of his professors. To tell you the truth, I forgot about the dictation in the shock of

143

his death. I suppose we could go now to see if it's still there.''

''Why not? I was only going to sleep tonight anyway.'' I drove her the few miles to Malcolm's old apartment.

Even Uptown quiets down in early morning. There were some drunks on the street, and an old man walking his dog, both moving cautiously on slow arthritic legs. But no one bothered us as we went into the stale lobby and climbed the three flights to Malcolm's door.

''I'm going to have to do something about this place,'' Lotty commented, fishing in her purse for the keys. ''The lease runs for another month. Then I suppose I'll have to clean it out. I don't know why he named me executor. I'm not particularly good at that kind of job.''

''Get Tessa to do it,'' I suggested. ''She can decide what she wants to keep and then throw everything else out. Or leave the door open. Things will evaporate quickly enough.''

Over the appalling mess of Malcolm's life now lay the stale smell of abandoned rooms. Somehow the smell, and the layers of dust, made the carnage more bearable. This was no longer a place where a real person lived. Just a wreck, something you might find at the bottom of the lake.

Lotty, usually fiercely energetic, stood passively in the doorway while I searched. She'd had too many shocks lately—Consuelo's death, Malcolm's death, the ravaging of her clinic, and now this malpractice claim. If it weren't so farfetched, I could almost believe all the events had been engineered by someone with a grudge against Lotty—perhaps Dieter Monkfish, madman that he was, attacking her most vulnerable spots to force her to retire. I sat back on my heels to consider it. That would mean collusion between Fabiano and Monkfish, which was hard to believe. And that Monkfish hired muscle to batter Malcolm, which was ludicrous.

I got to my feet.

''It's not here, Lotty. Either it's in some Clark Street pawnshop, or Malcolm left it in his car. We could check there if you have the keys.''

''Of course. My brain is not functioning these days. We

should have looked there first—he always did his dictation in the car if he couldn't finish it at the hospital.''

Even reform-minded Harold Washington isn't much interested in Uptown. Only a few streetlights functioned, and we had to go slowly up the street, looking at each car. The arthritic man and dog had gone home and the drunks were mostly sleeping, but a couple was arguing under one of the streetlamps near the end of the block. Malcolm's blue Dodge, dented and rusty with age, was parked close to them. It fit into the neighborhood well enough that no one had bothered it—the wheels were all still attached, windows intact, trunk unforced.

I unlocked the driver's door. The interior lights didn't work. I used the pencil flash on my key ring, saw nothing on the seat or in the glove compartment, and felt under the car seat. My fingers closed on a small leather case, and I pulled out Malcolm's recorder.

We walked back down the street to my car. Lotty took the machine from me and snapped it open.

''It's empty,'' she said. ''He must have done something else with the tape.''

''Or he had it in his apartment and his killers stole it—they took all his stereo tapes.''

We were both too exhausted to speak anymore. As we drove home, Lotty sat silently hunched over in the corner, her face in her hands. I've known her for many years, seen her in many moods, but never so depressed or lethargic she could neither think nor act.

It was almost four when we got back to her apartment. I helped her upstairs, heated up some milk, and poured in a large slug of brandy, the only alcohol she keeps in her place. It was a measure of her dejection that she drank it without protesting.

''I'm calling the clinic,'' I told her, ''leaving a message on the machine that you won't be in until late. You need sleep now more than anything else.''

She looked at me blankly. ''Yes. Yes, you are possibly right. You, too, Vic. You should sleep. I'm sorry to have kept you up all night. Lie down in the spare room if you want. I'll turn off the phones.''

I crawled under the thin, lavender-scented sheets on Lotty's spare bed. My bones ached and I felt gritty. The jumbled events of the day churned over and over in my brain. Monkfish. Dick's fee. The IckPiff files. Where was Malcolm's tape? Where was Consuelo's file?

The baby had them. She was sitting on a high bluff overlooking Lake Michigan, a manila folder in her tiny purple fingers. I was trying to climb up the dune to get to her, but my feet slipped on the scorching sand and I kept falling down. Hot and thirsty, I staggered to my feet. I saw Peter Burgoyne come up behind the baby. He grabbed at the folder and tried to take it from her, but her grip was too strong. He let go of the file and began strangling her. She made no sound, but watched me with piteous eyes.

I woke sweating and choking, disoriented. When I realized I wasn't in my own bed I panicked for a few seconds until the events of the previous night returned. I was at Lotty's. The little travel clock on the elegant bedside table hadn't been wound. I fished around for my watch in the clothes I'd thrown on the floor. Seven-thirty.

I lay back down, trying to relax, but I couldn't do it. I got up and took a long shower. I cracked open Lotty's door. She was still asleep, a frown drawing her heavy brows together. I closed the door softly behind me and left her apartment.

I knew something was wrong as soon as I started up the stairs in my building. Papers were strewn on the steps, and when I reached the second-floor landing I saw a spot of something that looked like dried blood. I had my gun out without thinking, running up the last sixteen stairs.

Mr. Contreras lay in front of my apartment. The door itself had been taken out with an ax. I wasted a minute making sure the place was empty, then knelt down next to the old man. His head had bled fiercely from a scalp wound, but the blood had clotted. He was breathing, short stertorous breaths, but he was alive. I left him for a minute to crawl through the ax hole. Called for the paramedics, called the police, dragged a blanket from my bedroom to wrap him in. While I waited, I felt him gently. The wound to his head seemed to be the only injury. A pipe wrench lay about a yard from his crumpled body.

The fire department arrived first—a young man and a middle-aged woman in dark-blue uniforms, both muscular and short on words. They listened to what I knew while hustling Mr. Contreras onto a stretcher; they got him down the stairs in less than a minute. I held the doors for them and watched them slide him into the ambulance and head for Beth Israel.

A few minutes later, a couple of blue-and-whites squealed to a halt in front of the building. Three uniformed men leaped out; one stayed in the car manning the radio or calling in reports or something.

I went out to greet them. "I'm V. I. Warshawski. It was my apartment that got broken into."

One of them, an older black man with a potbelly, wrote my name down slowly while they followed me up the stairs. I went through the routine: what time I'd come home, where I'd spent the night, was anything missing.

"I don't know. I just got back here. My neighbor was lying comatose in front of the door—I was a lot more concerned about him than I was about a few stinking belongings." My voice was unsteady. Anger, shock, the goddamned fucking last straw. I could not cope with this break-in or the injury to Mr. Contreras.

The youngest of the trio wanted to know about Mr. Contreras. "Boyfriend?"

"Use your head," I snapped. "He's in his seventies. He's a retired machinist who thinks he's still the muscleman he was forty years ago and he's set himself up as my foster father. He lives on the ground floor and every time I come or go in the building he pops out to make sure I'm okay. He must have followed whoever did this up the stairs and tried to take them out with the pipe wrench. Goddamned old fool." To my horror I felt tears springing to the corners of my eyes. I took a deep, steadying breath and waited for the next question.

147

"He expecting someone?"

"Oh, a couple of weeks ago I had an encounter with Sergio Rodriguez from the Lions—Detective Rawlings knows all about it—over at the Sixth Area. Mr. Contreras thought he ought to keep a lookout to see if they'd try to come in the night for me. I told him if he heard anyone he should send for you guys at once, but I guess he still thinks he ought to be a hero."

They all chimed in at once, wanting to know about Sergio. I gave them my standard Sergio story, about how he bore this long grudge against me for his prison sentence. One of them called on his radio down to the relay man in the car asking him to phone Rawlings. While they wrote up notes and waited for the detective, I wandered through my apartment, looking at mess. Something was wrong in the living room, but I wasn't sure what. My television was still there; so was the stereo, but all my books and records had been heaved onto the floor in a vast, sprawled mountain.

A few minor, portable items seemed to be missing, but the only things I really care about—my mother's wineglasses—were still standing in the dining-room cupboard. The little safe in the hall closet hadn't been touched; it held her diamond pendant and earrings. I couldn't imagine wearing such delicate jewelry myself, but I would never dispose of them. Who knows—I might have a daughter of my own someday. Stranger things have happened.

"Don't touch anything," the young white cop warned me.

"No, no. I won't." Not that it mattered. With nine hundred or so murders a year to solve, and aggravated batteries and rapes by the yard, a burglary wasn't going to get high priority. But we would all pretend that the burglary squad's fingerprinting and searching would really accomplish something.

The only thing I would just as soon they didn't look at too closely was the IckPiff ledgers. I went back into the living room to take a surreptitious look for them and realized what was wrong.

My coffee table is usually piled high with old copies of

The Wall Street Journal, mail that I haven't got around to answering, and miscellaneous personal items. Peter had stacked the ledgers and the membership file on the newspapers. When I left yesterday morning I had perched the name files precariously back on top. Now, not only were they gone, all the papers were missing. Someone had bundled up everything, newspapers, letters, magazines, an old pair of running socks I should have put away, and made off with them.

"What's wrong?" the potbellied black cop asked. "Something missing in here?"

I couldn't afford to talk about it. Not even to say my old newspapers were gone. Because if someone stole your old newspapers, it had to be because they thought you were hiding something in them.

"Not that I know of, Officer. I guess it's just starting to really hit me."

XX

Family Ties

Rawlings showed up around nine with an evidence team. He questioned the uniformed men, then sent them away and came into the living room. I had moved from the floor to the couch.

"Well, well, Ms. W. Didn't think housekeeping was your strong suit when I was here before, but this mess is pretty special."

"Thanks, Detective. I did it just for you."

"That so." He wandered over to the south wall, the one opposite the windows where I'd installed a wall unit for records and books. These were scattered on the floor, records partly out of jackets, books heaved every which way. He picked up a couple of volumes at random.

"Primo Levi? What kind of a name is that? Italian? You read Italian?"

"Yeah. The uniformed men told me not to touch anything until the evidence team came through."

"And then you'd have a sudden housekeeping fit and clean it all up. I hear you. Well, they have my prints on file. And I presume they have yours. They get a brainstorm or run out of work and take to dusting all these books and records, they can sort ours out from the burglars'. What were they looking for?''

I shook my head. ''Damned if I know. I'm not employed right now. I'm not working on anything. There's nothing for anybody to look for.''

''Yeah, and I'm the King of Sweden. Anything missing?''

''Well, I haven't been through all the books. So I don't know if my copies of *Little Women* and *Black Beauty* are still here. My mother gave them to me for my ninth birthday and it'd break my heart if someone stole them. And my old Doors album—the one with 'Light My Fire' on it, or *Abbey Road*— I'd sure hate to find they were gone.''

''So what would someone think you have, babe?''

I looked around me. ''Who you talking to?''

''You, Ms. W.''

''Not when you call me 'babe,' you ain't.''

He made a little bow. ''Excuse me, Ms. Warshawski. Ma'am. Let me rephrase the question. What would someone think you have, Ms. Warshawski?''

I shrugged. ''I've been going round on that one ever since I got home. All I can think is that it was Sergio. I went to see little Fabiano a couple of days ago. That boy knows something he isn't saying; he got upset at my questions and started to cry. Yesterday he found some sleazebag to sue Dr. Herschel for malpractice. So I was with her last night, trying to cheer her up a little. Maybe the Lions decided to avenge Fabiano's alleged manhood by coming through here.''

Rawlings pulled a cigar from his inside jacket pocket.

''Yes, I mind if you smoke that in here. Besides, it'll screw up the evidence team.''

He looked at it longingly and put it away. ''You didn't beat the boy up, by any chance?''

''Not so's it'd show. He telling people I did?''

''He isn't telling anyone anything. But we saw him all black-and-blue after his wife's funeral. What we heard was he was in a car accident, but unless it fell over on top of his head, I don't see it.''

''Honest and truly, Detective—that wasn't me. I wondered,

too, but all I heard was he hit his head on the Eldorado wind-shield.''

''Well, sister—excuse me, Ms. Warshawski—let's all pray for the recovery of your neighbor. If it was Sergio, that's the only way we're going to nail him.''

I agreed with him soberly and not just because I wanted to nail Sergio. Poor Mr. Contreras. It was only two days since they'd taken out the stitches where the fetus worshipers had hit him. Now this. I hoped to God his head was as hard as he always claimed it was.

After the evidence team finished their ministrations and I signed a zillion or so forms and statements, I called our build-ing super and got him to board up the front door. I'd go in and out the back way until I had a new door installed.

I'd have called Lotty, but she had too many troubles of her own right now. She didn't need mine, too. Instead, I wandered aimlessly through my place. It wasn't that the damage was irradicable. Some of the piano strings had been cut, but the instrument wasn't harmed. The things on the floor could all be put back. It wasn't like Malcolm's place, where everything was smashed to bits. But it was still a violent assault, and that is numbing. If I had been here . . . The noise of the door being smashed open would have woken me up. I probably could have shot them. Too bad I hadn't been home.

I went back to bed, too depressed to try to clean up. Too worn out by the combined assaults of the last few weeks to do anything. I lay down, but I couldn't get back to sleep for the thrashing in my head.

Say old Dieter discovered in the general mayhem of his office that the card catalog of members was gone. And he figured, as he'd said to the *Herald-Star*, that it was the evil abortionists who'd done it. And he hired someone—say the cute college kids I'd seen throwing rocks at Lotty's—to smash in my door and create havoc so as to get the ledgers and card catalog back but make it look like burglary. Or just to get even.

It was plausible. Even possible. But he'd have to guess I had the files; he didn't know for certain. The one person who def-initely knew I had them was Peter Burgoyne.

Who had he really been phoning from the restaurant? He'd

said it was personal—maybe he had an ex-wife stashed in an attic someplace. And he'd gotten me out of the city for the day. But if he was behind the break-in, why? And who could he get on a moment's notice to do something like this?

Round and round I went, my brain exhausted, my body worn out, the little slashes on my face and neck aching with tension. I could call him, of course. Better to see him. On the phone he might deny it, but he had such an expressive face that I thought I'd know he was lying by looking at him.

I could call Dick. See if there was some reason why Friendship or Peter Burgoyne didn't want me having the IckPiff files. Dick might well represent Friendship. But why would they care about a poor old lunatic like Dieter Monkfish? I could imagine the reception I'd get from Dick, too.

Action. What every detective needs. I got up and phoned Peter's house. I thought he sounded a little nervous at my voice.

"You okay?"

"Sure. Sure I'm okay. Why do you ask?" I demanded aggressively.

"You sound edgy. Something happen with Dr. Herschel—her malpractice suit?"

"Nothing more on that. Can I come out to Barrington today, pick up a copy of that record for her? You know, Consuelo's file from the hospital?"

"Vic. Please. I told you I'd look it up on Monday. Even if I could persuade the hospital to release it today, there's nothing she could do with it this weekend."

I tried to set up a date with him for the weekend, but he said that he wouldn't have any free time until after his conference was over—he had taken Friday off and that was his last play day until next weekend.

"Well, don't forget that record for Lotty. I know it's not as important as your conference, or getting sued yourself, but it matters a lot to her."

"Oh, for God's sake, Vic. I thought we'd thrashed all that out last night. I'll get on to the damned records office first thing Monday morning." He broke the connection with an angry snap.

I suddenly felt embarrassed at my suspicions and my rudeness and quelled an impulse to call Peter back with an apology. Since I wasn't in the humor to clean and wasn't able to sleep, maybe I'd stop by Beth Israel to check on Mr. Contreras.

I was dressing for a trip to the hospital when the phone rang; it was Dick, anticipating my thoughts. When we'd been in law school together a hundred years ago or so a call from him could make my heart flutter. Now it turned my stomach.

"Dick! What a surprise. Does Stephanie know you're calling me?"

"Goddamn it, Vic, her name is Terri. I swear to God you call her Stephanie just to annoy me."

"No, no, Dick. I would never do anything just to annoy you. There has to be some other good reason, too—it's a little rule I made for myself when we were married. Do you want something? I'm not behind on my alimony payments, am I?"

He said stiffly, "My client's office was broken into two nights ago."

"Which client? Or do you only have one these days?"

"Dieter Monkfish." He spat the name out. "The police say that the area winos broke into it. But the door wasn't broken open—the lock was picked."

"Maybe he forgot to lock it. People do, you know."

He ignored my helpful suggestion. "He's missing some items. A membership roster and his account ledgers. He tells me you were by earlier on Thursday looking at them, that he shooed you out. He thinks you have them."

"And you think I might have picked his lock, and so on. Well, I don't have anything that belongs to Dieter Monkfish. Not even his wandering wits, let alone his ledgers. I swear to you on my honor as an ex–Girl Scout that if you got a warrant and searched my home, my office, or the premises of any of my close or distant friends you would find neither hide nor hair of any papers belonging to Dieter Monkfish or his crazy pals. Okay?"

"Yeah, I guess," he said grudgingly, not sure whether to believe me or not.

"And now that you've called and virtually accused me of burglary, which is slanderous and actionable, let me ask you something: Which one of your clients is paying Monkfish's bill?''

He hung up on me. Dick's manners are always so testy, it's hard for me to see how he was elected partner in a firm that counts so heavily on public image. I shook my head over it and went over to Beth Israel.

The police had not bothered with a guard. They figured that Mr. Contreras had surprised home invaders in the act and had been coshed as a side effect—no one was gunning for him personally. Or bludgeoning. I didn't disagree, just thought it would be good to have someone with him if he recovered enough to identify the marauders.

At the hospital they told me that he was still unconscious, in intensive care, but with good vital signs. In the little waiting room for the intensive-care unit, the resident on call informed me that head injuries are tricky. He might wake up at any moment, or remain unconscious for some time. And no, I couldn't see him, the only people allowed into intensive care were family members, one at a time, fifteen minutes every two hours.

I've argued with Lotty about these rules a thousand times or so. You most need a warm and soothing presence when your life is on the line. Perhaps technology can save your body, but not your spirit. If I couldn't move Lotty, who is a maverick in most medical matters, I wasn't going to budge the resident—he had all of Institutionalized Medicine to lean on. He ended the argument by going back through the doors separating me from Mr. Contreras.

I was about to leave when an over-madeup woman in her mid-forties came in. She carried about thirty extra pounds, which made her look like an inflated rubber doll. Two boys followed reluctantly in her wake, one around twelve, the other a few years older. They wore clean jeans and white shirts with wornout sneakers—today's uniform for a boy dragged to formal events by his parents.

"I'm Mrs. Marcano," she announced in the harsh nasal voice of the South Side. "Where's my dad?"

Of course. Mr. Contreras's daughter, Ruthie. I'd heard her

voice wafting up the stairwell numerous times but had never actually met the lady.

"He's in through there." I jerked a hand at the door leading to the ICU nursing station. "The receptionist can get the doctor for you."

"Who are you?" she demanded. Mr. Contreras's wide brown eyes had been transplanted into her face, but without the warmth.

"V. I. Warshawski. His upstairs neighbor. I found him this morning."

"So you're the lady that got him into so much trouble. I might've guessed. He got his head cut open for you two weeks ago, didn't he? But that wasn't enough, was it? You had to try to get him killed, too, didn't you?"

"Ma, please." The elder of the two boys was suffused with the embarrassment only a teenager can feel when his parents make public fools of themselves. "She didn't try to kill Gramps. The detective said she saved his life. You know he did."

"You're going to believe a cop before you'll listen to me?" She switched her attention back to me. "He's an old man. He should be living with me. I got a good home. In a safe neighborhood, not like this Uptown or whatever, where he's going to be attacked every time he sets foot outside his door.

"I'm his only daughter, aren't I? But he has to go following you around like a sheep. Every time I go see him, it's Miss Warshawski this, Miss Warshawski that, till I'm ready to throw up when I hear your name. You like her so much, you marry her, that's what I said. The way you talk, you might as well not have a family, that's what I told him. Joe and I suddenly aren't as good as this college-educated lawyer, is that it? Ma wasn't good enough for you? Is that what you're trying to tell us?"

Her son kept bleating "Ma, please" to no avail. He and his brother shrank as far away from her as they could, looking around them with the doubtful expressions people often have in hospitals.

I was reeling under the flow of words. She'd certainly inherited her dad's oratory style.

"They won't let me go in to see him, but if you tell the receptionist you're his daughter, she'll get the resident in charge to take you in. Nice to meet you."

I fled the hospital, half laughing, but unfortunately she'd put into words the guilt I'd been feeling. Why the hell hadn't the old man minded his own business? Why had he gone barging up the stairs to get brained? He had been injured trying to look after me. Swell. That meant I damned well had to find out who had broken into my place. Which meant competing with the police on a task for which they had all the resources. The only thing I knew about that they didn't was the missing IckPiff files. I had to find out who was paying Dick's bill.

If I wasn't so well known to the partners at Crawford, Meade I'd try getting hired as a secretary. As it was, I didn't think I could suborn any of the office staff. Too many of them knew me by sight; if I started asking questions it would get right back to Dick.

I wandered out to the back of my building and climbed the stairs to the kitchen entrance. My apartment seemed unbearably dispiriting. It wasn't just the wreck; without Mr. Contreras popping his head out the door the building felt empty, lifeless. I stood on the back porch, watching the Korean boys play ball. They were running through the tomatoes now that the guardian was away. I took the splintered wood that had been my door and carried it down to the little garden. As the solemn-eyed brothers watched, I built an impromptu fence around the plants.

"Now, your playground is outside the fence. Got it?"

They nodded without speaking. I climbed back upstairs, feeling better because I'd made something, put some order into life. I started thinking again.

XXI

Well-Connected

Mr. Contreras recovered consciousness late on Sunday. Since they were keeping him in intensive care for another twenty-four hours, I couldn't see him myself, but Lotty told me he was vague about the accident. He could remember making supper and going line by line through the racing results in the paper—his evening ritual—but he could not remember climbing the stairs to my apartment.

Neither she nor the neurologist she'd gotten to look at him could offer the police any hope that he would ever remember his assailants—that kind of traumatic episode was frequently blocked by the mind. Detective Rawlings, whom I ran into at the hospital, was disappointed. I was just thankful the old man was going to make it.

Monday morning my pal from the Downers Grove box factory decided he was ready to pay my tariff; someone had smashed a forklift truck into the side of the building Saturday morning, doing about five grand in damage. The supposition was that the driver was toked out of his mind on crack. The owner balked when I told him it would be another week before I could be there personally, but he agreed in the end to start with the Streeter brothers. Two of them were available to go to Downers Grove the next day.

Fixed now with a paying customer, I turned my attention to my own problems. My suspicions of Peter embarrassed me, and when I thought of our last phone conversation I squirmed a bit. But my questions wouldn't go away. I needed to demonstrate clearly to myself that he'd had nothing to do with lifting the IckPiff files from my living room.

Dick's secretary. I lay on the living-room floor in the midst of the books and records and shut my eyes. She was in her forties. Married. Slender, polished, efficient, brown eyes. Regina? No. Regner. Harriet Regner.

At nine, I dialed Friendship's number in Schaumburg and asked for Alan Humphries, the administrator. A woman's voice answered, announcing that I had reached Mr. Humphries's office.

"Good morning," I said in what was supposed to be a pleasant, earnest, busy voice. "This is Harriet Regner, Mr. Yarborough's secretary at Crawford, Meade."

"Oh, hi, Harriet. This is Jackie. You have a good weekend? You sound a little under the weather."

"Just hay fever, Jackie—that time of year." I put a tissue to my nose to make my voice more snuffly. "Mr. Yarborough needs one small piece of information from Mr. Humphries. . . . No, you don't need to put him on—you can probably tell me yourself. We weren't sure if the billing for Mr. Monkfish was to go on to the Friendship corporate account, or to be listed on a separate invoice and sent to Dr. Burgoyne directly."

"Just a minute." She put me on hold. I lay on my back, looking at the ceiling, wishing there were some way I could be present if Dick learned about the conversation.

"Harriet? Mr. Humphries says he went through all that with Mr. Yarborough—that the bill is to come directly to him, but here at the hospital. He wants to talk to you."

"Sure, Jackie—oh, just a second, Mr. Yarborough is buzzing me—can I call you right back? Great."

I cut the connection. So now I knew. Or had it confirmed. Friendship was paying Dieter Monkfish's bill. But why, for heaven's sake? Maybe Alan Humphries was a fanatical member of the so-called right-to-life movement. But presumably Friendship performed therapeutic abortions; many hospitals do, at least in the first trimester. Maybe Friendship did and Humphries writhed in anguish over it: this was his conscience money. After all, he was paying Dieter's bill himself, instead of slipping it in with the hospital account.

But that left a painful question unanswered. What was Peter's connection with this? The only reason I'd checked out Friendship was because Peter had been at my place the night I'd brought home the IckPiff files. But why did he care? Beyond an ethical dislike of burglary, that is.

Reluctantly, I phoned his office at Friendship. His secretary informed me that he was in surgery—was there a message?

I could scarcely say, "Yeah, I want to know whom he hired to beat up Mr. Contreras," so I fell back on asking for Consuelo's hospital record.

"Doctor didn't leave me any instructions about this," she said dubiously. "What's your name?"

Receptionists calling the doctor "Doctor" are like grown-ups who talk about their fathers as "Daddy." Like he's the only one in the world, you know. God didn't leave me any instructions.

I gave her my name and asked her to have Peter call me when he came back from surgery. After hanging up, I paced tensely around my ravaged apartment, wanting to act, but not sure how. Not sure I wanted to find out anything else.

Finally I returned to the phone to call Murray Ryerson, head of the crime desk at the *Herald-Star*. The paper had done a small story on the Monkfish robbery in the "ChicagoBeat" section. When the news of my break-in came through the crime desk on Friday, Murray had called me with high hopes of a major story, but I'd told him that I wasn't working on anything.

This morning I reached him at the city desk. "You know that burglary at IckPiff headquarters?"

"You're confessing," he said promptly. "That's not news, V. I. Everyone knows you're a great second-story woman."

He thought he was being funny; I was just as glad he couldn't see my face. "Dick Yarborough at Crawford, Meade is Dieter's attorney—you know that? I looked into my crystal ball a few minutes ago, and it told me that Dick will have the missing files sometime today. You might call and ask him.''

"Vic, why the hell are you telling me this, anyway? IckPiff losing some files is not a big deal. Even if you did steal them and are planting them at the lawyer's—what's his name? Yarborough?—it's not interesting.''

"Okay. I just thought it might be a fun little paragraph, rounding out the burglary story. I don't have the stuff, by the way, and I don't know who does. But I think Dick will have it by tomorrow at the latest. Bye-bye."

I was about to hang up when Murray suddenly said, "Hey, wait a minute. Monkfish led a mob into Lotty Herschel's clinic a few weeks ago, didn't he? And Yarborough's the guy who bailed him out. Right. Got it here on the screen. And then *his* place was broken into. Come on, Warshawski, what's going on?"

"Hey, Murray. IckPiff files are not a big deal. If I may quote you on that. Sorry to bother you. I'll call the *Trib*." I laughed into his squawking voice and hung up.

I went over to the clinic to see how Lotty was holding up. Business had been slow for the first few days after she reopened, but this morning every seat in the waiting room was taken. Children, mothers with screaming infants, pregnant women, old women with their grown-up daughters, and one lone man, staring stiffly at nothing, his hands trembling slightly.

Mrs. Coltrain ran the place like an expert bartender with a nervous crowd. She smiled at me professionally, and her panic of a few weeks earlier slid from my memory. She said she would tell Dr. Herschel I was here.

Lotty saw me on the fly, in between two waiting rooms. She must have lost five pounds over the weekend; her cheekbones jutted out sharply below her thick black eyebrows.

I told her about my efforts to get the Friendship records. "I'm trying Peter again this afternoon. If he doesn't deliver, do you want to get Hazeltine to call?" Morris Hazeltine was her real lawyer.

Lotty grimaced. "He isn't representing me on this—I have

to go through the insurance company and use the lawyer they come up with. I'll mention it to them—they're most annoyed with me for losing the records.''

She suddenly smacked her forehead with the palm of her hand. "Strain is making me lose my wits. The state—the Department of Environment and Human Resources—they make an on-site, unannounced visit to any hospital where there's been a maternal or infant death. They should have some report on Consuelo and at least what Malcolm did.''

"What do you do—call up and ask for it?'' My experience with the state didn't lead me to think they'd be too helpful.

Lotty looked smug. "Ordinarily not. But I trained the woman who's now an assistant director there—Philippa Barnes. She was one of my first residents at Beth Israel. A very fine one, too—but that was in the early sixties—it was hard for women to go into private practice, and she was black to boot. So she went to work for the state. . . . Look—I've got at least four hours of patients to see here. If I called to tell her to expect you, would you mind going to see her?''

"Be a pleasure. I'd like to think there was something active I could do—I feel like the two of us have been those little ducks they used to line up for you to shoot at in Riverview.'' I told her about Dick and Dieter Monkfish. "What do you make of that?''

Her thick black brows snapped together to form a line across her nose. "I never did understand why you married that man, Vic.''

I grinned. "Immigrant inferiority complex—he's the complete WASP. But why Friendship?''

She echoed my earlier thoughts. "Maybe conscience money for doing abortions there—people are strange.'' Her mind was clearly back in the examining room. "I'll call Philippa now.''

She squeezed my arm briefly and moved back down the short corridor to her office—like a cat—so quickly she was there one instant and gone the next. It was a relief to see her back to her old self.

XXII

Public Health

My friends and I have financed one of the worst monstrosities known to woman on the northwest corner of the Loop. That is, we kicked in the revenues through our tax bills, and Governor Thompson allocated $180 million of them to a new State of Illinois building. Designed by Helmut Jahn, it is a skyscraper made of two concentric glass rings. The inner one circles a blockwide open rotunda that runs the height of the building. So not only did we get to finance the construction, we get to pay to heat and cool a place that is mostly open space. Still, it won an architectural award in 1986, which I guess proves how much the critics know.

I rode a glass elevator to the eighteenth floor and got out onto the corridor that circles the rotunda. All the offices open onto it. It looks as if the state ran out of money when they got to the doors, so working space flows into the hallways. You're supposed to think this creates a feeling of openness between state employees and the people they serve. But if you had private documents or had to work late—you'd probably like a little more protection between you and the lunatics who roam the Loop.

I went into the open space marked Department of Environment and Human Resources and gave my name to the middle-aged black receptionist. "I think Dr. Barnes is expecting me."

The receptionist gave the sigh of one asked to perform work beyond the call of duty and dialed the phone. "Dr. Barnes will see you in a minute," she announced without looking at me. "Have a seat."

I flipped through a pamphlet describing the symptoms of AIDS and what to do if you suspected you might have it and read another on teenage pregnancy—a noncommittal piece, since the state isn't allowed to advocate birth control—before Dr. Barnes appeared.

Philippa Barnes was a tall, slim woman of around fifty. She was very black; with her hair cropped close to the head on her long slender neck she looked like a swan. Her movements flowed as though water were her natural element. She shook my hand, looking at a gold watchband floating on her left wrist.

"Ms. Warshawski? I just talked to Dr. Herschel. She told me about the dead girl and the lawsuit. I'm trying to squeeze you in between two other appointments, so forgive me if we rush. I want you to talk to Eileen Candeleria—she's the public health nurse who actually schedules our on-site inspections."

We were about the same height but I almost had to jog to keep up with her long, smooth stride. We went back away from the corridor through a maze of offices and half-private cubicles to a room overlooking the Greyhound Bus Terminal on Randolph. One hundred eighty million hadn't paid for much soundproofing; the noise easily traveled the eighteen stories up to us.

Dr. Barnes's desk was a piece of working furniture. Made of scarred oak, it was covered with papers. She sat behind it in a leather swivel chair, moved some of the documents to one side to create a blank place for working, and spoke into an intercom, asking for the nurse.

While we waited, she gave me a rapid rundown on the department. "The Department of Environment has an enormous responsibility, which ranges from approving and certifying hospitals to making sure schools aren't contaminated with asbestos. I'm in the Health and Human Services division. I trained with Lotty—Dr. Herschel—in obstetrics, but in fact my responsibility is for state-run clinics and hospitals. We have another assistant director who is in charge of the whole hospital certification program. Nurse Candeleria works for both of us—she heads investigative teams that go into hospitals and clinics when we feel the need for an inspection.''

Nurse Candeleria came in on cue. She was a plain white woman around Dr. Barnes's age, with a strong, intelligent face brightened by a hint of humor in her brown eyes. She carried a thick file, which she shifted to her left hand so she could shake hands with me when Dr. Barnes introduced us.

"Cindy told me you wanted to talk about Friendship Hospital, Phil, so I've pulled their file. What's the question?''

"They had a maternal and neonatal death out there—when, Ms. Warshawski?—four weeks ago tomorrow. Have you sent a team out there yet? Can I see the report?''

Ms. Candeleria tightened her lips. "I got the report of the death"—she looked in the file—"fifteen days ago. I was scheduling a site visit for later this week. Tom told me he would take care of it himself, to cancel my team. I've diaried it to talk to him tomorrow, but I don't think he's been out there.''

"Tom Coulter,'' Dr. Barnes said. "He's in charge of hospital certification programs—master's in public health, not a doctor. MDs make him feel inferior and he's not madly in love with professional women.''

She quickly punched the buttons on her phone. "This is Dr. Barnes—let me talk to Mr. Coulter, Cindy. . . . Tom—can you stop into my office for a moment? I've got a question about Friendship. Yes, I'm busy, too. I'm backing up two people who flew in from Carbondale just to see me, so you could make their lives easier by getting this over with quickly.''

She hung up. "The bureaucracy in a place like this just about kills you. If I had charge of the whole program, instead of just a piece of it—'' She folded her lips, cutting off the sentence. We all three knew that having a sex-change operation—and perhaps dying her skin—was the only way that would happen.

To prove he wasn't responding to the demands of a woman who was merely his organizational equal, Tom Coulter made us wait ten minutes for him. Eileen frowned through the Friendship file. Dr. Barnes used the time to go through a stack of mail, making quick notes on some documents, tossing others. I sat on the uncomfortable vinyl chair trying not to fall asleep.

Coulter eventually breezed in in a lightweight summer suit, a brown-haired white man a good fifteen years younger than the two women.

"What is it, Phil?"

"The maternal and neonatal mortality at Friendship Five in Schaumburg three weeks ago, Tom. When are we going to see a report on the causes?"

"Well, Phil, it's hard for me to understand why you want to know."

She made a Pavlova-like gesture toward me. "Ms. Warshawski is an attorney representing one of the defendants in a suit involving the dead girl. They have an arguable interest in our report."

Coulter turned his impudent smile on me. "Lawsuit, huh? Has Friendship been sued?"

I did my best imitation of Dick's stuffy-attorney manner. "I have not conferred with any representatives of the hospital, Mr. Coulter."

"Well, Phil—I haven't been out there yet. But don't worry, we've got it under control."

She gave him a withering look. "I want a date. Before the end of the day."

"Sure, Phil. I'll talk to Bert about this right now, tell him you want a date."

A pencil snapped in her long fingers. "Do that, Tom. I guess that's all we need to discuss."

He ignored her to look at me. "So who's your client?"

Before I could speak, Dr. Barnes interrupted. "I'll tell

Ms. Warshawski how to find your office if you want to talk to her before she goes.'' She spoke with such finality that Coulter was forced to give in and leave.

He flashed his impudent grin at me. "I'm around the corner to the left—stop in before you leave."

I looked at the doctor's tight-lipped face. "What's the story?"

"Bert McMichaels is our boss—Tom's and mine. He's a good old boy and Tom's his drinking buddy. I don't know why Tom's dragging his rear end over this hospital visit, but there's no way I can promise Lotty any kind of report in the near future. . . . I'm sorry to have to rush you, but I'm behind on my appointments. Give Lotty my apologies."

I got up and thanked the two of them for their time. Wherever I go, good cheer and fellowship follow in my wake. I grimaced, and turned left around the corner to find Coulter.

The contrast to Philippa Barnes's office was striking. Modern furniture—the great slabs of wood that vibrate with masculine authority—stood on a Scandinavian rug shot through with blacks and reds. Coulter was the kind of executive who follows the old adage that the desk, like the mind, should be completely blank.

He was on the phone, his feet crossed at the ankle on the blond wood in front of him. He waved a cheerful hand at me and beckoned me to sit down. I made a big play of looking at my watch; when he continued to impress me with his importance for three minutes, I got up and told him he could get my number from Dr. Barnes.

I was leaving the receptionist's office when he caught up with me. "Sorry, Ms.—uh—didn't catch your name with Dr. Barnes. She kind of mumbles, you know."

"I hadn't noticed. Warshawski."

"Whom do you represent, Ms. Warshawski? Not the hospital, I presume."

I smiled. "My clients wouldn't have much reason to trust me if I blabbed their affairs in public, would they, Mr. Coulter?"

He slapped my arm playfully. "I don't know. I'm sure they'd forgive a pretty lady like you anything you did."

I continued to smile. "You've put me on the spot, Mr. Coulter. I hardly like to deny an allegation of prettiness. On the other hand, when you are fantastically beautiful, you have to be careful not to use it to dazzle people into overlooking the law. Wouldn't you agree? Or would you?"

He blinked a few times and laughed a little. "Why don't I buy you some lunch and you tell me about it?"

I looked him over. What did he want to know? "A quick one."

He bustled down the hall to the elevator with me, his coat skirts whirling around his hips in his eagerness. On the way to the ground-floor parking lot he explained (wink) that there wasn't any place private to go to in the building—how about some little restaurant a few blocks away?

"I don't need to be private with you, Mr. Coulter. And I don't have endless amounts of time. The only thing I'm really interested in is your postmortem on the death of Consuelo Hernandez at Friendship Five in Schaumburg. Or failing that, the reason you don't propose doing one."

"Now, now." He took my arm as the elevator doors opened and started to steer me toward the exit. I gave my shoulder bag, weighted by the Smith & Wesson, a little tap with my free hand, making it swing casually into his stomach. He dropped my arm, looked at me suspiciously, and moved on to the Clark Street exit.

The State of Illinois building has as neighbors the City-County building, an old concrete pillbox occupying the block to the south, and the Greyhound Bus Terminal, with a predictable coterie of winos, hustlers, and lunatics. Neither was likely to contain the slick kind of restaurant I thought would appeal to Tom Coulter. I wasn't surprised when he suggested we hop into a cab and head north.

I shook my head. "I don't have that kind of time. One of the Loop delis will do me fine."

We walked a couple of blocks east, Coulter chattering brightly the whole way, and turned into a dark little restaurant on the corner of Randolph and Dearborn. Sound reverberated from the walls, and cigarette smoke thickened the air.

Coulter cupped his hands against my ear. "Sure you don't want to head north?"

I turned to face him squarely. "Just what do you want, Mr. Coulter?"

His impudent grin came again. "I want to find out what you're really doing coming into E and HR. You're a detective, not a lawyer, aren't you, Ms. Warshawski?"

"I'm a lawyer, Mr. Coulter. I'm a member of the Illinois bar in good standing—you can call the bar association and find that out. And what I really want is the report on the death of Consuelo Hernandez and her infant daughter."

A harassed waitress in a stained uniform took us to a table in the middle of the small floor, plopped menus and water in front of us, and hurried on. Another waitress, laden down with plates of french fries and corned-beef sandwiches, bumped into my chair. My favorite lunch: grease, starch, and nitrosamines. Guessing by the waistlines of the city employees around me, they liked it, too. I decided to have cottage cheese. When we'd ordered, Coulter continued grinning at me.

"But you don't practice law, do you? So you're detecting something. I want to know what."

I nodded. "I'm trying to find out why you care." I also wanted to know how he knew I was a detective, but if I asked that I could expect a pleased smirk and little else.

"Oh, that's easy. Ours is a confidential agency. I can't have you trying to get information from my staff without looking into it."

I raised my eyebrows. "I wasn't aware Dr. Barnes worked for you."

He looked briefly uncomfortable, then recovered. "Not her. Eileen Candeleria."

"I have a client who has a pertinent interest in your investigation of Friendship Hospital. If your file on them is not available under the Freedom of Information Act, I believe I could get a subpoena for it. The fact that you canceled Nurse Candeleria's on-site visit and haven't scheduled one of your own is interesting. It raises grounds for all kinds of speculation. I imagine I could even get one of the newspapers interested in it. Not too many people know that the state has an obligation to look into maternal and infant mortality, but motherhood is always a hot topic and I bet the *Herald-Star* or the *Tribune* could make it look really good. It's a pity your face is so round—it won't show up well in newspaper photos.''

Our waitress slapped plates in front of us—cottage cheese and iceberg lettuce for me; BLT and fries for Coulter. He picked at his food for a few minutes, then looked at his watch and gave a sketch of his grin.

"You know, I'm glad you vetoed the North Side. I just remembered I'm supposed to see a guy. Nice talking to you, Ms. Warshawski.''

He walked out of the restaurant, leaving me to pay for his lunch.

XXIII

Connective Tissue

At two o'clock I tried Peter Burgoyne again. He'd emerged from surgery but was on another call, the secretary said with no great interest. I told her I'd wait.

"He's going to be a long time," she warned.

"Then I'll wait a long time." I was in my office with a stack of unopened mail to handle; I used the wait to sort the offers of insurance, computers, and management-training seminars from the four or five pieces of legitimate mail.

When Peter finally came on the line, his voice was hoarse and sounded exhausted. "I don't have time to talk now, Vic. I'll call you later."

"Yeah, I kind of got the feeling you didn't want to talk to me. But this won't take long. Consuelo's record. Can you get that called up today? I'd hate to have to tell Lotty she needs a court order to see it."

"Oh." He sounded tireder. "We got our own summons this morning in that lawsuit. Consuelo's record has been impounded. I'm afraid the only way Dr. Herschel can see it at this point is through legal action."

"Impounded? You mean the state or someone came and locked it up?"

"No, no," he answered impatiently. "We do it ourselves, take it out of the records room and lock it up so no one can get at it and alter it."

"I see. Sorry to bother you. Sounds like you ought to be in bed."

"I should. I should be anyplace but here. I'll—I'll call you, Vic. In a few days."

"Oh, Peter—before you go—how well do you know Richard Yarborough?"

He delayed answering a bit too long. "Richard, did you say? What was the last name? I'm afraid I've never heard of him."

I hung up and stared thoughtfully in front of me. Impounded, huh? Abruptly I called Lotty.

"Are you free for dinner this evening? I'd like to talk to you—about Consuelo's file."

She agreed to meet me at Dortmunder's, a little restaurant–cum–wine cellar in the basement of the Chesterton Hotel, around seven.

I threw out my mail. As I was shutting the door, the phone rang. It was Dick, having a temper tantrum.

"What the hell do you mean, setting the papers on me?"

"Dick, it's so exciting to hear from you. You haven't called me this often since you wanted to copy my con-law course notes fifteen years ago."

"God damn you, Vic! You told that damned Swede from the *Herald-Star* that I had the IckPiff files, didn't you!"

"Seems to me it was only five or six hours ago you were calling accusing me of having them. So why does it upset you if someone asks you the same question?"

"That's not the point. My clients' files are confidential. As are their identities and their problems."

"Yes. Confidential to you. But, sweetheart, I'm not a member of your firm. Nor of your person. I have no obligation—legal, mental, physical, or ethical—to protect their privacy."

"Yeah, and while we're on the subject of confidentiality,

did you call Alan Humphries at Friendship Hospital this morning claiming to be Harriet?"

"Harriet? I thought you keep telling me her name is Terri. Or are you on number three now?" I thought I smelled burning enamel coming through the wire from his teeth and smiled.

"You know damned well Harriet is my secretary. Humphries called at noon wanting to know why she hadn't gotten back to him this morning. And we figured out after some confusion that she'd never called him to begin with. Jesus, would I like to see your ass in court for stealing those IckPiff files."

"If you think you have any earthly way of proving it, by all means. I'd also love to see Friendship Hospital on the stand testifying about their role in returning the stuff to you," I continued enthusiastically. "And the papers would have an absolute field day, you prosecuting me while one of your senior partners was defending me. Or would Freeman have to disqualify himself? Why don't you switch me to him and I'll check on it while—"

He slammed the receiver down on me midsentence and I laughed happily to myself. I waited for a few minutes, staring hopefully at the phone, and sure enough it rang.

"Murray," I said into the mouthpiece, before the caller could speak.

"Vic, I don't like it. I don't like it when you pull the strings that make the puppets dance. How did you know it was me?"

"Psychic powers," I answered airily. "Actually, my beloved ex-husband just called. He was a bit on the peeved side about your questions—referred to you in his graceful way as 'that damned Swede.' "

"Yarborough's your ex-husband? Christ, I never knew you'd been married. And to a prize asshole like that? Is that why you sicced me on him? To get your revenge for a bad alimony settlement?"

"You know, Murray, I ought to hang up. That was tasteless. Alimony my Aunt Fanny. Anyway, we've been divorced more than ten years now. I hardly ever think of the guy. Only when I'm constipated.''

"You know more than you're telling, sweet pea. Yarborough has the IckPiff files—didn't take much of a newspaperman to get that out of a secretary who isn't used to the press. But I want to know what's going on. His reaction was just all out of proportion. Besides, he accused you of swiping them to begin with. You want to comment before I transmit my story?''

I thought for a second. "Ms. Warshawski, the eminent private investigator, was reached in her office late in the day. On hearing of the allegations from Crawford, Meade, she replied in classical Latin, *'Ubi argumentum?'* and suggested that her learned colleague blow it out his ears.''

"Vic, come on. What gives with IckPiff? Why is a two-hundred-dollar-an-hour man like Dick Yarborough representing a lowlife like Dieter Monkfish?''

"The Constitution guarantees a right to counsel,'' I began sonorously.

Murray cut me off. "Don't dribble legal shit at me, Warshawski. I want to talk to you. I'll meet you at the Golden Glow in half an hour.''

The Golden Glow is the closest place I have to a club. It's a bar in the south Loop for serious drinkers. Sal Barthele, who owns it, stocks twenty brands of beer and almost as many of whiskey, but she doesn't do happy hour, little quiches, or anything else exotic. After holding out for two years she reluctantly brought in a supply of Perrier; if someone asks for it they get waited on by the barmaid, not by her.

Sal was sitting behind the horseshoe mahogany bar when I came in, reading *The Wall Street Journal*. She takes her investments seriously, which is why she spends so much time in the bar when she could retire to the country. Sal tops my five eight by a good four inches and has a regal bearing to match. No one behaves in an unseemly fashion at the Golden Glow when Sal is there.

I went over and chatted with her until Murray arrived. He and Sal had hit it off from the first time I brought him in four or five years ago. She stocks Holsten beer just for him. He came over to the bar to say hello, his face flushed with heat underneath his curly reddish beard. I've been with him places where the kids think he's Rick Sutcliffe, the Cubs pitcher—he's about the same size and color. And the same amount of sweat.

We took our drinks—two bottles of beer for him, a glass of water and a double whiskey for me—over to one of the little tables lining the walls and switched on the tabletop lamp. The shade, made of genuine Tiffany glass, spread a mellow color around us—the golden glow of the bar's name.

"Jesus," Murray said, wiping his face. "Next Monday's Labor Day. Is this damned heat ever going to let up?"

I drank the water before taking any Black Label, then felt a welcome warmth spread through my arms and fingers. "It'll be winter soon enough. Enjoy it while you can." No matter how hot it gets in Chicago I savor the summers. I guess my mother's hot-weather Italian genes dominate my dad's ice-bearing Polish ones.

Murray nearly emptied his first bottle with a swallow. "Okay, Ms. Warshawski. I want the truth, the whole truth, and nothing but—not such little crumbs as you may choose to hand out."

I shook my head. "I don't have it. I don't know it. Something mighty weird is going on and I'm just beginning to get the hang of part of it. If I tell you, it is definitely off the record and if you can't promise that, we might as well talk about those clowns posing as ballplayers up in Wrigley Field. Someone ought to tell the commissioner about them anyway. I wonder if it's a crime to impersonate a major-league athlete?"

Murray took a genteel sip from the second bottle. "Off the record for forty-eight hours."

"Off the record until I have a better idea about what's going on."

"One week. And if the *Trib* or the *Sun-Times* have it first you will never get as much as another photograph out of our morgue."

I didn't like it, but it was all I was going to get and I

needed some help. "Okay. A week. Four P.M. Labor Day . . . It's like this. You know Dieter-baby spearheaded the drive into Lotty's clinic a few weeks ago. I went to night court to intercede for my downstairs neighbor, a misguided Don Quixote named Contreras. And I saw Dick bailing out Dieter Monkfish.

"As you so cogently grasped on the phone, Dick is way out of old Dieter's price range. And my curiosity was piqued." I took a larger swallow of the whiskey. Not a hot-weather drink but it felt good.

"Some angel had to be paying his bill and I wanted to know who. I tried getting the information by calling Crawford, Meade. And I went around to IckPiff and asked them. No one was telling me anything, so I went in and removed the files with a hope of getting the answer—I was then going to return the files."

Murray was nodding intently. He knows when I mean what I'm saying and doesn't interrupt with wisecracks.

"Two people knew I had the files because they saw me come home with them. My neighbor, Mr. Contreras. And a doctor from a hospital in the northwest suburbs whom I've been dating. Doctor did not like my breaking, entering, and stealing files. He invited me home with him. When I returned early Saturday morning, my apartment had been searched, Mr. Contreras lay concussed, and the IckPiff stuff was missing."

"The doctor. Or perhaps it was Mr. Contreras, being tripped up by his co-conspirators?"

"You'd have to meet him. He's seventy-five or so, a retired machinist, and his idea of finesse is hitting someone with a pipe wrench. It had to be the doctor. So this morning I impersonated Dick's secretary, called the hospital, and got the scoop—they are Crawford, Meade clients. And they are paying Dieter Monkfish's bill."

Murray's fuzzy red eyebrows crinkled together. "Why?"

"That's what I don't know. And there's something else." I sketched out the story about Lotty's suit and her need to see someone else's file on Consuelo. "So I went down to Big Jim's mausoleum this morning and learned that they aren't scheduling an investigation into Consuelo's death, which they do for all maternal and infant mortalities. But I don't know if the guy who squashed the investigation—smooth MBA type named Tom Coulter—knows the people at Friendship. Nor why that would matter, anyway.''

I swallowed the rest of my drink, but shook my head at Sal when she came over with the bottle. I still had to meet Lotty for dinner and she doesn't like it when I show up drunk. Murray took another Holsten. But then he's ten inches taller and ninety or so pounds heavier than I—he can drink more.

''So what the hell is going on? Is there some connection between the IckPiff stuff and Monkfish and the state non-investigation? Or what?''

Murray looked at me seriously before starting his third bottle. ''Yes. I see. Until we get this doped out there's no point in telling only a little bit of the story.''

I was glad to hear the ''we''—I needed two extra feet. ''How about if I go out to Friendship and try to figure out what's going on at their end and you find out if Tom Coulter knows Peter Burgoyne? And why he'd do him any favors.''

''You have only to speak, O She-Who-Must-Be-Obeyed. I'll do it myself. I don't want anyone getting a whiff of this before it breaks.''

XXIV

Garbage Disposal

Lotty was waiting for me at the Dortmunder. I'd gone home to shower and change and had finished by making up for three of my lost hours of sleep before I knew I was lying down. I quickly put on a silk shirt and a light skirt and headed for the restaurant. The walls of the basement of the Chesterton Hotel are lined with racks of wine; perhaps a dozen wooden tables sit in the middle of the floor. Somehow the whiskey in the middle of a hot day had spoiled my taste for drink and I skipped the wine.

Lotty grinned at me wickedly. "You must be unwell, my dear. This is the first time I've seen you willingly do without alcohol."

"Thank you, Doctor. So good to see you've recovered your spirits."

I hadn't eaten much of the cottage-cheese plate in the deli at lunch so I indulged myself with a veal chop and the special potatoes the Dortmunder makes, double-fried so they're crisp on the outside and soft and fluffy inside. Lotty ordered a seafood salad and coffee. But then, she's smaller than I am; she burns fewer calories. Or so I rationalized.

After we'd eaten I told her what I learned during the day. "What I want to know is—is that right? Would they impound the record of a patient over whom they were being sued?"

Lotty pursed her lips. "They might well. Every hospital does things differently. I've never been involved in the adminstrative end of one: I could call Max Loewenthal at Beth Israel and ask him, if you'd like." Max was the executive director there.

I shrugged. "What I really want to know is, if I go looking for Consuelo's record, where will it be—in their medical-records room or will it really be locked up somewhere like Alan Humphries's office?"

"Then I'd better call Max—and don't worry: I'll just tell him it's for my own interest in Consuelo."

She went over to the phone in the corner. Lotty really wanted Consuelo's file badly. Ordinarily she takes the moral high road when I go after evidence without a warrant and here she was, aiding and abetting. I absentmindedly ordered hazelnut torte for her and a raspberry tart for myself. I'd eaten my own dessert and was contemplating hers when she returned.

"It's quite plausible. They may well have it under lock and key. But something occurred to me, Vic. You probably don't know how to find the record if it's still filed in with the others."

"What—don't I just look them up in alpha order?"

She shook her head. "Most hospitals file by terminal digit. You need to know the patient's number—the number they give you when they admit you. The last two digits are what they sort by. So if you don't know Consuelo's number, you wouldn't be able to find her record. Not without going through all of them, and that would take weeks."

I rubbed my eyes. "They probably do what—assign patient numbers randomly by computer? So I need to be able to query the system, find out what her number is. So all I need to do is crack their system. That sounds like it would take me longer than going through all the files by hand."

She nodded sagely. "I know you, Vic. You'll think of something."

"Thanks, Lotty. In my current doddering state, any votes of confidence are accepted with gratitude."

We drove over to the hospital after paying the bill. Lotty went up on the patient floors with me so that I could see Mr. Contreras even though visiting hours were over. His scalp was wrapped in white, but he was sitting up in bed and watching the Cubs play a night game in Houston. When he saw me, his face lighted up and he switched off the set.

"What a relief to see you after watching those bums, doll. I'm telling you. Know what they need to do? They oughtta fire them all and bring in some real players. Heck, they could find nine guys from my old union team who could play better than that and do it for ten percent of the salaries these hotshots collect.

"So how are you? I really let you down, didn't I, doll? You left me on guard and I blew it. Might as well have been that pansy doctor you been palling around with."

I went over to the bed and kissed him. "You didn't let me down. I'm the one who feels like a heel—letting you take a blow to the head trying to defend my stupid apartment. How are you feeling? You must have got the boys in Local Ten-oh-three to install a stainless-steel skull for you when you retired, to take two head blows in two weeks without flinching."

He brightened. "Oh, yeah. This was nothing. You shoulda seen me in 'fifty-eight. We were on strike then, nothing like anything you ever saw before. They tried sending some scabs in. I'm telling you, World War Two wasn't nothing by comparison and I was on Guam. I was concussed, broke my leg and three ribs. Clara thought for sure she was going to collect on my life insurance that time."

His face clouded over. "How could a woman like Clara produce a kid like Ruthie? I ask you. She was the sweetest woman ever born and here's this daughter of mine like a tub of pickles. She's trying to make me go home with her. Says I'm not fit to live by myself and she's going to get a court order or something, or that damned Joe Marcano she married is going to do it. Goddamn fruitcake is what he is, working in a women's dress store. Course, he doesn't have any balls, anyway. Letting himself be bossed around by a loudmouth like Ruthie, even if she is my daughter. Whatever you say, dear. Hah. If you're an old man they treat you like you was a little kid.''

I smiled at him. ''Maybe Dr. Herschel and I can help you with that one. If the hospital says you need to have someone looking after you for a while you can come home with me. If you don't mind a few dirty dishes.''

''Oh, I can wash the dishes for you. I never did a lick of housework when Clara was alive, always thought it was women's work, but tell you the truth, I kind of enjoy it. I like to cook. I'm a good cook, you know. Putting a recipe together is kind of like getting two plates to fit together just so.''

The nurses arrived to put a stop to the flow. The fact that two of them came showed how popular he was—nurses like to hang out with the more agreeable patients, and who can blame them? They joked with him about how he needed to go to sleep, not for his own sake but so that the other patients on the floor could get some rest. I kissed him goodnight, found Lotty outside the maternity ward, and bade her good-bye.

I made my way cautiously up the backstairs to my kitchen door. If my apartment had been invaded to find Monkfish's papers, then I wasn't in any real danger, but it would be stupid to take any chances. I had my gun in my hand all the way up. No one interrupted my climb. When I got to the top, I found the little marker I'd put in the metal grill just where I'd left it.

I went to bed and fell instantly to sleep, hoping that Lotty's confidence would be justified by the appearance of some brilliant idea in my dreams. Whether inspiration shone in the night I had no way of telling. Before I could wake up in the slow way that helps you remember your dreams, my sleep was shattered by the telephone. I stretched out an arm and looked automatically at the clock readout: six-thirty. I was getting more sunrises this summer than I'd had in the last ten years put together.

"Ms. Warshawski. Not waking you, am I?" It was Detective Rawlings.

"You are, but I can't imagine anyone I'd rather have do it than you, Detective."

"I'm at the corner. Since your front door doesn't work I figured it was easier to phone than ring the bell. I want to see you."

"You been waiting up all night just for that?"

"I've been up a lot of the night. You just weren't at the top of my list."

I stumbled into the kitchen and put on water for coffee. While the water boiled I washed up and slipped on jeans and a T-shirt. Because it was the cops I put on a bra—better not to be too informal.

Rawlings pounded on the kitchen door just as I was grinding the beans. I put them into the filter and went over to unlock the bolts. He didn't need to tell me he'd been up most of the night; I'm a detective and I could tell. His black face was tinged slightly with the gray of fatigue and he'd clearly put on the shirt he'd worn the day before, badly wrinkled when he'd taken it off. Or maybe, like me, he threw his clothes on a chair where they tend to get a little more disheveled than they do in a closet.

I raised my eyebrows. "You don't look too swell, Detective. Coffee?"

"Yeah, if you can promise me the cup's been washed with soap." He slumped down in a chair and said abruptly, "Where were you between eleven last night and one this morning?"

"My favorite kind of question. Justify yourself for no particular reason." I turned to the refrigerator and started hunting for food. It was a dismal prospect.

"Warshawski, I know all about how you and Lieutenant Mallory interact. You clown and he gets red and starts blustering. I don't have the patience for that. And I sure as hell don't have the time for it."

I found a pint of blueberries that could have saved the

world if we'd run out of penicillin, and took them over to the garbage.

"If that's what you think, you don't know *all* about how we interact. You guys in the police get into habits. You get so used to having people shiver and answer whatever you choose to ask that you forget you don't have a right to ask, or at least you don't have a right to demand answers with no explanation. So when someone with a little more legal sophistication happens along, you get pissed because we stand more on our rights.

"If you have some creditable reason for wanting to know where I was last night, I'll be glad to tell you. But for all I know, my ex-husband is trying to slander me and you're helping out. Or you have the hots for me and are jealous of anyone else I might be dating."

He shut his eyes and rubbed his forehead before taking another swallow of coffee. "Fabiano Hernandez was shot dead last night. The ME thinks it happened in that time window. I'm asking everyone who I know had a grudge against the little prick where they were. So where were you?"

"Gang shooting?"

He shrugged. "Could be, but I don't think so. Doesn't have the right signature. He was shot at close range, once, as he was leaving the bar he hung out at—El Gallo. Someone he knew. Might've been Sergio. We're pulling him in. Might've been the dead Alvarado girl's brothers. We're talking to them. You and he weren't too tight. I want to know if it was you."

"I confess. Enraged with him for suing my good pal Dr. Herschel I shot him dead in the hopes his family would not realize the suit was part of his estate and that they could continue the action on his behalf."

"Yeah, laugh, Warshawski. Someone should have a good time when there's a dead punk and the police are up all night. It might as well be you. If I seriously believed you might've shot him, I'd be talking to you at the station, not drinking your coffee with no witnesses. Good coffee, by the way."

"Thanks, Viennese roast. I was here. Asleep. A rotten alibi, since I was asleep alone. No one called me."

"You are early-to-bed, early-to-shine? Doesn't fit your character."

"Normally I am not," I said formally. "But owing to the stresses of the last several days I've been short on sleep. I turned in at nine-thirty and slept until the phone rang."

"You carry a gun, don't you? What make?"

"Smith and Wesson nine-millimeter semi-automatic."

He looked at me quietly. "I need to see it."

"I won't make you tell me why. I can guess. Fabiano was shot with a Smith and Wesson nine-millimeter semi-automatic."

His gaze held mine a fractional second longer, then he nodded reluctantly.

I went to my bedroom and brought it out to him. "It hasn't been fired in days, not since I took it down to the range to practice last week. But you'll want to see that for yourself. May I have a receipt?"

He wrote it out gravely and handed it to me. "I don't have to tell you not to leave town, do I?"

"No, Detective. Least, not as long as you mean the Chicagoland area, not just the city limits."

He turned a smile into a grimace. "Lieutenant Mallory doesn't know the half of it. Thanks for the coffee, Warshawski."

XXV

Medical Supplies

I was pretty sick of the garbage in my kitchen. No breakfast there unless you were a rat or a cockroach and not too picky in your habits. I locked the back door and went over to the Belmont Diner. So what if I'd had fried potatoes for supper last night? I ate blueberry pancakes, a double order of bacon, lots of butter and syrup, and coffee. After all, once you're dead, you've got all eternity in front of you to diet in.

Fabiano Hernandez shot. Like Stewart Alsop said, he should have died herebefore. It was too late now to do anyone any good. I read about it in the *Herald-Star*, but they didn't give it much play—a little paragraph in "Chicago-Beat," not even the front page of the section. At least one teenager gets killed every day in Chicago and Fabiano hadn't been a basketball star or a prize scholar for whom tear-jerking copy could be written.

Between the last of the pancakes and my third cup of coffee I figured out an approach for Friendship. It wasn't exactly a work of genius, but I hoped it might do. I paid my bill and returned home. If the police were following me to breakfast and back, they were welcome. I didn't care if they knew I wasn't starving from guilt or grief.

I changed into a pale-olive summer suit with the gold silk shirt I'd had on the night before. Brown leather slingbacks, a leather portfolio, and I looked like the model for a middle-management training guide.

I was not happy to be without my Smith & Wesson. If Fabiano had been killed by a single shot at close range, it could not be palmed off as random violence. Not like Malcolm's death. Fabiano might have been involved in all kinds of scummy activity I knew nothing about. But he'd been connected with the Lions, he'd been suing Friendship, and both of those outfits knew me and didn't seem susceptible to the love mixed with awe I usually inspire. I would have to be doubly cautious now. Perhaps check into a hotel for a few days. And certainly make sure Mr. Contreras stayed in the hospital. The last thing I needed was for him to run between me and a bullet.

Climbing gingerly down the backstairs in nylons and heels, I was glad my normal business attire was jeans. In the summer heat, pantyhose clings to the legs and crotch, cutting off air to the skin. I was feeling slightly baked by the time I got to my car.

I didn't think the police would bother to tail me—the law thinks of me as reasonably responsible and even though the same make of gun as mine had killed Fabiano, Rawlings didn't seriously suspect me. Still, just in case, I drove over to the clinic and asked Lotty if we could trade cars for the day.

She greeted me in a subdued, almost fearful way. "Vic, what is going on? Now Fabiano is dead. You don't think Carol's brothers would have killed him trying to protect me?"

"God, I hope not. Besides, if they did, it wouldn't really help you. The law regards a juicy lawsuit like this as an asset and his estate inherits it. Probably the only thing he had to leave besides that Eldorado. The Alvarado boys are too sensible—I don't think they'd jeopardize their futures just for the fleeting satisfaction of knocking off Fabiano. And no, I didn't kill him.''

She blushed faintly under her olive skin. "No, no, Vic. I didn't really think you might have. Of course you can take my car.''

I followed her to her office to trade keys with her. "Can I borrow one of your lab coats, too? Or one of Carol's—it'd be more my size. Also a pair of your nifty little plastic examining gloves.''

Her eyes narrowed. "I don't think I want to know why, but certainly.'' She took a clean white jacket from her office closet and took me to an empty examining room where she pulled out a box of gloves and handed me two pairs.

Her venerable Datsun was parked in the alley behind the clinic. She went with me, giving me a worried, most un-Lotty-like good-bye.

"You must be careful, Vic. This summer has been very rough on me. I could not bear it for anything to happen to you.''

We're not usually so demonstrative, but I pulled her to me and kissed her before taking off. "Yeah, I'm a little nervous myself. I'll try to talk to you tonight, but it'll probably be late before I get back. If—well, if I'm stupid or careless, tell Murray where I've been, okay?''

She nodded and returned to her patients. Her narrow shoulders were a little stooped, and she looked her age.

Lotty fancies herself as Sterling Moss and drives her car fast and recklessly. Unfortunately her intrepidity isn't matched by her skill and over the years she's stripped the gears on the Datsun. Shifting up and down in the city traffic took patience and enough attention that I couldn't be sure my back was clean until I got onto the Northwest Tollway. After going a couple of miles, I pulled onto the shoulder and watched the cars sweep past. Nobody slowed, and when after five minutes I reentered the swarm of traffic, I didn't see anybody dropping back to tag me.

The heat hung heavier in the northwest suburbs. Being away from the lake adds a good fifteen degrees to the air in the summer. Lotty's no-frills approach to life didn't include car air-conditioning. I shrugged out of my suit jacket, but the armpits of the silk shirt grew sodden as the morning progressed. When I exited onto Route 58 and headed south toward the hospital I looked as though I'd been heading across Death Valley on foot for three or four days.

I parked in the visitors' lot and came in through the hospital's main entrance. Alan Humphries and the admissions clerk were the only people who'd met me when I'd been here before. That had been three weeks ago and I'd been in jeans. If they passed me this morning they'd assume I was a visitor and probably not spare me a second glance.

I found a rest room where I washed my face and neck, combed most of the Tollway dust from my hair, and tried to restore some semblance of professional demeanor. When I'd done the best I could, I returned to the information desk in the main lobby.

A neat, white-haired woman wearing the pink coat of a volunteer smiled at me and asked me how she could help.

"Can you direct me to the medical-records office?"

"Straight down this hallway, then turn left, go up the first flight of stairs and you'll find it easily at the top of the stairs."

"This is a little embarrassing—I have an eleven o'clock appointment with the director and forgot to put the name in my pocket diary."

She gave me an understanding smile—we all do these silly things from time to time. She flipped through her directory. "Ruth Ann Motley."

I thanked her and headed down the hallway. Instead of going up the stairs, I went on down to the emergency entrance where I'd brought Consuelo four weeks ago. I pulled Lotty's white doctor coat out of my portfolio, slipped it on, and immediately became part of the hallway furniture.

To one side of the entrance was the emergency-admissions office. Unlike a city hospital's emergency room, which is always packed with the people who use it in lieu of a family doctor, only one woman was sitting in the waiting area. She looked up at me as I walked briskly past, seemed about to speak, and sat back down.

A beige internal phone was mounted on the wall near the outside doors. I used it to call the hospital operator, asking her to page Ruth Ann Motley down to the emergency-room office. After a short wait I heard Motley's name echoing from the loudspeaker.

I stood in the doorway, where I could view the hall and the entrance to the emergency room. After perhaps five minutes a tall, lanky woman appeared, moving at a fast trot. She looked to be in her mid-forties, with dark hair done in a disheveled perm. She wore a light-blue seersucker suit that showed too much of her bony wrists and fleshy thighs when she walked. After a few minutes she reappeared, frowning in annoyance, looked around, and trotted back down the hall.

I followed her at a discreet distance. She took the stairs to the second floor. I watched her go into the records room and settled down with my portfolio in a chair about twenty yards up the hall.

I seemed to be in an outpatient area; ten or so other people, mostly women, were scattered against the wall in the cheap vinyl chairs, waiting their turns to see the doctor. I took off the white coat, folded it, returned it to the little briefcase, and bent over a stack of papers I'd stuck into it at random.

Around twelve-fifteen, when the cadre in the hall had turned over completely, Ruth Ann Motley reemerged from the records room. She came up the hall toward me but apparently intended to go to the bathroom rather than accost me. When she came out, she headed back down the stairs. I gave her five more minutes and figured she was at lunch.

I strolled down the hall to the records room, looking as official as I could. Inside was the busiest setting I'd yet seen in the hospital. A half-dozen desks stood piled high with files. On each desk sat a computer terminal. Beyond lay the records, row on row of shelves packed with color-coded folders.

Only two people were at work, covering the place during the lunch hour. Both were women, one perhaps my age, the other a young girl handling her first post–high school job.

I went to the older one, an overweight, uncertain-looking person in a salmon-colored shirtwaist dress.

I gave the brief smile of someone in a great hurry. "I'm Elizabeth Phelps, State of Illinois. We're doing some surprise inspections around the state to make sure medical records are secure."

The woman blinked watery blue eyes at me. Hay fever or a cold seemed to be attacking her. "You—uh—you'd have to talk to the director about that. Ruth Ann Motley."

"Great," I said briskly. "Take me in to her."

"Oh. Oh, she's at lunch right now. She'll be back in forty-five minutes if you'd like to wait."

"I wish I could, but I've got to be in Downers Grove at one o'clock. I don't want to see any patient records, just see whether patient confidentiality is protected here. Why don't you look up a patient record for me. I brought some names with me of people who've been admitted here."

I flipped through the portfolio. "Oh, yes. How about Consuelo Hernandez. You don't think Ms. Motley will object to your just showing me the system is secure by looking up one patient, do you?"

The two clerks looked at each other. Finally the older one said, "I guess it can't do any harm. What we do is, we access the system through a password. Each of us has her own password, and I can't tell you mine because I'm not supposed to let anyone else know it."

I came around and stood behind her. She typed a few strokes that didn't show up on the screen—a protected password. A menu came up.

"I can only get at two menu functions. Patient number by name, and file location. Do you want to spell the name of the person you're looking for?"

I obligingly spelled out Consuelo's name for her. She slowly typed it in and hit the return key. After a few seconds lines of type moved across the screen: Consuelo's name, her admission date, and the record number: 610342. I memorized it and asked if she could show me file status.

She typed a few more commands and the screen responded: File charged out on 8-25 to Administration.

"Thanks very much," I smiled. "You've been most helpful, Ms."—I squinted at the nameplate on her desk—"Digby. I don't think we'll have to come back here. You can tell Ms. Motley we're impressed with the management of security here."

I made my way briskly down the stairs and back out of the hospital. It was only twelve-forty-five. I had a good long time to wait before I could go on with my agenda and I wasn't much in the mood for more food. I drove around aimlessly for a while and happened on a public swimming pool, a beautiful, Olympic-length facility.

I went into one of the malls that dot the suburban countryside and bought a bathing suit, a towel, and a few toilet articles, including a heavy sunscreen for my face, which still needed protection against midday rays. With these and the latest junk book from the best-seller rack, I was ready to while away the afternoon in best suburban style.

XXVI

A Matter of Records

At eleven o'clock I returned to Friendship. In the dark the star-shaped building loomed like a giant sea monster, the few lighted windows, its malevolent eyes. The visitors' lot had emptied out and I could park close to the front entrance, the mouth of the beast.

I slipped on Lotty's white coat and walked in, frowning, moving quickly: Doctor is worried about a patient and shouldn't be disturbed. Few people were about. The information desk where I'd sought directions in the morning was vacant. A couple of orderlies chatted quietly in one corner. Ahead of me a janitor moved desultorily with a mop. With the bright neon lights, the periodic announcements over the inter-com, and the empty halls it reminded me of O'Hare in the middle of the night. There is no more desolate place than an empty building that is normally crowded.

The administrative offices where I'd talked with Mrs. Kirkland and Alan Humphries lay near the stairwell I'd taken this morning to the records room. The door leading to the suite of offices was locked, an ordinary push-button lock. I pulled out my collection of keys, found one of the right make, and fiddled in the door with it. It turned after an agonizing few moments during which I expected one of the orderlies to notice me or a nurse to pass by and accost me.

Mrs. Kirkland's little office lay directly in front of me. A black plastic label etched with white letters announced her name and title: Director of Admissions. I slipped on a pair of Lotty's gloves and tried the doorknob out of curiosity; her room was locked. The corridor to Alan Humphries's office ran parallel to her cubicle, with his office suite at its end. Two other doors, also locked, led off the hallway to the right.

The privacy of the hallway made it possible to relax; I opened Humphries's office suite easily. A small outer room was clearly the secretary's—Jackie Bates, to whom I'd spoken yesterday morning. She had a utilitarian desk, a state-of-the-art word processor, and her own photocopy machine. The back wall was lined with filing cabinets. If Consuelo's file wasn't in Humphries's office I'd have to bite the bullet and go through every drawer.

The door to Humphries's inner sanctum was made from a heavy slab of real wood, perhaps rosewood. Once I had the lock undone and was inside, I felt I was truly in the for-profit part of the hospital.

Instead of the general-issue linoleum, real wood parquet covered the floor. On top of that lay a rug, Persian by the looks of it, big enough to let you know it had cost a whole bunch, but not too large to obscure the inlaid wood. Astride the rug stood an antique desk, the double-sided kind, soft red leather inset into the top, gold marquetry all down the legs and in the drawers. Brocade drapes covered the glass that separated his office from the parking lots outside.

The desk drawers weren't locked, a relief since forcing them might damage the beautiful old wood. I sat in a spacious leather chair and carefully worked my way through them, trying hard not to disturb the order in which papers lay. For someone of my untidy habits, the invisible-search part of the detective's job was perhaps the most difficult.

Consuelo's file was not among Humphries's open papers, but I did find the organization and ownership of the hospital. Behind it was a folder labeled "Monthly Operating Reports."

I pulled both into one thick stack. I was tempted to steal it rather than spending the time on photocopying, but virtue triumphed and I went to Jackie's antechamber and switched on the machine.

While waiting for it to warm up, I turned my attention to the discreet wooden filing cabinet built into the wall behind Humphries's desk. This was locked, but like all the Friendship locks it yielded easily. When you live in Schaumburg and don't expect to be burglarized, you make the detective's job infinitely simpler.

Consuelo's file was in the front of the cabinet's top drawer. I sucked in a breath and opened it. I was expecting something dramatic—Lotty's missing records or some striking statement about Consuelo's treatment. Instead, a few skimpy pages announced her arrival at the hospital: female Hispanic patient, aged sixteen, presented on July 29 unconscious and in labor. . . . From there it deteriorated into medical jargon, which Lotty would have to interpret. The three pages were typed, apparently from Peter's dictation, and dated and initialed by him.

I weighed the file in my hand, frowning. Somehow I'd expected more than this. I went slowly to the antechamber, where I copied both it and the massive documents relating to the hospital organization. When I was putting the three sheets back into the folder I noticed a small piece of paper stuck inside, one of those desk sheets that's labeled "A memo from," in this case Alan Humphries.

The only thing on it was a phone number, no area code, so presumably 312, and no name or address. I copied it, then restored everything to its original upright position, carefully switched off the machine, turned out the lights, and headed back to the main part of the hospital.

At the door leading back to the hallway I paused for a moment, listening to make sure no one was standing on the other side, then slipped into the main wing. Two nurses were walking toward me, deep in conversation. They didn't seem to notice that I'd been where I oughtn't, and didn't give me even a cursory glance. I headed on up the hallway to the obstetrics wing.

It was always possible that Peter was making a late-night delivery. Better to be safe than sorry. I found a pay phone in a waiting area and dialed his home number. He answered the phone immediately, so he wasn't asleep. I hung up without saying anything, just the usual annoyance call we all get from time to time.

I had never been to Peter's office, but knew from his conversation that it was in the same general area as the labor and delivery rooms. These were on the second floor of the wing where Consuelo had been treated. I climbed the stairs, only to be faced with a double door informing me that I had to be gowned and masked to pass that point. I returned to the ground floor and walked down the corridor until I came to another stairwell. This one entered the second floor on the other side of the restricted zone.

The hall here was deserted, lighted dimly by occasional emergency bulbs. I had arrived in an office area; with luck no one would appear before morning. A large Xerox machine stood at about the halfway point of the floor.

Peter's office was the fourth door down. His title, Director of Obstetrics, was lettered neatly below his name on the glass door. I unlocked it and went in.

Like Humphries, Peter had a small suite for a secretary and himself. While Jackie and her boss lived in opulent tidiness, here everything was bright colors and chaotic. A rack of gaily colored brochures invited me to make Friendship my full-service obstetrical care provider. Pictures of beaming mothers nestling wholesome infants stared at me from the walls. A poster with an illustration of a stork perched happily on top of the starfish shaped hospital showed what a great place this was to give birth.

A little row of keys hung next to the desk. One was labeled "Dr. Burgoyne's office"; another was for the photocopier. The secretary's desk was crammed with patient files and other documents. A row of filing cabinets was covered with paper as well. I gave them a jaundiced look before taking the key to Peter's office door.

Parquet apparently was an executive perk at Friendship—secretarial linoleum ended abruptly at Peter's office door and the expensive wood began. The floor looked funny at the join, but we can't let the hired help forget their place. And with his door shut, you couldn't tell. Peter had not furnished his office with the opulence favored by Humphries. An ordinary modern wooden desk, also covered with stacks of paper, was in the middle of the room. A few plain chairs were placed for patient consultations; his own was a standard-supply vinyl-covered swivel chair. A large picture of his retriever made the sole personal contribution to the decor.

Once more donning my rubber gloves, I started through the papers on the desk top, skimming them briefly to make sure they held no reference to Consuelo. Finished with the top layer, I made my way through the drawers.

Peter kept everything—mementos of infants he'd delivered, correspondence with drug companies, reminders from MasterCard that his bill was overdue. In a file marked "Personal Papers" I found the original agreement between him and Friendship five years earlier. I raised my eyebrows at the terms—no wonder it had been more attractive than a perinatology residency at Beth Israel. I put it to one side for photocopying.

A report on Consuelo lay at the bottom of the last drawer. It was written in a tiny, illegible hand—his, I presumed—I'd never seen his writing. To my untutored eye it was incomprehensible:

> *At 1430 called Dr. Abercrombie*
> *At 1500 began IV administration of mg. sulf.*

I scanned the difficult script and saw where the baby had been born, efforts to revive it, death at 1810. Then Consuelo's death the following day at five-thirty.

I frowned with incomprehension. One more for Lotty. I debated whether it would be better to take the originals, running the risk that Peter would miss them, or stand at the machine in the hallway with the possibility that a nurse or doctor might come by and question me. Reluctantly I decided this was my one shot at burglarizing the files. I couldn't very well return them in the mail.

I stopped at the secretary's desk to get her key to the photocopier, then turned out the lights and closed the doors behind me without locking them. The hallway was still deserted when I went over to switch on the community copier. A half-dozen unlabeled locks in the back of the machine presumably belonged to the different offices on the floor. I tried the key in each; it turned in the fourth slot and the machine came to life.

A dead photocopier can take five or more minutes to warm up. While I waited for this one, I hunted in the hallway for a bathroom. The women's room was next to the stairwell. I was just opening the door when I heard someone coming up the stairs. I couldn't very well go back to turn off the machine; nor did I wish to be found standing in the hallway with a fistful of Friendship files. I moved into the bathroom, not turning on the light.

The footsteps came past me without halting and headed down the hall. A man, by the weight of the tread. I cracked the door and looked out. It was Peter. Why the hell was he coming into the hospital this time of night?

I watched tensely while he inserted his key in the lock. He turned it absentmindedly, couldn't get the door open, frowned at the lock and turned the key again. His thin shoulders shrugged and he went inside. I saw the bars of light come on around the edges of the door. I waited for what seemed an endless amount of time. Would he call security when he found his own office unlocked as well?

I ran through "Batti, batti" from *Don Giovanni* — that takes me about five minutes. I carefully mouthed the words twice. Ten minutes and no action. Ignoring the impulse that had sent me to the bathroom to begin with, I slunk down the hallway, retrieved the key to the photocopier, and went back down the stairs to the main wing of the hospital.

I went briskly down the corridor to the main entrance, got into the car, and circled around the building until I found the staff parking lot. In the suburbs, if you work you drive to get there. The parking area was filled with the night shift's cars. I couldn't drive into the area without a plastic card to open the gates, but I went in on foot and finally located Peter's car at the far end.

I returned to the car and moved it down the road where it would be inconspicuous, but where I could see the lot entrance. At three o'clock, Peter finally emerged. I watched him into the lot, waited until the Maxima came out, and followed it at a discreet distance until I was sure he was heading for home.

My silk shirt was again wet with sweat. You are so dumb, I admonished myself. Why will you persist in wearing silk on difficult errands in midsummer?

By this point I was past caring whether anyone intercepted me. I boldly made my way back to Peter's office wing. It was still deserted. Once more, I used his secretary's key to bring the Xerox machine to life. When the "ready" light was on, I copied the papers, stuck them in my portfolio, reopened Peter's office, and restored what I'd taken.

As I hung the keys I'd borrowed back on the little hooks by the secretary's desk, I saw what had brought him into his office: work on his amniotic-embolism conference. A note in his cramped handwriting lay on top of a stack of papers: "Okay now for typesetting and 35 mm. Sorry to bring it down to the wire for you." The conference was this coming Friday—he'd left his poor secretary with two working days to get his slides together.

On impulse I picked up samples of the brightly colored brochures and stuffed them with the other papers into my now-bulging portfolio. I carefully locked the doors behind me and left.

It was time for whiskey, bath, and bed. Near the entrance to the tollway I found a Marriott, which even at this late hour was willing to provide me with all three. I took a double Black Label from the bar up to my room. By the time I'd finished soaking in the narrow tub I'd drunk all the whiskey. Practice makes perfect in these precision-timed exercises. I fell into bed and slept the perfect sleep of the honest laborer.

XXVII

The Fading Trail

I woke up at eleven, refreshed and relaxed. I lay stretching in the king-size bed for several minutes, not wanting to break my mood of lazy well-being. They say completing a successful criminal enterprise often leaves this feeling in its wake—the people I used to represent for the county weren't successful, so I never saw it firsthand.

At last I swung out of bed and went into the bathroom to wash. The walls were covered with mirrors, offering me a complete and unappetizing view of my stomach and hips—time to lay off the pancakes and double orders of bacon. I sent down to room service for fresh fruit, yogurt, and coffee before phoning Lotty at the clinic.

"Vic! I've been debating the last half hour whether I should ring Murray Ryerson. Are you all right?"

"Yes, yes. I'm fine. I didn't get done at the hospital until close to four this morning, so I checked into a hotel out here. I'll be back later this afternoon. Are you free this evening? Can we go over some papers?"

We agreed to meet at the Dortmunder again at seven. I phoned my answering service next. Murray Ryerson and

199

Detective Rawlings both wanted to talk to me. I tried Murray first.

"So what've you got?" he greeted me, after I'd waited on hold for five minutes.

"I won't know until after Lotty's looked at it tonight. We're meeting at the Dortmunder for supper and powwow—want to join us?"

"I'll try. . . . Hang on a second."

As he put me back on hold, a knock on the door heralded my breakfast. I hadn't planned ahead and was still naked. I looked around me dubiously—the only clothes I had were what I'd worn yesterday. I put on the skirt to the suit and wrapped a towel around my top and let in the waiter.

When I got back to the phone, Murray was bellowing into it. "Jesus, Vic—I thought maybe a mysterious foreigner had given you knockout drops. I didn't even know where to send the marines."

"Schaumburg. Any luck on your end?"

"It would help if I knew what I was looking for. If your pal Burgoyne is a good old buddy of Tom Coulter's in the public-health arena, there isn't any evidence I can turn up on it. No one in Coulter's office seems to have heard of Burgoyne. Coulter's wife doesn't know him. In fact she was pretty shirty on the question of her husband's friends. Seems he goes drinking six nights out of five with his boss, Bert McMichaels. The two of them go back a ways."

"Who's McMichaels?" I asked as sharply as I could through a mouthful of berries.

"I just told you, Warshawski: Tom Coulter's boss. Schaumburg addling your brains? And don't eat while you talk, or vice versa—didn't your mother teach you the basics?"

"Yeah, yeah." I hastily washed the berries down with a mouthful of coffee. "I mean, what's McMichaels's position?"

"Oh." Murray stopped a moment to consult his notes. "He's deputy director of health regulation. Reports to Dr. Strachey, who heads up the Human Resources part of the department."

"And how do these guys get their jobs? They're not elected, are they?"

"You want Civics One-oh-one? No, they're appointed by the governor and approved by the legislature."

"I see." I studied the rest of the fruit. I had an inkling of an idea. It would mean going back to Friendship tonight to check out . . . unless . . . let your fingers do the walking.

"You still there?" Murray demanded.

"Yeah, and the unit charges are ticking away. Look, someone recommends these people, right? I mean, does Big Jim call the state medical society and say, tell me who your ten best people in public health are and I'll pick one to be king of Human Resources?"

"Get real, Warshawski. This here is Illinois. Some hack down in Springfield who's on the public-health committee, or whatever legislative name they give it, has a pal who wants a job and he—" He broke off, suddenly. "I see. The lumbering Swede catches up finally with the nimble-brained Polack. I'll try to see you tonight at Dortmunder's."

He hung up without another word. I smiled sardonically and dialed the Sixth Area Headquarters. Rawlings came on the line immediately.

"Where in hell are you, Warshawski? I thought I told you not to leave the jurisdiction."

"Sorry—I went to the burbs last night and stayed up too late to drive home. Didn't want one of your pals in traffic patrol prying my body away from a lamppost on the Kennedy. What's up?"

"Just thought you'd like to know, *Ms*. Warshawski, that since your gun hasn't been fired lately we don't think you used it to kill Fabiano Hernandez."

"What a relief. It's been keeping me up nights. Anything on Sergio?"

He made a disgusted noise. "He's got an airtight alibi. Not that that means anything. But we took his little place on Washtenaw apart. Found enough crack to maybe get a judge to agree he ain't a model citizen, but no Smith and Wesson."

I remembered the little place on Washtenaw all too

clearly. I wished I'd been able to help strip it and said as much to Rawlings.

"I didn't realize I had anything to be thankful for until just now. Anyway, come by the division and pick up your gun if you want it. And in the future, if you're spending a night away from Chicago, I want to know about it."

"You mean, forever and ever? Like if I go to England in the spring, you want to know about—" The receiver slammed in my ear before I could finish the sentence. Some people, nothing you do can please them.

I smelled the shirt I'd been wearing yesterday. If I put it back on again I wasn't sure I'd be able to stand the drive home. Marriott's little guide to hotel services listed a "Galleria of shops." I chose a sportswear store and explained my predicament.

"Could you send someone up with two or three tops—medium, or size twelve? Red, yellow, white—anything in those colors?"

They were happy to help out. Half an hour later, dressed in a white ribbed T-shirt and black jeans, with my smelly business clothes stuffed into a laundry bag, I settled the bill and headed back to the city. My night's rest and all the little extras came to over two hundred dollars. Thank goodness for the box factory in Downers Grove—something was going to have to come in before the American Express bill arrived.

My first stop in town was to pick up my gun at the police station. Rawlings wasn't in, but he'd left word with the desk sergeant. I had to show three pieces of identification and sign a couple of receipts, which suited me fine. I didn't want anyone and his dog Rover able to pick up a handgun at whim. Especially my handgun. Although someone apparently had—or at least its twin brother.

I was still wearing high heels and pantyhose under my new jeans, so I stopped at home to change into running shoes. I took a few extra minutes to arrange for a cleaning service to come straighten out my place, then headed downtown—I couldn't concentrate on my work in the middle of such squalor.

My office faces east. It was relatively cool in the midafternoon heat. Instead of turning on the air conditioner, I opened a window to let in the city air and smells. The clattering roar of the Wabash L underneath made a pleasant backdrop for my work. Before getting started, I dialed the number I'd copied from Alan Humphries's file on Consuelo. No answer.

I pulled the papers from the portfolio briefcase and divided them into neat piles: the medical material for Lotty, the financial and administrative documents for me. As I sorted, I sang snatches of "Whistle While You Work," which filled me with the happy industry of Snow White and her pals.

I went through Peter's employment agreement first, since that was only a few pages long. A base salary of $150,000 a year to join Friendship as their top obstetrics man. Plus two percent of all profits accruing from the hospital's obstetrics service. Plus profit sharing from the Schaumburg facility as a whole—at a rate to vary based on his own contributions to the hospital and the total number of staff. And, as a sweetener, a little chunk of change from the national franchise. Nice work if you could get it.

The letter was signed by Garth Hollingshead, chairman of the national company. In a concluding paragraph, Hollingshead commented:

"Your recommendations from Northwestern tell us you were the top man to graduate in your year. They offer similar comments on the skill you showed in three years of obstetrical residency. We at Friendship can all understand your desire to spend additional time training in perinatology, but believe the facilities we can offer you to do your training on the job, as it were, will not be equaled anywhere in the country."

Well, gosh. If someone wrote me a letter like that, offering me that kind of money, with profit sharing thrown in, I'd have a hard time turning it down. Ms. Warshawski, as an unparalleled thorn in the side of the police, with deductive capabilities well above the average, we would like you to be a private detective for twenty or thirty thousand a year, plus no health insurance, plus getting your face cut open and your apartment burglarized every now and then.

I turned to the material I'd taken from Humphries's office. These documented the formal organization of the hospital. Humphries was head of Friendship V, with a salary and bonus guaranteed to equal two hundred thousand in any given year in which the hospital met its profit targets. Profit sharing kicked in for any amounts above plan. I pursed my lips in a silent whistle.

Friendship was a closely-held corporation. Most of its hospitals were in Sunbelt states where certificates of need were not required. In the Northeast and Midwest, most states required their approval before anyone—town, corporation, or anyone else—could start a new hospital or add a major new facility to an existing hospital. As a result, Friendship's Schaumburg facility was its first in the Great Lakes area.

As the afternoon wore on, I picked up a miscellany of useful knowledge. Friendship V, the chain's eighteenth hospital, was the fifth it had built from scratch. When it acquired an existing facility it apparently kept the original name.

Every hospital department had separate sales and profit goals set by an administrative committee made up of Humphries and the department heads. The national parent set overall goals for each facility. It was hard to keep reminding myself that sales in this context referred to patient care.

Humphries sent out periodic administrative memos to the departments telling them how to work within federal guidelines, which set average lengths of stay and care for different conditions. Where Medicare or Medicaid reimbursement was involved, it was important that they not exceed the guidelines, since the hospital paid the difference.

I wouldn't have thought there'd be too much in the way of government-insured patients in the affluent northwest, but they apparently treated a fair number of older people. Humphries had detailed month-by-month statistics on who ran over and under the maximum reimbursed stay, with a note to one offender, heavily underscored, to "Please remember we are a for-profit institution."

By the end of the afternoon I had made my laborious way through the stack of files and reports I'd brought with me. I'd marked a few questions for Lotty, acronyms and special jargon, but for the most part the documents were comprehensible corporate reports. They presented an approach to the practice of medicine that I personally found unappetizing, since it seemed to place the health of patients second to that of the organization. But Friendship didn't seem involved in any direct malpractice, or any overt illegal finances—such as billing the government for more expensive procedures than it was performing.

So Friendship was honest. That should please me in a world filled with corruption. Why wasn't I happy? I'd gone on a fishing trip. I'd found Consuelo's record for Lotty, even if it wasn't a copy that could be used in court. What else had I expected? Blackmail by IckPiff that would make the hospital pay my ex-husband's bill? Or did I just want a scapegoat for the frustrations and disasters of the last month?

I tried to shrug away a faint sense of depression, but it stayed with me as I packed up the papers and headed north to the Dortmunder.

XXVIII

Falling to the Bottom Line

Lotty brought Max Loewenthal, executive director of Beth Israel, to the Dortmunder with her. A short, sturdy man of sixty or so with curly white hair, he had been a widower for a number of years. He was in love with Lotty, whom he'd met after the war in London—he, too, was an Austrian refugee. He had asked her several times to marry him, but she always replied that she wasn't the marrying type. Still, they shared season tickets to the opera and the symphony every year and she had traveled around England with him more than once.

He stood up at my entrance, smiling at me with shrewd gray eyes. Murray hadn't arrived yet. I told them we might expect him.

"I thought Max could answer administrative questions if any arose," Lotty explained.

Lotty rarely drinks, but Max was knowledgeable about wines and pleased to have someone to share a bottle with. He picked out a '75 Cos d'Estournel from the bins along the walls and had it opened. Max waved away the waitress, who knew Lotty and me well and was disposed to talk. None of us wanted to eat until we'd been through my cache.

"I have Friendship's file on Consuelo, although if you're going to have it admitted in court you'll have to order a copy through proper channels." I pulled the two records on Consuelo from my briefcase and handed them to Lotty. "The typed one was the one locked in Humphries's office and the handwritten one was in Peter Burgoyne's desk file."

Lotty put on her black-rimmed glasses and studied the reports. She first read the typed copy, then went through Peter's handwritten notes. Her heavy brows drew together and deep lines etched themselves around her mouth.

I found I was holding my breath and reached for the wine. Max, equally intent, didn't try to stop me from pouring before it had breathed properly.

"Who is Dr. Abercrombie?" Lotty asked.

"I don't know. He's the person in the report Peter says he tried calling?" I thought of the brochures I'd picked up in Peter's office and fished them from my portfolio. They might list hospital staff.

"Friendship: Your Full-Care Obstetrics Service" proclaimed a slickly printed piece. They had spent a lot of money on it—four-color, letterpress with photographs. The cover showed a woman nestling a newborn infant, a look of ineffable joy on her face. Inside, the copy proclaimed: "Giving birth: the most important experience of your life. Let us help you make it your most joyful experience as well." I skimmed through the copy. "Most women give birth without complications of any kind. But if you need extra help before or during birth, our perinatologist is on call twenty-four hours a day."

At the bottom of the page, a serious but confident man held what looked like an electric blanket control against the abdomen of a pregnant woman. She gazed up at him trustingly. The caption read: "Keith Abercrombie, M.D., board-certified perinatologist, administers ultrasound to one of his patients."

I handed it over to Lotty, indicating the picture with my finger. "Translate, please?"

She read the caption. "He's using sound waves to make sure the baby is still moving, checking the heartbeat to make sure it's normal. You can also estimate height and weight with these gadgets. Late in pregnancy you can usually tell sex as well.

"The perinatologist is an obstetrician with a specialty in treating the complications of pregnancy. If your baby is born with problems, you'd get a specialist pediatrician in, a neonatologist. Consuelo needed a perinatologist. If he'd shown up, then little Victoria Charlotte might have made it long enough to get to the neonatologist, who also didn't seem to be there."

She took off her glasses and laid them on the table beside the papers. "Dr. Burgoyne's problem is obvious. Why he didn't want me to see his case notes. What I don't understand is why he didn't throw them out—the typed report is explanatory without revealing overt negligence."

"Lotty. It may be obvious to you, but it isn't to us. What are you talking about?" Max demanded. Unlike her, he still spoke with a pronounced Viennese accent. He reached for the reports and started looking through them.

"In the typed report, they explain that Consuelo showed up as a nonambulatory emergency. She was beginning labor and she was comatose. They administered dextrose to try to restore her blood sugar and raise her blood pressure. They say in the typed report that they used ritodrine to try to retard labor. Then it became a trade-off on whether they could stop labor without killing her, so they went ahead and took the baby. Then she died, of complications of pregnancy. But Burgyone's handwritten notes tell a much different story."

"Yes, I see." Loewenthal looked up from perusing Peter's handwritten notes. "He spells the whole thing out, doesn't he?"

I thought I might scream with impatience. "Spell it out for me!"

"What time did you get to the hospital?" Lotty asked me instead.

I shook my head. "I can't remember—it's been almost a month."

"You're a detective, a trained observer. Think."

I shut my eyes, recalling the hot day, the paint factory. "We got to the plant just at one. Fabiano's appointment was at one and I had an eye on the dashboard clock—we were cutting it close. It might have been a quarter hour later that Consuelo started in labor. Say I spent fifteen minutes in the plant getting instructions on what hospital to use and how to find it. Another fifteen to drive there. So it must have been around one-forty-five when we got to Friendship."

"And yet at three o'clock they were just calling Abercrombie," Max said. "So a good hour went by in which they didn't do anything for her."

"So when I talked to that impossible woman in admissions, they *weren't* treating her," I said. "God damn it, I should have made a bigger stink at the time. They must have kept her waiting on that gurney for an hour while they debated treating her."

Lotty ignored that. "The point is, they say they gave her ritodrine. That's the drug of choice today, and certainly what this Abercrombie should have done, if he'd been there. But Burgoyne's notes say he gave her magnesium sulfate. That can cause heart failure; it did in Consuelo's case. He notes that her heart stopped, they took the baby and revived Consuelo, but all the shocks her system had had that day were too much—her heart stopped again in the night and they couldn't revive her."

Her brows furrowed together. "When Malcolm got there, he must have known what the problem was. But maybe he didn't know right off that they weren't using ritodrine. If the IV bag wasn't clearly labeled . . ."

Her voice trailed off as she tried to visualize the scene. The bins of wine bottles rotated around me and the floor seemed to swoop up toward me. I clutched the edge of the table. "No," I said aloud. "That's just not possible."

"What is it, Vic?" Max's sharp eyes were alert.

"Malcolm. They wouldn't have killed him to stop him reporting what he'd seen. Surely not."

"What!" Lotty demanded. "This isn't a time for jokes, Vic. Yes, they'd made a serious mistake. But to kill a man, and so brutally? Anyway, when he talked to me, he told me they were using the right drug. So maybe he didn't know. Or maybe he questioned the nurses later. Maybe that's what he told me he wanted to check on that night—before he wrote his report. What I don't understand is where this Abercrombie was. Burgoyne says he tried calling him, more than once, but he never showed up."

"I guess I could try to find Abercrombie's office," I said unenthusiastically. "See if *he* left any telltale case notes lying around."

"I don't think that will prove necessary." Max had been studying the brochure. "We can use logic. They just say he's on call twenty-four hours a day. They don't say he's part of the hospital staff."

"So?"

He grinned. "Here's where my specialized knowledge becomes important. You wonder why Lotty brought me. You say to yourself, why is this senile old man interrupting my great detection—"

"Knock it off," I said. "Get to the point."

He became serious. "In the last ten years, there's been a shift in the age at which educated women give birth—they're having their first babies much later than they used to. Because they're educated, they know about the risks, right? And they want to go to a hospital where they know an expert will be on hand to treat them if they have complications."

I nodded. I have a number of friends agonizing over the various stages of conception, pregnancy, and delivery. The modern pregnancy—gone through with the care we used to reserve for buying a car.

"So by now enough people are worrying about these issues that hospitals that want to be competitive in obstetrics have to have a perinatologist on hand. And they have to have a full complement of fetal monitors and neonatal intensive-care unit and so on.

"But to make something like that pay, you need to be delivering at least twenty-five hundred to three thousand infants a year." He grinned wolfishly. "You know. Bottom line. We can't offer unprofitable services."

"I see." I did. I saw the whole picture with amazing clarity. Except for a few little pieces. Like Fabiano. Dick and Dieter Monkfish. But I had an idea about them, too.

"So is Dr. Abercrombie a chimera?" I asked. "They just hire an actor to pose with a fetal-monitor machine?"

"No." Max spoke judiciously. "I'm sure he's real. But is he really attached to the hospital? Friendship Five is in an upscale neighborhood, correct? They do not typically treat high-risk pregnancies—the type of patient that Consuelo was—young, bad diet, and so on. If one of your Dr. Burgoyne's patients seemed to be prone to complications, he'd get Abercrombie over to see her. But why pay a quarter of a million dollars a year for someone whose work you need only once a month at best?"

He poured more wine into my glass and tasted his own. He nodded absentmindedly, a fraction of his attention on the wine.

Lotty frowned. "But, Max. They're advertising a full-service obstetrics service. Level Three care, you know. That's why we told Vic to take Consuelo there. Carol spoke with Sid Hatcher, asked him where they should go in that part of the suburbs. Sid had seen the advertisements, had heard their service discussed at some meeting he'd been to. That's why he recommended Friendship."

"So if they didn't have this Abercrombie really on staff they couldn't advertise?" I asked skeptically. Truth in advertising is the law, sure, but only if you get caught.

Lotty leaned forward in her intensity. "The state comes in and certifies you. I know this, because I was the perinatologist at Beth Israel when we got our original certification. Before I went into family medicine and opened my clinic. They came in and put us through a major review—equipment and everything."

I emptied my glass. I hadn't eaten since the virtuous fruit and yogurt I'd had for breakfast. The rich, heavy wine went straight from my stomach to my brain, warming me. I needed a little warmth to deal with what I was learning.

"If Murray shows up I think he'll have the answer to that." I held out my right hand and rubbed my first two fingers against my thumb, the Chicago city symbol.

Lotty shook her head. "I don't understand."

"Payoffs," Max explained to her kindly.

"Payoffs?" she echoed. "No. It wouldn't happen. Not with Philippa. You remember her, don't you, Max? She's with the state these days."

"Well, she's not the only person with the state," I said. "She has a boss who's in charge of health regulation. She's got an obnoxious young prick of a colleague who's on the make. The two of them are good drinking buddies. Now all we need to find out is what state rep they drink with, and we'll be all set."

"Don't joke about it, Vic. I don't like it. You are talking about the lives of people. Consuelo and her baby. Who knows what others. And you are saying a hospital and a public official would care more about money. It is not a joke."

Max put a hand over hers. "That's why I love you, Lottchen. You have survived a horrible war and thirty years of medicine without losing your innocence."

I poured more wine, my third glass, and pushed my chair back a bit from the table. So everything falls to the bottom line. Humphries and Peter are part owners of the hospital. It's important to them personally that every service make a profit. More important to Humphries, perhaps, since his potential take is bigger. So they advertise their full-care service. They get Abercrombie on a part-time basis and figure that's all they need because they're in a part of town where they won't have a lot of emergencies.

The emergency room at Friendship. After all, I'd been there twice—yesterday, and earlier when I came in with Consuelo. No one used it. It was just there to be part of the full-care image, to keep the paying guests walking in the door.

And then Consuelo and I showed up and put a spanner

in the works. It wasn't exactly that they thought she was indigent that they didn't treat her. That might have been part of it, but the other part was they were trying to locate their perinatologist, Keith Abercrombie.

"Where was he?" I asked abruptly. "Abercrombie. I mean, he must be in the neighborhood someplace, right? They couldn't expect to use him if he was at the University of Chicago or some other remote place."

"I can find that out." Lotty got up. "He'll be in the American College Directory. I'll call Sid—if he's at home he can look it up for us."

She went off to use the phone. Max shook his head. "If you're right . . . What a horrible thought. Killing that brilliant young man just to protect their bottom line."

XXIX

A Good Wine with Dinner

Murray arrived just as Max finished speaking. His red beard glistened with sweat. Sometime during the day he'd discarded his tie and jacket. His shirt, which he had custom-tailored to cover his large frame, had come out of his trousers on one side; as he came up to the table he pushed at it ineffectually, trying to get it back into his pants.

"What brilliant young man?" he demanded by way of greeting. "You hadn't given me up for dead, had you?"

I introduced him to Max. "Murray's friends worry about him—he's too shy and modest, they say. How can he survive in the raw world of journalism?"

Murray grinned. "Yeah, it's a problem."

The waitress sauntered over. Murray ordered a beer. "In fact, bring me a couple. And something to eat—one of your cheese and fruit plates. You guys didn't wait, huh?"

I shook my head. "We've been too busy to eat. I guess we'd all like something—you, Max?"

He nodded. "Lotty won't want much. But let's have some pâtés to go along with the cheese."

After the waitress had brought Murray a bottle of Holsten, Max and I recapitulated our conversation for him. Murray's eyes began to gleam with excitement. He drank the beer left-handed, jotting madly in his notebook.

"What a story," he said enthusiastically when we'd finished. "I love it. 'Profit Motive Ices Teenager: What Price the Bottom Line?' "

"You're not going to print that." That was Lotty, who'd returned to the table, flat-voiced and angry.

"Why not? It's terrific copy."

Lotty's objections centered on not wanting to violate Consuelo's privacy. I waited for her to finish speaking before turning to Murray, who was looking blandly unconvinced.

"It's a great part of a great story," I said as patiently as I could. "But we don't have any admissible proof."

"Hey, I'm not taking this to court—I'm quoting a reliable source. A usually reliable one, that is." He wiggled his eyebrows provocatively.

"You're not taking it to court. But Lotty is. She's been sued for malpractice, for failure to treat Consuelo. Her file on Consuelo was stolen during the great abortion raid—"

I broke off. "Of course. How simpleminded can I get? Humphries got Dieter to organize a protest. Then he had someone break in for him and steal the file. Whoever took it didn't have time to be picky—he just grabbed everything with the Hernandez name on it. He was looking for Malcolm's report, of course. That's why Friendship's counsel is representing Dieter Monkfish. It doesn't have anything to do with Humphries's feelings about abortion. It's part of his debt to the guy."

"Then the attack on Malcolm?" Max asked, his eyes troubled.

I hesitated before speaking. I couldn't imagine either Humphries or Peter actually battering someone to death. And Malcolm had been badly beaten. But if it was true, if Friendship was covering up for failure to deliver the obstetrics care they were promoting . . . I turned abruptly to Murray.

"What did you find out today?"

"Nothing as hot as you've come up with, kid." Murray flipped back through his notebook. "Bert McMichaels. Associate director of Environment and Human Resources, responsible for hospital regulation. Fifty years old. Been in state government for a long time. Was with the state environmental-protection agency, got a promotion into the health side in the last round of appointments. No particular background in public health or medicine, but a lot of savvy with state agencies, administration, finance, that kind of thing."

He stopped to drink more beer, wiping his mouth on his hand, like Sutcliffe after a sweaty pitch. "Okay. What you want to know is, his pals in Springfield. He's tied in with Clancy McDowell."

He turned to Lotty and Max, who were looking at him in puzzlement. "McDowell is just an average hack state rep—Northwest Side district. He has pals who go out and get votes for him and in return he gets them jobs, that kind of stuff. So McMichaels is a big vote deliverer and he has had steady employment with the State of Illinois."

Lotty started to object. Murray held up a hand. "I know. It's awful. It's shocking. A guy like that shouldn't be in a position to decide whether a hospital gets built or an obstetrics service gets licensed, but alas, this isn't Utopia or even Minneapolis—it's Illinois."

He didn't sound particularly depressed about it. How could you bother getting depressed, or angry, about a situation so entrenched that schoolchildren routinely learn about it as part of their civics lesson? I mean, Mayor Daley's control of city and county had been in my eighth-grade government textbook.

Murray was going on. I don't know why he looks at his notes when he talks—he knows it all by heart, but somehow he can't talk without the prop, the thumbing—maybe that's how he convinces himself he's really a journalist.

"Anyway, your pals at Friendship made a nice little contribution to Clancy's reelection campaign in '80, '82, and '84. About ten thousand each time. Not spectacular amounts of money, but it doesn't take much to elect a state rep, and after all, it's the thought that counts."

He closed his notebook with a flourish. "I want some-thing to eat. And I want more beer."

The Dortmunder is not famous for its speedy service. That's why it's a good place for a supper meeting. The staff doesn't hover trying to kick you out. In exchange for that, you don't complain when it takes an hour to get your food.

Lotty was seriously upset. "I know you and Vic think this is commonplace. But I cannot accept it so lightly. How can they do that—buy off a politician just to save a few dollars. And then put someone's life at risk. It is treating medicine like—like an automobile company deciding to put a faulty car on the streets!"

No one said anything for a few minutes out of respect for Lotty's feelings. It hurt her badly to find corruption in the profession she'd chosen to cure those injustices she'd suf-fered as a child. She would never develop a shellac of cyn-icism to protect herself against it.

Finally Max said hesitantly to me, "Perhaps the people in Springfield, the friends of this Clancy, might have tried killing Malcolm? Rather than have their part in the certifi-cation come to light? Or you know, it might really have been what the police are saying—a random break-in."

I shook my head. "I don't think so. And I doubt that Bert McMichaels would care, at least not care to the point of murder, if Friendship's dereliction came to light. After all—he can claim he accepted the hospital's submission about its facilities in good faith. No, the ones who have something at stake are the people at the hospital. They couldn't afford for Malcolm's report on Consuelo to get to Lotty. When they didn't find it at his apartment, they staged the raid on the clinic. But where on earth is it? We found his recorder, but it was empty."

And who actually killed Malcolm? I added to myself. I still couldn't see Alan Humphries doing such dirty work. And Peter, with his sensitive conscience? He'd be in a strait-jacket by now if he'd battered someone's head in.

Max turned to Lotty and took her hand again. "My dear, how many times have I begged you to come to me when you are in difficulty? I know where the report is."

The rest of us broke in in a chorus, demanding an answer. The waitress chose that moment to arrive with a towering tray of cheeses, salamis, pâtés, and fruit. Murray took the opportunity to order more beer and I told Max I was game for more wine if he was.

Max agreed amiably. "But not Clos d'Estournel, Vic. I can't stand to watch you gulping it like Kool-Aid."

He got up and made his leisurely way to the wine bins.

"How maddening," Lotty said. "Why did you ask for more wine, Vic? You should have known it would slow him down ten minutes."

I broke off a piece of country pâté and ate it with mustard and cornichons. Lotty nibbled at a slice of apple; tension makes it hard for her to eat. Murray had already consumed most of a half-pound wedge of Brie and was starting in on the cheddar.

Max returned to the table with a house Bordeaux. While the waitress opened it and poured, taking her time in the hopes of getting to join the party, he discoursed gently on the proper way to drink fine wines.

"You are in the wrong profession," Lotty informed him when the waitress finally ambled away. "You should be an actor—bringing people to the brink and then making them wait. Now this is serious, Max. If you have Malcolm's final dictation, why have I not seen it?"

He shook his head. "I didn't say I had it, Lotty. I know—or I suspect—where it is. Malcolm brought his dictation to Beth Israel for typing. I'm surprised you didn't think of it. It's probably sitting in the Medical Transcription room in an envelope with his name on it, waiting for him to pick it up."

Lotty wanted to go to Beth Israel at once, but I restrained her. "We want to know what Dr. Hatcher said about Abercrombie," I reminded her. "And Murray is going to agree not to run this story until we say it's okay."

Murray's blue eyes flashed angrily. "Look here, Warshawski. I appreciate the tip and the scoop. But you don't run my head or my paper. With what I've found out today, and the story you three are fleshing out, this has banner headlines and a weeklong exposé written all over it."

"Come on, Murray. They say Polacks are dumb—jeez, use your head! Here's Lotty, being dragged into court for malpractice. We have illegally obtained copies of evidence showing that all the negligence was out at the hospital. You print the story, they destroy the original of Peter's notes, deny like hell, and what kind of defense does she have?"

I paused to drink some of the new wine. It wasn't as full-bodied as the Cos d'Estournel, so I was less inclined to gulp it like Kool-Aid. Not that I've ever liked Kool-Aid well enough to gulp it. I got back to my argument.

"There's a chance that they've kept Lotty's file on Consuelo. If you run your story, that will disappear faster than democracy in Chile. I want to take them by surprise."

"Oh, all right." Murray was grumpy for a minute or two, but his basic good nature won't let him carry a grudge. "What do you propose doing, Nancy Drew?"

"We-ll, I've got an idea." I ignored Murray's Bronx cheer and ate some more pâté. "Max, they know Lotty's name, but I bet they don't know yours. They're giving a conference this Friday. Amniotic-something-or-other. Can you call tomorrow and sign up? You'll want to bring—you coming, Lotty? Murray?—four people with you."

Max smiled. "Certainly. Why not? I will speak with my heaviest accent and tell them I am calling from New York, flying in just for the day."

"You don't have to show up. Just get five spaces reserved. Maybe we'd better all have pseudonyms in case Peter checks the attendance roster. He knows Lotty and me. He won't know Murray's name, of course. Or Detective Rawlings."

"Rawlings?" Murray asked. "Why bring in the police? They'll spoil everything."

"I don't know if he'll come," I said impatiently. "But I'd like him to see the story with his own eyes. It's too unbelievable otherwise. Will you do it, Max?"

"Certainly. And I want to be there in person. If there are to be fireworks, why should I not see them? Anyway, this will be a fine opportunity for me to watch you at your detective work. I have always been curious.''

"It's not the thrill you're expecting, Loewenthal," Murray said. "Vic favors the Dick Butkus approach to detection—hit the offense hard—you know, just so they know they met you at the line of scrimmage—then see who's left on the ground when she gets done. If you're looking for Sherlock Holmes or Nero Wolfe doing some fancy intellectual footwork, forget it."

"Thank you for the testimonial," I said, bowing over the table. "All are appreciated and may be sent to our head office in Tripoli, where an appropriate response will be generated. Anyway, Murray, you don't have to come. I was just asking Max to include you out of courtesy."

"Oh, no. I'm coming. If this story is going to start breaking on Friday, I want to be there. Anyway, I'm going to have the thing keyed in, ready to transmit, the moment your pal Burgoyne looks at you with his honest but troubled eyes and says, 'Vic, you've persuaded me to turn myself in.' Or does he just call you 'sweetheart' or 'Victoria' or 'She-Who-Must-Be-Obeyed'?''

XXX

Voice from the Grave

When we got to Beth Israel and went down to the Medical Transcription center, finding Malcolm's dictation was almost anticlimactic. The night operators were startled to see Max come in. The laughter and raucous comments we'd heard while walking down the hallway stopped immediately and everyone turned to her machine with the intensity of radarwomen looking for incoming ICBMs.

Max, behaving as if it were the most natural thing in the world for the hospital's executive director to show up at ten at night, asked the lead operator for Malcolm Tregicre's output. She walked over to an opened filing cabinet, thumbed through to the T's, and pulled out a manila envelope with Malcolm's name on it.

"We wondered why he hadn't come for it—it's been sitting here for close to a month."

I took a look at Lotty, who appeared to be controlling herself with maximum effort.

"He's dead," she finally said, her voice coming out harshly. "Perhaps you missed the news and the announcement here at the hospital."

"Oh, gee—I'm sorry. He was such a nice man to work for."

When Max started to walk away with the folder, she said hesitantly, "Uh, look, Mr. Loewenthal. We're not supposed to let dictation go out to anyone but the person who did it. So could you write a little note for my supervisor? You know, explaining Dr. Tregiere is dead and all and you're taking responsibility for the papers?"

"I had no idea I ran such a tightly organized hospital," Max murmured ironically. But he obediently took a piece of paper and scribbled a few lines on it.

We followed him out of the room, trying not to act like tigers surrounding a gazelle. Max pulled a stack of papers out of the envelope and riffled through them, continuing to walk toward his office. We trailed behind him.

"Yes, here it is. Consuelo Hernandez. 'At Dr. Herschel's request I drove to Friendship Hospital on July twenty-ninth where Consuelo Hernandez had been admitted at thirteen hundred fifty-two. According to the nurse on duty, she had arrived unconscious and in labor. . . .' " He handed the sheaf of papers to Lotty.

"I don't understand," Murray said, gazing hungrily at Lotty. "If you're right that the boys at Friendship wanted this badly enough to kill for it, why didn't they simply do what you did just now—come in here and get it?"

Lotty looked up briefly from her reading. "They didn't know he was on staff here. They knew he was my associate. That was all. I didn't think of it myself. My secretary, Mrs. Coltrain, typed his dictation about patients he saw at the clinic. It never occurred to me that he didn't give all his notes to her. I know that was stupid. But between the shock of his murder and the shock of the attack on the clinic, I haven't been thinking too clearly this last month. I didn't even remember to expect his report on treating Consuelo at Friendship until I got notice of that claim last week."

We had reached Max's office and waited while he unlocked the door and turned on the lights. It was a comfortable room, not furnished with the opulence of his counterpart at Friendship, but filled with the artifacts of a long, cultivated life. The desk, scarred from years of use, sat like Alan Humphries's atop a Persian rug. This one was old and worn in places—Max had bought it himself when he was twenty-five, in a secondhand store in London. The shelves were filled with books, many on hospital management and finance, but many also on the Oriental art he liked to collect.

Lotty sat on a faded couch to finish her reading. Murray watched her intently, as though he expected to absorb the material by picking up her brainwaves. Fatigue had hit me, a combination of too much wine, too little food, and my unpleasant reflections on Peter Burgoyne. I sat in an armchair apart from the others, my eyes closed. When Lotty finally spoke, I didn't open them.

"It's all here. The failure to treat her for close to an hour. It must have been when you told them Malcolm was coming that they started the magnesium sulfate, Vic."

I didn't move at the mention of my name and she went on.

"He says they'd told him they were using ritodrine. He told me that on the phone. But he'd got there shortly after her first cardiac arrest and it kept worrying him, what had caused it. So he called the head nurse when he was back at Beth Israel and got the truth out of her—she was worried about Consuelo's condition and was eager to talk. . . . Abercrombie showed up right before Malcolm left. At six."

"Abercrombie?" That was Murray.

"Oh, yes. You don't know, do you?" Lotty answered. "He is the perinatologist they advertise as being on their staff. Actually, he's part of Outer Suburban—that big teaching-hospital complex in Barrington. He just takes a retainer to fill in at Friendship when they call him."

No one said anything for a few minutes. Then I forced myself to sit up, think, open my eyes.

"You have a safe?" I asked Max. At his nod, I said, "I'll feel better if these things are under lock and key. But let's get photocopies first—Murray, can you make thirty-five millimeters of Malcolm's report as well as Burgoyne's notes?"

"I kind of felt that coming," he said. "This is going to cost a fortune—twenty-four-hour turnaround on . . . we'll have to split these pages in four to make the text readable . . . twelve slides. You got six hundred dollars, Warshawski?"

I didn't, as he knew damned well. Max spoke up. "I'll get our darkroom here to make up the slides, Ryerson."

I got to my feet. "Thanks, Max. I appreciate it. . . . I'm going home. Too long a day. I'm past thinking."

"You'll come with me, my dear." That was Lotty. "I don't want you driving. And I don't want you going home to that wreck of an apartment. Besides, whoever broke in may think you have more to reveal. I'll feel better if you're safe with me."

No one could feel totally secure facing a drive with Lotty at night, but the offer cheered me. The thought of that solitary climb up the backstairs to my kitchen door had been hovering unpleasantly at the back of my mind.

We waited while Max went down the hall to copy the papers. He had a little wall safe behind his desk, put in by the trustees to safeguard his personal papers—"an absurd response to urban crime," he called it, but useful tonight.

Murray, almost slavering like a bloodhound, took the copies. I nearly laughed watching his face fall as he tried to read them. Nothing like someone else's jargon to make you feel completely ignorant.

"Damn," he said to Max. "If you and Lotty weren't swearing these were life-threatening documents I sure as hell would never guess it. I hope Nancy Drew Warshawski here knows what she's doing—I wouldn't leap up and yell 'I'm sorry—I killed Malcolm Tregiere' if someone confronted me with them."

"Then isn't it good that you're not exploding this in the *Star* without all the facts," I said nastily. "Anyway, I don't think Peter Burgoyne killed Malcolm. I don't know who did."

Murray faked astonishment. "There's something you haven't figured out?"

Max was watching us with patent amusement but Lotty

didn't find the interchange particularly funny. She bustled me out the door and down the hall, scarcely waiting for Max's good-bye.

Once buckled into Lotty's passenger seat, I let exhaustion take over. If Lotty was going to pick this night to ram into a streetlamp, my fear wouldn't stop her.

Neither of us tried speaking during the ride. I supposed, from the remote shell of my fatigue, that she needed comfort. With her skill and experience, Lotty could have commanded any price she wanted to name at any hospital in the country. But her major goal was to make her art as accessible as possible to the people who needed it most.

Sometimes when Lotty gets me angry I goad her by accusing her of thinking she can save the world. But I suspect it really is her goal—to somehow cleanse herself of the evils she's lived through by making people healthy. I don't have such grand ideals as a detective. Not only do I not think I can save the world, I suspect most people are past redemption. I'm just the garbage collector, cleaning up little trash piles here and there.

Like Peter Burgoyne. No wonder he'd been so obsessive about Consuelo's death and Lotty's reaction. Because he knew he'd let her die. Whether the treatment he'd given her had contributed, I wasn't competent to evaluate. But by agreeing to work in an environment where he was promising a service he couldn't deliver, he had created the situation that caused her death.

He'd been a good doctor once, with lots of promise. That was what the chairman of Friendship indicated his references said about him in the letter offering him the position at Friendship. That's probably why he'd kept his case notes on Consuelo: laceration. He knew what he should have done, if he'd been the kind of doctor Lotty was. But he didn't have the guts to admit he was wrong. So he could torment himself in private, without having to confess in public. Mr. Contreras was right. Peter was a lightweight.

XXXI

Midnight Projectionist

As I was falling asleep between Lotty's lavender-scented sheets I remembered the phone number I'd found in Alan Humphries's papers. I struggled awake and dialed it again. It rang five times; I was going to hang up when a sleepy-voiced woman answered.

"I'm calling from Alan Humphries," I said.

"Who?" she asked. "I don't know who you mean." She spoke with a Spanish accent; in the background a baby began to cry.

"I want the man who's been helping Alan Humphries."

There was momentary pause. From the muffling of the receiver, I thought she might be conferring with someone. When she spoke again, she sounded worried, or helpless. "He—he's not here right now. You must try later."

The baby's cries sounded louder. Suddenly, in the total relaxation fatigue induces, a fragment of an old conversation swam up in my memory. "Oh, I'm a married man now, Warshawski. Got me a nice wife, a little baby. . . ."

No wonder she felt worried or helpless. Sergio's angelic beauty might have swept her off her feet. But now she had a small baby and a husband who was gone much of the time, who had frequent conversations with the police, who brought home large amounts of money whose source she wasn't supposed to ask about.

"Can I reach him here tomorrow, Mrs. Rodriguez?"

"I don't know. I—I suppose so. Who did you say is calling?"

"Alan Humphries," I repeated.

I barely remembered to hang up the phone before falling down the well of sleep. When I woke up, the August sun was streaming around the edges of Lotty's oatmeal-colored curtains. As I came to, a feeling of dismay gripped the pit of my stomach. Oh, yes. Peter Burgoyne. A goodly apple rotten to the core. But it was Humphries, not Peter, who'd been calling Sergio. Getting him to break into Malcolm's apartment and hunt for the dictating machine. Maybe bludgeoning Malcolm to death had been Sergio's added touch, not included in the original price of admission.

I picked my watch up from the bedside table. Seven-thirty. Too early to reach Rawlings. I got up and went to the kitchen where Lotty already sat with her first cup of coffee and *The New York Times*. Lotty never exercises. She maintains her trim figure through sheer willpower—no muscle would dare go flabby under that stern gaze. She does have rigorous ideas on diet, however—fresh-squeezed orange juice, no matter what the season, and a bowl of muesli constituted her invariable breakfast. She had already eaten; the empty bowl and glass were rinsed and neatly placed on the draining board.

I poured myself a cup of coffee and joined her at the table. She put her paper down and cocked her head at me.

"You're doing all right?"

I smiled at her. "Oh, yeah, I'm okay. Just a little bruised in the ego. I don't like having affairs with people who are using me. I thought I had better judgment than to let it happen."

She patted my hand. "So you're human, Victoria. Is that such a bad thing? Now what do you do today?"

I grimaced. "Just wait. See if Rawlings will come to Friendship's conference. Oh—one thing you could do if you would. Can you see that they don't discharge Mr. Contreras until after this weekend? His daughter is hot for him to go home with her, away from the dangerous city. He doesn't want that at all, and he's nervous the doctors will insist on it. I said I'd bring him home with me if they want someone looking out for him, but I don't want to have to spend half my time worrying that he's fending off Sergio Rodriguez while I'm away.''

She promised to take care of it during her morning rounds. Looking at her watch, she gave a little exclamation and took off—Lotty goes to Beth Israel to see patients before starting her day at the clinic.

I wandered moodily around Lotty's apartment for a while. Human, huh? Maybe she was right, maybe not such a bad thing. Maybe if I learned to accept my own fallibility I'd be easier on other people. It sounded good—a page out of Leo Buscaglia. But I didn't believe it.

I walked from her apartment to the clinic to pick up my car, then headed to my own place to change clothes. At ten o'clock Max's secretary called me there to say everything was set for me to go to the Friendship conference on Friday. "He registered you as Viola da Gamba." She spelled it dubiously. "Could that be right?"

"Yes," I said grimly. "We'll hope that they're as stupid as he thinks they are. Who's Lotty going as?"

She sounded more doubtful than ever. "Domenica Scarlatti?"

I decided my nerves couldn't take very many collaborations with Max, told the secretary to thank him but remind him that the sharpest people often cut themselves.

"I'll give him the message," she said politely. "The conference will be held in the Stanhope Auditorium on the second floor of the main wing out at Friendship Hospital. Do you need directions?"

I told her I could find it and hung up.

Rawlings was in when I tried him. "What do you want, Ms. W.?"

"You free Friday morning?" I asked as nonchalantly as I could. "Want to go on a field trip?"

"What are you up to, Warshawski?"

"There's a medical conference out in Schaumburg on Friday. I think they may cover some interesting morbidity and mortality statistics.''

"Morbidity and mortality? You're trying to snowball me, but I know you're talking about death. You know something about Fabiano Hernandez's death. You have evidence and you're concealing it, that's a felony, Warshawski, and you damned well know it.''

"I'm not concealing anything about Fabiano." I'd forgotten him. I paused a minute, trying to work him into my equation, and couldn't. Maybe Sergio had shot him, thinking he was being double-crossed. "Malcolm Tregiere. And I don't know anything—I'm just guessing. They're going to present a paper that may or may not reveal the truth about what happened to him.''

Rawlings breathed heavily into my ear. "May or may not? And what might that be? Or not?''

"Well, that's why I thought you'd like to go to Schaumburg. Just on the chance, I had you registered for the conference. It starts at nine, coffee and rolls at eight-thirty.''

"Damn your ass, Warshawski. For two cents I'd run you in as a material witness.''

"But then you'd miss the conference, Detective, and you'd go to your grave wondering if you'd ever really have found out about Malcolm Tregiere.''

"No wonder Bobby Mallory turns red when he hears your name. His trouble is, he's too much of a gentleman to try police brutality. . . . Nine o'clock in Schaumburg, huh? I'll pick you up at seven-thirty.''

"I'm going to be out there already. Why don't you arrange to go with Dr. Herschel? She can help you find the place.''

"Mighty white of you, Ms. W.,'' he grumbled.

"Always happy to do my citizen's duty of helping the police uphold the law, Detective,'' I said politely. He slammed the receiver in my ear.

After that, there was nothing else I could do but wait. The cleaning service I'd called sent over a crew around noon. I told them to pick everything up and put it away someplace and scour and wax every surface. Why not have it completely clean once a year? I called the friend who'd made my extra-thick front door for me originally and commissioned another one. He apologized profusely when he heard it hadn't held up to an ax and offered to line the new one with steel, for an additional five hundred dollars.

I covered my face with extra-strength sunscreen and jogged over to the lake, where I spent most of the afternoon. Labor Day was around the corner, and usually about that time we have a big storm that turns the lake water over, making it too cold for swimming for the rest of the year. Time to make the most of it. I floated on my back, enjoying the sense of being rocked in the cradle of the deep, secure in the arms of Mother Nature.

Max's secretary called me at noon Thursday to tell me the slides were ready. I drove over to Beth Israel for them. Max was in a meeting, but he had left a neatly labeled packet for me.

Thursday night. Back in my business clothes with Lotty's white coat for disguise. This time I'd packed an overnight case and reserved a room at the Marriott. Lotty and Rawlings would meet me there at eight-thirty in the morning. Max and Murray were driving together and would join us at the hospital entrance.

At midnight I reached the hospital grounds. I made a circuit of the staff parking lot before going in, to make sure that Peter's Maxima wasn't there. Then, white-jacketed and, I hoped, professional, I went in through the main entrance and up the stairs to the second floor.

The Stanhope Auditorium took up the far end of the corridor overlooking the parking lot. The double doors were locked, but again they had used a standard model that turned back easily. I closed them behind me and shone a flashlight around.

I was in a small theater, ideal for this kind of meeting. Twenty-five or so rows of plush-covered, swivel seats were stair-stepped down to a stage. Just now its curtains were drawn. In front of them stood a large white movie screen, with a podium and microphone to one side.

The audiovisual equipment was in a projection room at the rear of the theater. I unlocked the door, my hands shaking a bit with nerves, and started examining the carousels full of slides.

XXXII

Mortality Conference

Max and Murray were waiting for us in the visitors' parking lot. In contrast to Lotty, whose dark face was pinched with worry, and Rawlings, who affected a heavy-policeman attitude, Max was ebullient. He wore a tan summer suit with an orange-striped shirt and a tie of darker umber. When he saw us, he bounded over radiating goodwill—kissing Lotty and me, shaking hands enthusiastically with the detective.

"You look very sharp, Vic, very professional," Max told me. I was wearing a trouser suit in wheat-colored linen with a dark-green cotton shirt. The jacket was loose, covering my gun, and I had on low-heeled shoes. I wanted to be able to move quickly if I had to.

Murray, whose shirt was already slightly rumpled from the hot drive, merely said grumpily that "this had better work." He joined spiritual forces with Rawlings, who cheered up slightly when he realized none of the party knew exactly what to expect—he had thought I might have brought him out to embarrass the police.

At eight-fifty-five we went into the hospital where we joined a large group going up the stairs to the auditorium. My heart was beating uncomfortably and I felt my hands turn cold and slightly damp. Lotty was lost in her own thoughts, but Max took my hand and gave it a friendly squeeze.

Max took charge at the auditorium door, where two cheerful young women were handing out name badges. Through the press of people I could make out Peter and Alan Humphries in the front of the room. They were talking with a small group of men. Peter's dark hair was combed sleekly back, showing his face white and strained. He stood tautly, not joining in the laughter of the small group.

Lotty and I hung back while Max got our name badges and programs. The five of us moved furtively into seats at the rear of the small auditorium. I devoutly hoped that the theater-style lights would block Peter's view if he looked up at the audience. The well-designed room gave everyone good sight lines to and from the stage.

Rawlings stirred nervously at my left. His tan polyester-blend sport jacket stood out in the crowd of six-hundred-dollar suit coats. " 'Amniotic Fluid Embolism: The Whole Team Approach'?" he muttered incredulously. "What the hell have you got me into, Warshawski?"

I was almost too nervous to speak. "Wait a few minutes."

I looked at the program. "Welcome," by Alan Humphries, MHA, Executive Director of Friendship V. "Introduction," by Dr. Peter Burgoyne, Chairman of Obstetrics at Friendship. Then a series of six talks on how to treat the embolism patient by various eminent specialists, some from Chicago, two from the east coast. "Lunch," followed by case histories and group discussion. "Breakup" at three in time to beat the rush-hour home.

I noticed that the registration fee was two hundred dollars. Max must have paid that. I leaned across Lotty to tap his arm and point to the spot in the program; he smiled and shook his head emphatically.

At nine-twenty, the auditorium was two-thirds full. Most of the guests had taken their seats. The bulk were men, I noted automatically, and Rawlings was the only black present. We children of the sixties do affirmative action head counts without thinking whenever we're in a public place.

With a last smile and gesture at the group he was talking to, Humphries got them to sit down and climbed up on the stage. Peter took a place in the front row close to the stage stairs.

"Hi. I'm Alan Humphries, Executive Director of Friendship Hospital. I'd like to welcome all of you here on such a beautiful day, when I know you'd rather be on the golf course—that is, treating your patients" (loud laughter). A quick joke about an obstetrics resident, a few serious words on the difficulty of treating the amniotic-fluid embolism, a skillful PR plug for Friendship's commitment to the whole patient, and Humphries introduced Peter.

"I'm sure most of you know him—his skill and dedication in the obstetrics field are not often found today. We at Friendship feel very fortunate to have him on our staff, heading up our team approach to full-service obstetrics care."

Polite applause as Peter got to his feet and started up the stairs to the podium. Humphries sat in the place Peter vacated. The houselights were turned down and the projector flashed the first slide up on the screen: the Friendship logo laid over a long shot of the starfish hospital. The knot in my stomach was so tight I was wishing I had skipped breakfast.

Using a hand control to move the slides forward, Peter quickly moved into the main theme of his talk. He started with a table of morbidity statistics in obstetrics for 1980–1985. The next slide, he said, broke down all deaths by known cause.

As he was talking, going through fetal hypoxia, rupture of the fetal membranes, and other technical material, the audience grew at first unnaturally quiet. Then a buzz swept through them, like a flock of birds spreading through a cornfield. Peter's fluent voice faltered. He turned to look at the screen and saw his own cramped handwriting, greatly magnified.

"Saw patient at 1458. . . . In the absence of Dr. Abercrombie, the decision was made to treat with 4 gms of mg. sulf. intravenously STAT and 4 gms/hour. At 1530 returned to patient, who was still comatose; no reflexes, no urinary output, dilated to 7 cm. Mg. sulf. continues intravenously."

Peter stood momentarily dumbstruck, then he pushed the forward button on the projector control. His own merciless exposition of the failure to treat Consuelo continued on the next slide.

I saw a shape get up from the front row and move hurriedly up the aisle. The projector-room door opened behind us. The screen went blank and the houselights came up. Alan Humphries's voice wafted through an intercom from the projection room.

"Excuse us just a minute, gentlemen. One of the secretaries apparently got the slides confused with those from an in-house mortality conference. Dr. Burgoyne, if you'll just join me back here for a second, we'll get these slides sorted out."

Peter didn't seem to hear him. Under the harsh glare of the stage lights his strained face looked faintly yellow. He paid no attention to the rising hum from the audience. He dropped the projector control and walked up the aisle. Past the projection booth. Out the double doors.

It took Humphries a moment or two to realize Peter wasn't coming into the booth. He recovered himself smoothly to suggest that the audience take a quick break. He gave them instructions on how to find the cafeteria, where coffee and rolls would be on the house.

As soon as Humphries left the theater, I nudged Rawlings. He was on his feet at once and the two of us beat the rush out the door. I could hear Murray calling to me querulously over the din, but I didn't stop. Rawlings kept pace with me as I jogged down the corridors to the obstetrics wing.

I'd forgotten the double doors barring entry to anyone who wasn't gowned and masked. I hesitated an instant, decided not to waste time going down the stairs and back up again on the other side, and pushed through. Rawlings was on my heels. An angry nurse tried to stop us, but we ignored her, ignored two women sweating in labor, paid no attention to the doctor who popped out of one of the side rooms to yell sharply at us.

We went on through the doors at the far end. The hallway, which had been deserted at two in the morning, was filled now with bustling figures. We shoved past them into Peter's office.

Peter's secretary was one of the fresh-faced women who'd handled registration. Her automatic smile of greeting changed to panic when we charged past her desk to her boss's door.

"He's not in there. He's in a meeting. He won't be in all day."

I opened his office door anyway and looked in. It was empty. The secretary bleated in the background, but she wasn't used to throwing people out and didn't know how to start.

"Now what," Rawlings demanded sharply.

I thought for a minute. "His house, I guess." I turned to the secretary. "Alan Humphries hasn't been in here, has he? No? I guess he's quicker on his feet than I am. Or knows Burgoyne better."

We left. I took Rawlings down the near staircase.

"You know this place pretty well," he said suspiciously. "You know where this Dr. Burgoyne lives?" When I nodded he added ironically, "You and the doc were kind of good pals, huh? So you're sure he ain't going to mind you barging in on him."

"I'm not sure of anything," I snapped, my nerves stretched to their tautest. "If this turns into a wild-goose chase, then I've cost the city of Chicago your salary for an entire morning and you can bill me."

"Hey, relax, Ms. W. If that's all that's worrying you, that's such a tiny sum it isn't worth thinking about. I'm having a good time." We had reached the front exit and were heading to the parking lot. "My car or yours?"

"Yours, of course. If one of the local boys stops you for speeding you can plead professional courtesy or something."

He laughed and moved over to his Monte Carlo at a pace that seemed smooth and relaxed but had me jogging slightly to keep step. He unlocked the doors and started the engine. The car was rolling before I had my door shut.

"Okay, Ms. W. I'm putty in your beautiful hands. Point me."

I gave him directions to Route 72. Rawlings drove rapidly but skillfully; I relaxed a bit. During the short ride I gave him a summary of my analysis of the cover-up in obstetrics and Malcolm's death.

He was quiet for a minute, thinking, then said cheerfully, "Okay, I forgive you. If you'd told me all that Wednesday I would have said you were blowing smoke. I ain't totally convinced yet, but those two guys hightailing it did have a suspicious aura to it. . . . You know anyone drives a Pontiac Fiero? It's been trailing us at least since we hit the highway."

I twisted to look at the road behind us. "Oh, that's Murray—I guess he saw us leave and didn't want to lose the end of his story."

Rawlings turned onto the side street leading to Peter's house and pulled into the driveway. Peter's Maxima was there and behind it a dark-gray late-model Mercedes. Burning a little rubber, Murray pulled in behind us.

"What the hell you mean, Warshawski, leaving me there when all hell broke loose?" he shouted angrily, slamming the car door.

I shook my head. It was too complicated to explain in twenty-five words or less.

Rawlings was already at the door. "Can it, Ryerson. Your hurt feelings don't count right now."

As we ran from the car to the house, Peppy came bounding up to us, her golden-feathered tail waving like a pennant in the summer sun. She recognized me and gave a short bark of delight, turning to race back to the yard where she picked up a tennis ball. She reached me again as we were opening the back door. Her pure joy in me and the day brought an involuntary catch to my throat. I blinked my eyes hard, petted her gently, and told her to stay. Rawlings and Murray followed me silently into the house.

We were in the kitchen, an electronic showroom that silently gleamed stainless steel in the summer sun. We moved quietly across the Italian tile floor into the hushed dining room, past rich dark chairs and modern statuary to the hall leading to Peter's study. The door was shut.

Rawlings jerked his head toward the wall on the blind side of the door. I took up position there. He swung the door open and rolled clear of the entrance. I had my Smith & Wesson in hand and followed him rapidly into the room. As well choreographed as if we'd practiced it for three years. When no shots sounded, Murray followed us in.

Peter was sitting behind his desk, a gun in his right hand, a replica of my semi-automatic. Alan Humphries sat in an armchair facing him. Peter's gun was pointed at Humphries; although Peter looked up when we crashed in, he didn't move the gun. His face was pinched and the whites of his eyes showed dangerously. Our surprise entrance didn't seem to startle him—he was in a state beyond shock or surprise.

"Oh, Vic, it's you."

"Yes, Peter. It's me. This is Detective Rawlings from the Chicago Police Department. Murray Ryerson from the *Herald-Star*. We want to talk to you about Malcolm Tregiere."

He smiled a little. "Do you, Vic? That's nice. I'd like to tell you about him. He was a good doctor. He was going to be the kind of doctor I should have been—Lotty Herschel's prize student in perinatology, healer of the sick, protector of the poor and innocent."

"Shut up, Peter," Humphries said sharply. "You're out of your head."

"If I am, it's a good place to be, Alan. You know, money isn't all it's cracked up to be. Or maybe you don't know that. When Tregiere showed up at the hospital, I knew the game was over. He took in everything we'd done—and hadn't done. He was too polite to say anything, just pitched in, did his best with the baby and the girl. But it was too late, of course."

He was speaking in a dreamy voice. I glanced at Rawlings, but he was far too shrewd a cop to interrupt the flow of a confession.

"I knew he'd be reporting back to Dr. Herschel, so I went to Alan to tell him we'd better get ready to face the music. But Alan didn't want to do that, did you, old boy? Oh, no, not to interrupt the future flow of capital, or whatever the shit the financial garbage says. So he stayed late at the hospital, trying to figure it out. That was before we lost the girl, Consuelo, of course, but she had gone under once because of the magnesium sulfate and her condition was pretty shaky. Critical, we say in the medical-industrial business."

He held the gun level at Humphries the whole time he spoke. At first the administrator tried to interrupt him, tried to signal to us to disarm Peter, but when he saw we weren't responding, he lapsed into silence.

"Then Alan had a little luck, didn't you, Alan? The girl's

husband showed up late that night. Alan's always been good at sizing people up, judging their strengths and weaknesses. He did a real fine job with mine, for instance. I mean, once I'd swallowed the Friendship financial bait, it was easy to push me each step of the rest of the way, wasn't it?

"Anyway, the girl's husband showed up. And Alan gave him five thousand dollars to keep him happy. And learned that he had some pals back in Chicago who were into some rather antisocial activities, who might do anything for a price. Like break into Malcolm Tregiere's apartment and steal his notes. And maybe bash his brains in. You said you'd told them to wait until he wasn't home—but that wouldn't have done you much good, would it? Because he could always reconstruct his dictation. No, you needed him dead."

"You're raving, Burgoyne," Humphries said loudly, his own face pale. "Can't you see, Officer, that he's out of his mind? If you'd get that gun away from him, we could talk sensibly. Peter gets carried away, but you look like an intelligent man, Rawlings. I'm sure we could work something out."

"Knock it off, Humphries," I said. "We know you have Sergio Rodriguez's phone number in your office. I could get the detective here to send an officer over right now and lay hands on it."

He sucked in his breath sharply, the first chink in his defenses.

Peter went on speaking as if there had been no interruption. "So Tregiere was dead. But we knew Warshawski was a detective. And her reputation was pretty good, so I stepped in to keep an eye on her. Young good-looking doctor, lots of money—plenty of women would fall for that, and maybe she would, too. Besides, Alan still didn't have the dictation. Perhaps Tregiere had given it to her when they were out at Friendship together. Easy enough to search her apartment while she was asleep."

He turned eyes which were dark holes of despair to me. "I liked you, Vic. I might have fallen in love with you if I hadn't been carrying the burden of death on my shoulders. I could tell you were getting suspicious and I'm not very good at hiding things, so I backed away from you. And besides, there was the whole business of those IckPiff files. . . ."

His voice trailed off. I took a deep breath to ease the tension in my throat. "It's okay, Peter. I know about those. Alan got in touch with Monkfish and convinced him to stage an anti-abortion rally outside Lotty's clinic. He had someone in the crowd to get Lotty's file on Consuelo. You couldn't know that Friendship's counsel, Dick Yarborough, was my ex-husband. I knew Monkfish couldn't afford Dick and I wanted to know who was paying him to get off the hook for destroying Lotty's clinic."

Humphries, seeing Peter's attention distracted, made a move to get out of his chair.

Rawlings pulled out his police revolver and waved him back. "Let the doctor finish, man. So you got Sergio to break into Warshawski's place to get the files, huh? And the old man who lives downstairs got his head bashed in, but fortunately didn't die. We can read that part. But what about Fabiano? How'd he come to die?"

"Oh, that." Peter looked down at the gun in his hand. "Alan had paid him to shut him up. We figured five thousand was more money than he'd ever get together and it wouldn't occur to him to sue. But then he got sick of being harassed by his dead wife's brothers, and by Vic here. Everyone knows how tight she is with Dr. Herschel, and Dr. Herschel's nurse is the dead girl's sister. So anyone who wanted to get back at Vic or the Alvarado family would do it through Dr. Herschel, right?"

Rawlings and I nodded without speaking.

"So Fabiano brought suit against Dr. Herschel for negligence in treating his wife while she was pregnant. He meant to keep his word and leave Friendship out of it—slime that he was, he had that much honor—but once you start a process like that, you don't have much control over it. Of course the lawyer he found soon saw where the deep pockets were. Out at Friendship.

"So we got our summonses. And Alan kind of lost his head. He got me to give him the model number of Vic's gun and went out and bought one just like it. Then he met Fabiano at his bar in the city for a friendly, fatherly chat. I came along for the ride. And the incrimination, right, Alan? So he put his arm around the boy and shot him in the head. Of course, he kept the bullet case. He figured the police knew Vic here would spring to Dr. Herschel's defense, and if they found Fabiano'd been killed with a bullet from her gun, why, they'd arrest her.

"He gave me the gun to keep. After all, he's got a wife and children at home. You can't keep a gun around the home, it isn't safe, is it, Alan?" He waved the pistol at Humphries and laughed a little.

Rawlings cleared his throat, started to say something about forensic evidence, then thought better of it. "Okay, doc. You didn't mean Warshawski any harm. You'd have brought her flowers in prison and got her a good lawyer. Maybe her old moneybags lawyer husband. Now I'm afraid I'm going to have to ask you to give me the gun. It's evidence in a murder case, you see, and I need to take it back to Chicago with me."

He spoke in a quiet, persuasive voice and Peter turned his dreamy gaze to him.

"Oh, yes, the gun, Detective." He held it up and looked at it. Before I realized what he was doing, he held it to his temple and fired.

XXXIII

Retriever in Mourning

The whine from the gun vibrated in the room. The smell filled the place, burnt gunpowder and blood. Maybe our noses are too blunted to smell blood anymore. But we could see it. See it. A bright crimson splash against the desk top. The white shards are bone. And the darker soft mass seeping out beyond the hair is the brain.

"You can't faint now, Ms. W. We got work to do."

A strong black hand seized my head and forced me to bend over, to tuck my head between my legs. The buzzing faded from my ears. The nausea rising in my throat receded. I stood up slowly, avoiding the desk. Murray had gone to the window where he stood with his back to the room, his big shoulders hunched over. Humphries got uncertainly to his feet.

"Poor Peter. He couldn't forgive himself for not saving that poor girl's life. He's been talking wildly for some time now—we've been very concerned about him. No offense to you, Miss Warshawski, but I didn't think it was sensible for him to see so much of you—it kept him brooding about the girl and the baby and Dr. Herschel's problems in a very unhealthy way.''

He looked at his wrist. "I don't want to seem callous, but I'd better get back to the hospital—see what I can do to break the news to the staff, see if we can get someone to cover Peter's patients for the next few weeks.''

Rawlings moved to the door, blocking the exit. "Seems to me you're the one talking a little wildly, Mr. Humphries. We need to go into Chicago together for a chat.''

Humphries's brown eyebrows went up to his carefully combed hairline. "If you need a statement from me, Officer, I'll dictate one this afternoon and send it to my attorney. With Peter killing himself, we're going to be under tremendous pressure. I need to talk to my secretary—the two of us will probably have to work the weekend.''

Rawlings sighed softly and pulled out a pair of handcuffs. "You don't understand, Mr. Humphries. I'm arresting you for conspiring to murder Malcolm Tregiere and for the murder of Fabiano Hernandez. You have the right to remain silent. Anything you say can and will be used in court. You have the right to talk to a lawyer for advice before we ask you any questions and to have him with you during questioning. You have the right—"

Humphries, who'd been struggling while Rawlings cuffed his hands behind him; bellowed, "You'll regret this, Officer. I'll have your commander bust you out of the force.''

Rawlings looked at Murray. "You taking notes, Ryerson? I'd like a verbatim record of everything Mr. Humphries has to say. I think the charges are now going to include threatening a police officer in the discharge of his duty.

"I guess we'd better notify the local people that there's a dead man out here, let them come and talk to us before we go back to town.''

Humphries continued to rail for a few minutes. Rawlings ignored him, going over to the desk to phone his watch commander in Chicago. When the administrator tried to walk out while Rawlings was at the desk, Murray and I blocked the door.

"I just want to find another phone," Humphries said haughtily. "I presume I'm allowed to call my lawyer?"

"Wait until the detective is through," I said. "And by the way, he'll probably be happier if you start calling him 'Detective' or 'Sergeant' instead of 'Officer.' Insulting the man isn't going to help your case."

"Look, Miss Warshawski," Humphries said urgently, "you saw a lot of Burgoyne the last few weeks. You know he wasn't himself—"

"I don't know," I interrupted. "I don't know what you think he was supposed to be like."

"But all of this crap he was spewing—about me and some Mexican—what did he call him? Sergio?—it'd be worth a great deal to me if you'd be willing to testify to his delusional state. It's a pity I never got around to asking our psychiatric guy to do a formal evaluation. Although he probably observed some changes at staff meetings. But think about it seriously, Miss Warshawski. After all, you're the person who probably saw the most of him the last few weeks."

"Gee, I don't know, Mr. Humphries. I wonder what a great deal means to you—the V. I. Warshawski wing out here at Friendship? Or Peter's profit-sharing for the year? What do you think, Murray?"

"Think about what?" That was Rawlings, very sharp.

"Oh, Mr. Humphries is going to dedicate a wing at the hospital to me if I testify that Dr. Burgoyne was off his head the last few weeks."

"That so? Pity you're only a private eye, Ms. W., or we'd be able to add attempted bribery to the charge sheet."

We moved into the living room to wait for the local people. Rawlings told Humphries he could call his lawyer when he'd been booked in Chicago. The administrator took that with good humor, keeping up a steady stream of cajolery. He'd decided, apparently, that sweet-talking would work better than threats, but Rawlings was impervious to both.

The local force showed up with three cars all flashing red, sirens howling. Five officers came running up the drive. Peppy took exception to the alarms and the uniforms; she chased them to the house, barking madly. I opened the door and held her collar while they came in.

"Good girl," I murmured into her soft ear after they'd gone inside. "You're a good dog. But what are you going to do now? Your boy is dead, you know. Who's going to feed you and play fetch with you?"

I sat outside with her, holding her against me, feeling the long, luxurious hair with my fingers. Made nervous by the flashing lights and uniformed men, she moved uneasily against me.

After about ten minutes an ambulance came squealing up. I directed the attendants into the house, remaining with the dog. A short time later they came out with Peter's body in a black bag. As soon as they reappeared, Peppy began trembling and whimpering. She strained against my hands, finally breaking free as the ambulance pulled away. She charged after it, barking frantically, a high, pained bark. She followed them down the drive and up the road. When they were out of sight, she came back slowly, her head and tail lowered, her sides heaving. She plopped herself in the driveway where it met the road, her head against the ground.

When Rawlings finally came out with Humphries and the local men, she lifted her head hopefully, but dropped it again when she saw Peter wasn't with them. We all got into cars—Murray and me together to go back to the hospital for Max and Lotty, one of the local men with Rawlings to escort Humphries to Chicago. We drove carefully around the dog. As we turned a bend in the road I could see her still lying there, her head against the blacktop.

Murray barely stopped long enough for me to get out of the car at Friendship before racing off to the city. Max and Lotty were waiting in the cafeteria. Lotty, annoyed at being left to cool her heels for two hours, switched rapidly to sympathy after a look at my face.

I told them briefly what had happened. "Let me drive you home now. I need to get over to the Sixth Area to make my statement."

Lotty took my arm and guided me gently to my car. We didn't talk much during the drive. At one point Max asked if I thought they'd be able to make charges against Humphries stick.

"I don't know," I said wearily. "His current line is that Peter was mad, that all the stuff about hiring Sergio to kill Malcolm was a delusion. It all depends, I suppose, on which way Sergio decides to jump."

I left them both at Lotty's apartment and drove on to the Sixth Area Headquarters. Before getting out of the car I locked my gun in the glove compartment—the police don't like outsiders carrying weapons into their stations. As I started up the station steps, a Mercedes sports car pulled up to the curb with a squeal of brakes. I turned and waited. My ex-husband came flying up the walk.

"Hi, Dick," I said sociably. "Glad to see Humphries got hold of you—he was really digging a pit for himself out in Barrington: threats, attempted bribery, the whole works."

"You!" Dick's face turned crimson. "God damn it, I might have guessed you were behind this!"

I held the door for him. "For once you're right: I figured it out practically all by myself. If not for me, your client would probably go to the grave without doing a minute's time for Malcolm Tregiere's death. I don't care so much about Fabiano Hernandez, but the state takes a dim view of murder no matter who's been killed."

Dick strode past me. I followed him into the building. He was trying to maintain an air of dignified outrage while covertly figuring out where to go—his typical clients don't bring him to the police station.

"Desk sergeant, straight ahead," I said helpfully.

He strode purposefully to the desk. I hovered in his wake.

"I'm Richard Yarborough. My client, Alan Humphries, is being held here—I need to see him."

When the desk sergeant asked for identification, then told him he had to be searched, Dick got angry.

"Officer, my client was denied the right to call counsel for well over an hour after his arrest. Now, am I to be humiliated as well simply because I want to restore his legal rights to him?"

"Dick," I murmured, "it's the way things are done

around here. They don't know you're pure beyond belief—there have been cases of lawyers less scrupulous than you smuggling weapons in to their clients. . . . Sorry, Sergeant—Mr. Yarborough's usual venue is La Salle Street."

Dick stood rigid with anger while he was searched. Letting the sergeant assume I was his entourage, I opened my handbag and was patted down myself. We got our visitor's passes and moved on.

"You really should have brought Freeman with you," I told him as we walked up the stairs. "He knows his way around these police stations. You can't antagonize the desk sergeant; he's your key for any information—charge sheets, how your client's doing, where he is."

Dick ignored me majestically until we got to the room where they were holding Humphries. Then he put on his heaviest face for me.

"I don't know what you did to make the police think Alan Humphries was guilty of murder. But you have created a very serious legal situation for yourself, Vic. Very serious. Whether we will bring slander charges depends on how forgiving my client feels."

"And how long he's put away for," I said brightly. "You know, Dick, Lotty Herschel keeps asking me how come I ever married you. And damned if I can see why. You couldn't have been this big an asshole when we were in law school together, could you?"

He turned on his heel hard enough to make the leather smoke and knocked on the door. A uniformed man looked out to see who it was. Dick showed him his pass and was admitted to the room.

After a couple of minutes Rawlings came out to talk to me. "You get the doc home okay? I'm going to need her to be an expert witness on this medical testimony. I've got a police doctor in there, but he doesn't know shit about birthing babies."

"I'm sure Lotty'll do it. She'd do damned near anything to clear up Malcolm's death. You're not trying to hold him on that, are you? What about Fabiano—that's cut and dried—he shot the guy."

Rawlings grimaced. "On Burgoyne's testimony. And Burgoyne is dead. I was hoping to get no bond, but now that slick piece of goods who represents him is here, I'm not so sure. He's looking to argue it was Burgoyne who bought and fired the gun. Of course we can check that, but not before the preliminary hearing, and this Yarborough looks like the kind who wines and dines the bench—just my luck some good old boy will be handling night court today. We need more of a case. Don't you have any evidence? I mean anything concrete?"

"You could bring in Coulter, the guy from the state Human Resources Department. But that would just get you collusion on the perinatal cover-up. How about Sergio?"

Rawlings shook his head. "I've got a warrant out for him. But that could cut both ways, you know. For a big enough chunk of change, Sergio'll say he never laid eyes on Humphries."

I thought about it. "Yeah. You got a problem. Let me make my statement and get out of here. Maybe I can come up with something."

"Warshawski! If you—" He broke off. "Never mind. If you've got an idea, I don't want to know about it until after you've executed it. I'll be happier."

I smiled at him sweetly. "See? I'm easy to work with, once you've figured out how."

XXXIV

Preliminary Hearing

I drove several blocks from the police station before stopping to find a pay phone. The nervous woman answered on the fifth ring, her baby crying again in the background.

"Mrs. Rodriguez? I called two nights ago. For Sergio. Is he there?"

"He—no. No, he's not home. I don't know where he is."

I paused a second and thought I heard an extension stealthily lifted. "It's like this, Mrs. Rodriguez: Alan Humphries is in jail. Right now. Over at the Sixth Area Headquarters. You could call and check it out if you wanted to. They're going to give him immunity—you know what that is?—immunity from prosecution. That means he won't go to jail. As long as he tells them that Sergio is the one who really killed Malcolm Tregiere and Fabiano Hernandez. Make sure Sergio gets that message, Mrs. Rodriguez. Goodbye."

I waited on the line after she hung up. Sure enough, a second click followed. I smiled grimly to myself, got back into my car, and returned to sit behind the police station.

By now the networks had gotten hold of the story. Channel 13 and Channel 5 both had mobile vans parked out front.

Around four-thirty there was a flurry of activity. The mobile units sprang to life as a crowd of uniformed men, surrounding a barely visible Humphries, came out the side entrance. They put him into a transport van, brought out three other handcuffed men for the van, and locked them all in. The networks made a great show of running footage of Humphries's removal. This would look like news at ten tonight: Mary Sherrod in front of the police van, speculating on what might be going on.

Dick came out a few minutes later. He pulled the Mercedes away from the curb with a great flourish of gear shifting. I started my Chevy and followed more leisurely, down Western Avenue toward Twenty-sixth and California where the criminal courts sit. Since the van could flash blue lights at the intersections, I quickly fell behind. I've spent enough time at criminal court that I wasn't worried about finding it. I was more interested in looking for any other escorts we might have picked up, but Dick's was the only car trailing the van; no one was following me.

The criminal-court building was put up in the 1920s. Its decorated ceilings, beautifully carved doors, and inlaid marble floors make a curious contrast to the crimes discussed there. At the entrance I was stopped for a thorough search—handbag emptied onto a countertop, including a bedraggled tampon, a fistful of miscellaneous receipts, and an earring I thought I'd lost on the beach. The bailiff remembered me from my trial days; we chatted about her grandchildren for a few minutes before I headed for the third floor where night court was held.

Humphries's preliminary hearing showed Dick at his finest. Pearl-gray suit jacket buttoned, his light hair combed as carefully as though he'd just left his dryer, he was the very picture of affluent power. Humphries, at his side, looked sober and puzzled, a law-abiding man caught in events he didn't understand, but doing his best to help straighten things out.

The state's attorney, Jane LeMarchand, had been well

briefed. She was a senior prosecutor, fluent and able, but the plea for no bond was denied, given the fact that the evidence of murder was all hearsay from a man now dead. The judge ruled that the state had probable cause to try Humphries, bond was set for one hundred fifty thousand, and the case was entered in the computer for assignment to a trial judge. Dick gracefully wrote out a check for ten percent of that, and he and Humphries exited to the chorus of popping flashbulbs. In a fit of pique I gave the reporters Dick's home phone number and address. Petty, but I hated to see him getting away with no inconvenience whatsoever.

Rawlings caught up with me at the courtroom exit. "We're going to have to build a mighty careful case, Ms. W., for when we come to trial."

"You mean for the first motion for continuance," I said bitterly. "This thing will come to trial in five years. Want to put money on it?"

He rubbed thick fingers tiredly across his forehead. "Forget it. We tried to get the judge to agree we could hold the dude twenty-four hours for questioning—I'd like to see him spend at least one night in jail, but your old man—ex-old man—was too slick for us. You want to get a drink someplace? Something to eat?"

I was surprised. "I'd like to—rain check, maybe? I have some stuff to do tonight. Might help the case." Or might destroy it, I added myself.

He narrowed his eyes. "You've had a long day, Warshawski. Think maybe you've done enough for the time being?"

I laughed but didn't say anything. We pushed our way through the crowds of cameras at the front entrance. Dick was standing with one hand lightly resting on Humphries's shoulder. He must have taken a course in television presence—he was at the top of the stairs for full dramatic effect.

"My client has had a long and trying day. I believe Ms. Warshawski, while a well-meaning investigator, probably got carried away by her emotional involvement with the doctor who unfortunately took his own life earlier today."

A mist covered my eyes. I felt the blood drumming in

my head as I shouldered my way past the cameras to Dick. When he saw me, he stiffened and pulled Humphries closer to him. I found a mike under my nose and mustered all my willpower to grin instead of grabbing it to bash Dick's brains out.

"I'm the emotional Ms. Warshawski," I said as lightly as I could. "Since Mr. Yarborough had to leave a golf game to race to the courtroom here, he unfortunately didn't have time for a full review of the facts. When he sees tomorrow's paper, and learns of the collusion between the State of Illinois and his client, he may wish he'd stayed on the links."

There was a ripple of laughter from the crowd. I ducked away on a tide of questions, glanced over my shoulder to see Dick fighting for self-control, and headed back for my car. I looked around for Rawlings, but he'd disappeared in the confusion.

Dick wrapped up the press conference quickly after that. He bustled Humphries into the Mercedes. They headed north to the expressways. I had to strain the Chevy to the limit to keep up with his fast-cruising sports car. Once on the Kennedy, headed toward O'Hare, he picked up speed, weaving in and out of traffic. It was almost completely dark now, a difficult time of day for tailing. Only the distinctive spacing of the sports car's taillights helped me keep him in view.

As we joined the tollway and headed on beyond O'Hare, I realized that a brown Buick Le Sabre had become my permanent escort. It held back behind me until I'd dropped my four dimes into the toll basket, then pulled in front of me. It paced the Mercedes for a few miles, pulled in front of it around Algonquin Road, then dropped back behind me, where it hung closely.

We were going over seventy by then. The little car was vibrating. If I had to stop suddenly, the Buick would run right over me. My hands were sweating on the steering wheel.

Dick took the I-290 exit without signaling. I swerved right, felt the wheels lose traction briefly as I turned, saw the Buick slide past two honking, braking cars to keep up with me, then was miraculously back in control, picking up the Mercedes's taillights about a half-mile up the road.

I patted the steering wheel. "Come on, old girl. Show that damned Kraut car what a Yankee can do. Come on, babe. Just because you cost forty thousand less doesn't mean you aren't as good." The Chevy continued to vibrate, but climbed up to eighty and closed the gap.

The Buick continued to hang about a hundred yards in back of me. My gun was in the glove compartment where I'd locked it before going into court. I didn't dare take one hand off the steering wheel to fiddle with the lock and get at it. I couldn't believe the state police were letting the three of us cruise this fast this far.

My hair was wet, my armpits dripping, when we slowed to fifty-five and turned onto the Northwest Highway. After that, progress was more sedate, interrupted by periodic traffic lights, with suburban police cruising ostentatiously in between. On one stop I was able to remove the glove-compartment key from my key chain. At the next I unlocked it, quickly pulled out my gun, and stuck it into my jacket pocket.

Humphries lived in Barrington Hills, a good fifty miles from the Loop. Thanks to Dick's driving, we pulled up in front of his driveway only seventy minutes after leaving the criminal courts. Dick turned in; the Buick and I moved on past. As soon as the Mercedes had disappeared, the Buick put on a rush of speed and pulled around past me, disappearing up the road.

I moved over to the shoulder where I sat with my head on the steering wheel, my arms wobbling. I needed food. It had been more than twelve hours since I'd last eaten, and the intervening time had used up all my blood sugar. If I had a partner, I'd be able to send her off for food while I continued to watch. As it was, I had to take a chance. I retraced our route until I came to a strip with takeout joints. I had a double hamburger, a chocolate shake, and fries. By then I was ready for sleep, not action.

" 'When duty whispers low, *Thou must*, the youth replies

I can,' '' I muttered encouragingly to myself, heading back for Humphries's house.

He had a good two- or three-acre spread. Nestled far back among the trees, the house was only partly visible from the road. In the dark, all I could see was the limestone front where a spotlight shone on it. I pulled over, waiting for—I wasn't sure what.

I leaned back in the driver's seat and shut my eyes briefly. When I opened them again, it was because a set of headlights had flashed in my eyes—the Buick, headed back up the road. It was pitch-black, with no streetlights to mark the way. I was cold and my muscles were stiff; I was barely able to turn the Chevy around and pick up the Buick before it turned back onto the main road.

We'd gone several miles when I realized we were heading for the hospital. I slowed down—no point in getting a ticket when I knew the destination, and my arms were too sore to relish another Grand Prix driving demonstration.

It was midnight on my dashboard clock when I pulled into the visitors' lot at Friendship. As I moved toward the entrance I kept one hand on the automatic in my pocket, scanning the rows of cars for the Buick but not seeing it.

The brightly lit, deserted hallways were becoming as familiar to me as my own office. I half expected the janitor leaning on his mop in the corner to greet me, or to find that the nurses walking down the corridor wanted to consult me about some patient's condition.

No one tried to talk to me as I made my way to the administrative wing. This time, the outer door was unlocked. I opened it cautiously, but the hallway in front of me was empty. I moved quietly down the passage, straining to hear but catching no sounds. The handle to Jackie's antechamber door also turned in my hand. No lights were on, but the parking-lot lamps shone brightly enough into the room that I could make out the furniture. Humphries's door fit flush with the floor; I couldn't tell if anyone was behind it or not.

Holding my breath, I slowly turned the knob and pushed

enough to crack the door. I couldn't see anything, but now I could hear. A husky voice was speaking.

"What we want to know, man, is what you're telling the cops. We don't give a fuck about your doctor pal and what he said. He's dead, that don't count. But my informant said, man, you were fingering me. Now tell me about it."

That was Sergio. I would know his voice anywhere. I thought frantically. I ought to call the police, but getting them to listen to me would be hard enough, let alone getting them to come without enough fanfare to announce the Second Coming. With the other half of my mind I was trying to figure out why Humphries had come back to the hospital to meet Sergio instead of settling it all on a deserted country road. And if that had been Sergio in the Buick, why hadn't he killed me while I lay asleep behind my steering wheel?

Humphries was answering. "I don't know who your informant is, or why he would know anything about the matter. But I can assure you that I have said nothing to the police. As you can see, they released me."

He gasped. Someone had hit him. Or they were holding his arms back, giving them a twist when he didn't say what they wanted to hear.

"I wasn't born yesterday, man. You don't walk on a murder rap. You walk when you tell the cops what they want to hear. And they be real glad to hear some spic taking the rap, letting a rich honky businessman off the hook. You dig?"

"I think we could talk more easily if you'd take that knife away from my neck."

I had to hand it to Humphries—he was cool under pressure.

"We have a slight problem, you see," he went on. "After all, you did kill Malcolm Tregiere—I didn't."

"Maybe we did, maybe not. But if we did, man, you ordered the hit. And that's conspiracy to commit murder. You go up for a lotta years on a rap like that, man. And believe me, we gonna take you down with us if we go. Besides that, there's a little matter of my man Fabiano. Oh, yeah. I know you offed him, man. Just the kind of dumb shit a honky like you would pull. So before you talk to the cops about anything, dig, just remember we ain't laying down and playing dead for you."

Humphries didn't say anything. Then he gave a small gasp.

"What the hell do you want?"

"Ah, my man. Now we're talking. What I want. I want to hear you say those magic words: I shot Fabiano Hernandez."

Silence, then another gasp.

"Come on, man. We got all night. Nobody's gonna hear you if you scream."

Finally Humphries said in a choked voice, "Okay. I shot the guy, but he was a punk, a loser, a wastrel. If you've come out here to avenge his death, you're wasting your lives on a worthless heap of shit."

I took a breath, pulled the gun out, pushed the door open, and rolled in behind it.

"Freeze!" I yelled, pointing it at Sergio.

He was standing in front of Humphries, his knife in his hand. Tattoo was behind Humphries, holding his arms. Two other Lions were lounging on the sidelines, holding guns. The long window behind the desk was shattered—they'd apparently broken in and surprised Humphries when he showed up.

"Drop your guns," I barked.

Instead of obeying, they turned them on me. I fired. One went down, but I missed the other. I rolled as he shot and the bullet went into the floor where I'd been kneeling. Sergio left Humphries. Out of the corner of my eye I saw his arm go back to throw the knife. A gun barked and he crumpled across the leather desk. I fired again at the other gunman. He dropped his weapon as soon as Sergio fell.

"Don't shoot! Don't shoot!" he screamed in a falsetto.

Rawlings picked his way past the broken window glass into the room. "God damn your eyes, Warshawski. Why in hell did you break in when you did?"

I sank back on my heels, arms shaking. "Rawlings! That

was you in the Buick! I thought—thought Sergio— And didn't you drive a Chevy this morning?''

The gold gleamed briefly. ''Buick's my own car—didn't think you'd recognize it. I figured you for the action type—thought I'd better come along to see which way you jumped. Why do you think you got by with doing eighty on the tollway? Police escort . . . Okay, Humphries. *Mr.* Humphries, I mean. I think we got enough to make it stick this time. Like I said a few hours ago, you got the right to remain silent. But if you give up that right—''

Humphries shook his head. Blood was trickling from the cuts Sergio had made on his neck. ''I know the patter. Knock it off. If you've been outside all this time, why in hell didn't you come in when that damned spic was threatening to cut my throat?''

''Don't worry, Humphries—much as I'd have liked to, I wouldn't let the guy kill you. I'm just like him, though—I wanted to hear you say those magic words. That you killed Fabiano Hernandez. Ms. W. heard them, too. So I think we got enough to please the judge.''

I went over to Sergio. Rawlings had hit him in the shoulder. A .38 in the shoulder creates a major mess, but the boy would live. The Lion I'd shot was lying on the Persian rug, moaning pathetically and spoiling the wool. Tattoo and the other guard were standing sullenly to one side.

''I don't know, Humphries,'' Rawlings said. ''Maybe just as well you'll be in jail—it'd probably break your heart to have to look at all those bloodstains on your rug and your desk every day. Now is there a doctor in the house?''

XXXV

Last Swim of the Summer

The late summer sun blazed in glory, heating the sand, dancing on the water. Children screamed wildly, knowing this was their last day of summer vacation. Husbands and wives shared picnic baskets, and enjoyed their final weekend on the beach. In the background, some had radios tuned to the Cubs, some to the local rock frequencies. Harry Caray and Prince fought with each other to control the airwaves. I stared blindly in front of me.

"What's the problem, doll? Why don'tcha go in the water? Might be your last chance before the weather changes."

Mr. Contreras lay on a plastic lounge chair under a large umbrella. He had come with me to Pentwater, a little town on the Michigan side of the lake, on the strict understanding that he would stay in the shade at all times. I'd hoped he'd been sleeping. As a convalescent, he was even more exhausting than he had been when he was healthy.

"You ain't still eating your heart out over that doc, are you, doll? Believe me, he ain't worth it."

I turned to face him, gestured with my right hand, but didn't speak. I couldn't put my feelings into words. I hadn't known Peter well enough to be eating my heart out for him. His bones and brains on the desk top flashed into my mind. Horrifying, yes. But not my personal burden.

By rights I should be on top of the world. Humphries and Sergio were both being held without bond, Sergio in the prison wing of county hospital while his shoulder healed. The weekend *Herald-Star* had had a field day with Dick, showing him at his most pompous. He had called to chew me out after we got Humphries down to Twenty-sixth and California for the second time in twenty-four hours. Maybe, as Lotty said, my reaction to him was childish, but I'd had a good time—he was in way over his head with criminal law and didn't want to admit he didn't know as much about it as I did.

Tessa had come to visit me Saturday morning before I left for the country, grateful I'd cornered Malcolm's murderers and contrite she'd ever doubted me. She'd arrived at the same time as Rawlings, who wanted to check up on me and work on our statements. I'd half hoped to take him up on his dinner offer, but he and Tessa left together to get lunch. That didn't really trouble me, either—Rawlings was amusing, but it's not good for a PI to get too sociable with the police. So why did I feel wrapped in a cocoon of lethargy, barely able to keep awake?

Mr. Contreras was looking at me anxiously. "Life goes on, doll. When Clara died, I thought, boy, this is it. And we'd been married fifty-one years. Yep. We were high-school sweethearts. Course, I dropped out, but she wanted to finish and we waited to have the wedding until she did. And we had some fights, cookie, fights like you never saw the like of. But we always had the good times, too.

"That's what you need, doll. You need someone tough enough to fight with you, but good enough to give you the good times. Not like that ex of yours. How you ever came to marry a guy like that I'll never know. No, nor that doctor, neither. I told you he was a lightweight. Told you the first time I laid eyes on him. . . ."

I stiffened. If he thought not having a husband was troubling me . . . Maybe I was just burned out. Too much city, too much time spent in the sewer with people like Sergio and Alan Humphries. Maybe I should get out of the detective business—sell my co-op, retire to Pentwater. I tried picturing myself in this tiny town, with twelve hundred people who all knew each other's business. A quart of Black Label a day might make it tolerable. The idea made me give a little snort of laughter.

"That's right, doll. You gotta be able to laugh at yourself. I mean, if I laid down and cried for every mistake I ever made, I'd a drowned to death by now. And look at the good side. We got a dog. At least, you got a dog, but who's going to walk her and feed her when you're out to all hours, huh? She'll be company—long as she don't pee on my tomatoes, huh, girl?"

When Peppy realized he was talking to her, she dropped the stick she'd been gnawing to lick his hand. Then she bounded back to the stick, picked it up, and dropped it next to me, her tail making a great golden circle in the sun. She nudged me hard with her wet nose, slapping me with her tail to make sure I got the point. I pushed myself up to standing. While the dog danced herself into a crescendo of ecstasy, I picked up the stick and hurled it into the setting sun.

About the Author

Sara Paretsky is the author of three previous novels: *Indemnity Only*, *Deadlock*, and *Killing Orders*, all published by Ballantine Books. Like V. I. Warshawski, she lives in Chicago.

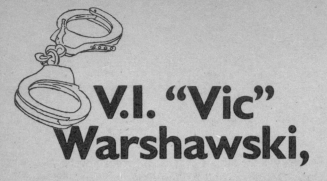

V.I. "Vic" Warshawski,

a tough Chicago dick ...who just happens to be a woman.